IT WAS A CREATURE
NEVER SEEN ON EARTH

Fitz thought that he was to make it across the plain without so much as sight of one of the monsters, for the sheen of sun upon the spring-fed pond at the plain's inland margin was in easy sight and he was headed toward it, angling a bit to the east in order to avoid a declivity some five or six feet deep, when suddenly, it was there. Up, out, over the lip of the hole it came with a bound, covered the intervening yards with but one or two racing, leaping strides, a black-skinned, five-fingered hand tipped with black, flat, blood-dripping nails reaching for Fitz.

Warned by his peripheral vision, the man swayed

Recognizing the value of predators in Nature's scheme of things, he tried a warning shot, hoping that the roar and muzzle blast of the Remington magnum would terrify the whatever-it-was into finding other prey.

It did stop for a brief moment, just long enough for Fitz to jack another round into the smoking chamber and eject the empty case, but then it came on, relentlessly. He set his jaws and compressed his lips in a tight line; there was no help for it, then, he'd have to kill the beast.

He saw dust puff up as the big, heavy slug struck the animal's body, some eight inches below the left shoulder. To his way of thinking, that should have been a true heart-shot ... but the Teeth and Legs obviously did not know it, for it just kept coming, gnashing its fearsome fangs, the cuspids looking to be big as a tiger's. So he worked the carbine's action, aimed and fired again at the same spot ... and with no better results. It now was only twenty-five yards away, if that.

"What the hell does it take to kill you, you bastard?" Fitz cried.

ROBERT ADAMS

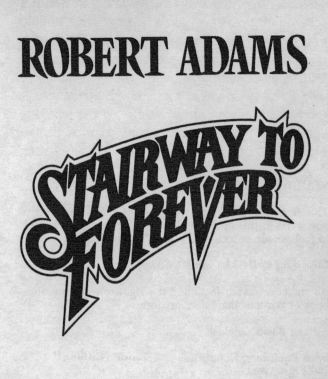

STAIRWAY TO FOREVER

BAEN
BOOKS

STAIRWAY TO FOREVER

This is a work of fiction. All the characters and events portrayed in this book are fictional, and any resemblance to real people or incidents is purely coincidental.

A Baen Books Original

Baen Publishing Enterprises
260 Fifth Avenue
New York, N.Y. 10001

First printing, September 1988

ISBN: 0-671-65434-9

Cover art by K.W. Kelly

Printed in the United States of America

Distributed by
SIMON & SCHUSTER
1230 Avenue of the Americas
New York, N.Y. 10020

PROLOGUE

Charity Mathews thought from the very beginning that it was a big mistake to give her eldest son, Calvin, a rifle for his twelfth birthday, but as usual her wishes were ridden over roughshod by her rude, crude, coarse and often brutal husband, Yancy. At her hesitant words, the tall, lanky, rawboned man only snorted in derision and popped open yet another beer, half of which he guzzled, prominent Adam's apple working, before he deigned to give her an answer.

"Shitfire, woman, you ain't got you the brains God give a piss ant, you know that? I was out a-huntin' with my own gun when I's eight, ten year old, not just no fuckin' BB gun, neither, like these dumbass city fuckers give they kids. Calvin, he gettin' on towards being a man soon, and it's high time he had him a real gun for to hunt varmints and all with.

"Now I don' wanta hear no more about it. You

1

want suthin to do, you git me another beer. You hear
me, Char'ty?"

Justly fearing her husband's ill-controlled temper
and his big, bony fists, Charity sped to the kitchen to
fetch him back another cold beer. Yancy just didn't
know but the one side of his sons, she thought. Both
Calvin and Bubba behaved themselves around the
father they feared, but otherwise they were about as
well-behaved as wild Indians, constantly in trouble
at school, with the neighbors in the decaying suburb,
and now and again with the sheriff and his deputies.

On the morning after his birthday—the afternoon
of which, Calvin and Bubba and their father had
spent at the county dump shooting at rats, bottles,
cans and anything else that seemed a good target—
Calvin waited until the rural mail carrier came along
in his rusty car. The lanky boy, trailed by his chubby
brother, stepped from behind a stretch of overgrown
privet hedge and leveled the pump rifle at old Mister Bartlett, saying in his nasal twang, "Thishere's a
stickup, Grandpa. Gimme all yore money . . . an' all
yore whiskey, too." Then, both boys sniggered.

But their plan worked only that far. Bartlett did
not cower and beg for his life; instead, he rolled out
of the car much faster than they would have thought
the old drunk could move. His hand clamped the
barrel of the rifle and jerked it away from Calvin so
hard and so fast that his grubby trigger finger was
both strained and barked.

While he worked the action repeatedly, ejecting
all fifteen of the long-rifle cartridges into the mud
and water of the roadside ditch, the letter carrier just
shook his head and muttered.

"Never did think your pa's long suit was brains
and this here just goes for to prove it. Any damn fool
would give a damn proved JD like you a damn .22

rifle to raise hell with is got to be God's gift to all
morons. Ain't you two nitwits ever heard tell what
the Fed'ral Gov'mint does to bastards as robs the
Yew-Ess Mails . . . or tries to, leastways? Won't for
your poor, long-suf'ring ma, I'd stuff you two in the
trunk and drive you over and turn you in to Sher'ff
Vaughan. It ain't bad enough she's got her a husband
like Yancy, but she winds up with a couple brats
who's jailhouse bound if ever any two kids was."

"You gimme my gun back, you old drunk!" demanded Calvin. "I's just a-joshin' you and you know
it, too. And I'm gonna tell my pa what-all you just
said about him and he's gonna stomp the shit outen
you."

"Oh, I'm scared," sneered Bartlett. "Can't you see
me shakin' all over? You tell Yancy any damn thing
you wants to, kid, he knows better'n to mess with
me. I think, though, that maybe I should oughta
phone him up tonight and tell him how you're running around pointing loaded guns at folks and saying
you holding 'em up."

"You gawdamn old fart, you," snapped the fat-
faced Bubba, "you do that and Calvin and me'll slash
the fuckin' tires on yore old rattletrap car like we
done las' year, too!"

Without a word, the man began to field-strip the
rifle, dropping the smaller parts into the puddly
ditch and heaving most of the larger as far as he
could into the weedy, roadside tangles of brush.
When only the barrel remained in his hands, he
jammed it, muzzle-down, with all his strength into
the soft mud.

And he squeezed back under the wheel, he admonished, "I'm gonna tell the sher'ff about all this
here. I'm also gonna have the Postmaster to send a
letter to your pa, 'cause if he don't rein you two

hellions in a mite, he can just start comin' and picking up his mail at the post office, is all. We don't gotta put up with vicious dogs or with vicious little brats like of you two, neither.

"Oh, and you better git the mud outen that barr'l fore you tries to shoot it again, elst it'll backfire and blow your damn head off, you li'l snotnose, and good riddance, I'd say."

CHAPTER I

He did not look his age, the man called Fitz, despite the dark circles under his eyes, the soul-deep sadness in those eyes and his careworn appearance. But just now he felt the full weight of every one of his fifty-five years.

In the last few years, fate had dealt blow after stunning blow to Fitz, and a weaker man would never have retained his sanity under such buffets, so much pain. But black-haired, blue-eyed Alfred Fitzgilbert had been noted since boyhood for both physical strength and strength of character. He was not a big man—only some five feet nine and lacking the massive bone structure that had characterized both parents and all his siblings—and his were not the rolling muscles of the iron-pumping body-builders, but his compact body and flat musculature held power unsuspected by any who had not personally experienced that power or at least witnessed the prodigies it could accomplish.

It had taken both varieties of strength to keep him alive during nearly three and a half years of Pacific Theater combat during World War Two. Although appalled and soul-sickened by the incredible amounts and degrees of slaughter and bloodshed attendant to the seemingly endless campaigns of one amphibious assault after another, Fitz had so proven himself and impressed his superiors with his leadership abilities and survival traits that he had several times over been offered the plum of a regular commission in the United States Marine Corps. And on each occasion, he had courteously but firmly declined, finally leading said superiors to settle by retaining him in a reserve commission when that war ended and Fitz went to college under the GI Bill, married and commenced building a family and a secure, peaceful existence for him and them.

But then, with his son only three years old and the ink still wet on his baccalaureate degree, he and his Marine Corps Reserve unit had found themselves activated, recalled to fight yet another war, this one on a stinking, God-cursed peninsula of the Asian landmass, called Chosen or Korea. By then, Fitz was looking back at his thirtieth birthday and went back across the vast Pacific wearing gold oak leaves, but again his strengths served him well and he survived that war also. At the stalemated conclusion of that one, however, he resigned his reserve commission and plunged into the world of business, not caring to take the chance of staying in the reserves and being force-fed yet a third helping of war in a few more years.

Bearing the cloth-wrapped bundle under his arm

and the rusty spade in his hand, Fitz carefully negotiated the loose, warped boards of the rotting porch, then tightly gripped the flaking iron banister with his free hand as he gingerly descended the crumbling, concrete steps down to the backyard. Once, long, long ago, it surely had been a green, tended lawn; now, there was but a weedy, trash-littered tangle through which the ground squirrels scurried . . . and how Tom had loved to stalk and chase the tiny, striped-brown creatures, although Fitz could never recall that the aged cat had ever actually caught one.

Tom, good old, gentle old Tom. He unconsciously hugged to his side the cold, stiff body enwrapped in the damp, threadbare towel. Tom had not deserved the hard, agonized death of a bullet in the lower belly that had been his lot. Somehow, despite his obscene pain, the cat had made it home, made it as far as the lowest step of the front stoop and, when Fitz found him, had been still warm, his green eyes only starting to glaze over.

But, warm body or not, Fitz knew death when he saw it, knew full well that there by then was nothing that the vet five miles away could do for the cat. He had backtracked the trail of blood and bloody feces, then searched in ever-widening circles around the beginning of that trail until he had found two shiny brass rimfire cases, caliber .22 long rifle.

He then had known almost for certain fact just who had murdered the inoffensive cat. The same cruel, bloodthirsty young brat who had to date shot at least three pet dogs, an inflatable wading pool, a succession of automobile and truck tires and the windshield of a rusty Volkswagen bug. Why any parent would give such a child a firearm to begin with was beyond Fitz's comprehension, and why said child had been left in possession of so lethal a weapon after all his misdeeds was beyond any semblance of rationality.

Pocketing the two cases, he had considered bearding the perpetrator and his parents in their nearby home, but had instead remembered Tom and his duty to the husk of the animal that had for so long been pet, friend and sole companion. Back in the decaying, rented bungalow, he had first laved off the mess of blood and serum and dung and urine from the furry body, then arranged and bound it so that it would stiffen in the feline posture of sleep, with feet tucked under and tail curled around. Weeping copious and completely unashamed tears, he had sought out the very best of his bath towels and carefully wrapped the body in it, then searched the spider-infested crawl space under the bungalow until he had found the spade he recalled seeing there.

But then, he had had to stop everything long enough for a drink, a half-water glass of the smooth, brownish-amber John Jameson's Irish Whiskey. His father had died of complications resulting from near-lifelong alcoholism, and two of his younger brothers and one younger sister were clearly headed toward that same end, so Fitz normally strictly limited his intake of the "creature," which was what his mother had called spirits of any kind. But he felt this drink and the one that quickly followed it to be, if ever a drink was such a thing, medicinal.

For poor Tom had constituted his last remaining tie with all the joy that once had been—with Janet and Kath and young Fitz, with success and fulfillment and a happy, comfortable life—all gone now, gone forever, irrevocably. And here, thanks to a savage, sadistic boy, Tom was gone, too.

Beyond the initial ten or fifteen yards of weeds

and rubbish, the backyard sloped abruptly upward to level off again some two feet higher than the rest of the property. The miniature plateau thus formed was roughly circular and sported not just weeds but a few scraggly bushes. It was beneath the centermost of these neglected shrubs that Tom had most often been found snoozing and that was where Fitz had decided to bury his dead companion, last member of his death-sundered family.

As he walked slowly up the slope to the site of the unpleasant task that he must perform, Fitz wondered for the umpteenth time just when and why and how the low mound had originated. The agent who had first shown, then rented him the ill-kempt, twenty-five-year-old tract house had scratched at the sparse growth of hair under his straw planter's hat, shrugged and grunted, "Hell, Mister Fitzgilbert, I dunno. Prob'ly it was a layout for crowket or suthin', one time."

But Fitz had even then doubted the verity of that sad excuse for an answer and he thought even less of it, now, after having lived on the place for two-plus years. For one thing, the flat, circular top was too small for such a purpose. Besides, considering the amount of labor involved in raising such a mound, a man would have had to have been absolutely 'round the bend to do so much simply for the occasional game of croquet.

Jefferson Bartlett, the letter carrier, had lived in the general area all his life, save for twenty years in the Army, since long before the former Dineen estate—of which this had been a part—was sold and subdivided and built upon in the late nineteen-forties. While sharing a tall iced tea and several short John Jamesons during the course of his rounds in Fitz's first summer of renting the decrepit house, the wiry little man had waxed most voluble with the latest in a long succession of tenants of the property.

"Thet ol' Mistuh Dineen, he won't from 'round here, you know. He's from England, I think. Leastways, he talked that funny, stilty kinda English what them folks all talks. He showed up away 'fore I's borned, o'course, musta been back in the 'eighties or 'nineties, but my paw, he tol' me all 'bout it.

"But it won't Mistuh Dineen what built thet mound, it's on some the ol' county maps from clear back to the sixteen hunnerds. I recollec', some fellers come down here from the University, during the Depression, that was, back in the thirties. They aimed to dig inta it, but ol' Mistuh Dineen he sent 'em both packin'. Dint give no reasons or nuthin', just tolt 'em to git off of his land or he'd have the sher'ff put 'em off.

"I heered them two fellers a-talkin' down to Bates's Store 'fore they got set for to drive their Model A back to the University. In between a cussin' ol' Mistuh Dineen and all, they allowed as how the mound had to be a Injun mound and the onliest one ever heered tell of in this part the country, too. Anybody could of told both them fellers was just a-itchin' for to get inta that mound and mebbe make a name for theyselfs and their university, too. But they fin'ly drove off and they never come back, neither."

"What became of Mister Dineen?" asked Fitz. "Did he die here?"

With an experienced flick of the wrist, the carrier threw down the two fingers of straight whiskey, then shook his head. "Nossir, don't nobody I ever talked to know just what did happen to the ol' genulman. I won't here, see; I jined up in thirty-seven, see. But seems like he was just gone one day when his ser-

vants went to wake him for his breakfast. The Sher'ff
and all, they looked all over the place for Mistuh
Dineen, but they never found hide nor hair of him.
Not only that, but they never could find no relatives
as could prove they was, so after 'bout ten years, the
state just auctshunned the place off for taxes and all
and some bunch of damn yankees bought it and
started puttin' up these here crummy little half-asted
houses on it.

"Why, yessuh, Mistuh Fitzgilbert, thank you
kindly." Bartlett had swabbed at his sweat-running
face with a faded, already-soggy bandana, while Fitz
refilled his whiskey glass. "Y'know, lotsa folks thinks
whiskey's no good in hot weathuh, but really ain't
nuthin' better, cause whiskey makes a body to sweat,
y'know, and the more you sweats, the cooler you
gets from the 'vaporation. Eny sawbones'll tell you
that."

Of course, the argument that Bartlett used for
non-abstinence in winter was that whiskey possessed
sovereign warming properties. Fitz had discovered
over a period of time that the letter carrier never
commenced his route but that a full half-gallon bottle
of bourbon reposed within easy reach on the floor-
boards of his asthmatic, rusty ranch wagon. And
Deputy Hagen attested that many was the time he
had chanced across that ranch wagon, engine still running, at the end of the mail run, with Bartlett "resting his eyes" in the driver's seat, the empty glass jug
tenderly cradled in his arms.

But Fitz would not, could not, force himself behind the wheel of a car otherwise than stone cold
sober. That was because of Janet . . . and Kath.
Indeed, he still frequently awoke from sleep in a
cold sweat, tears streaming down his cheeks, gasping

out wrenching sobs, at the terrible, unbearable memories of what he had seen that horrible night.

Choosing his spot for the feline's grave, he laid the cloth bundle to one side, spat on his hands and began to ply the spade, portions of it flaking away with each shovelful of dirt, while the warped, crooked handle wobbled loose in the socket.

It had not any of it been poor Janet's fault, not really, he mused darkly while deepening and widening the hole in the rich black soil of the mound. She just had never been a truly strong woman—a sweet and a loving wife, a faithful and a devoted mother, yes, but never really strong. The tragic loss of their only son, young Fitz, had started it, begun the disintegration of Janet, Kath, his life and everything he had once held dear.

"*. . . regrets to inform you that your son, Lance Corporal Alfred O'Brien Fitzgilbert III . . . died this day of wounds sustained through enemy action, while in the service of his country . . . the Commandant deeply and sincerely . . .*"

That, alone, would have been bad enough. But even more shattering to poor Janet had been that her son's bright, cheery letters had kept trickling in—one or two at a time—for long weeks after she had known that he was dead, that none of the plans he detailed in those letters could ever now come to fruition. The drinking had started during those torturous weeks.

At first, it was only Fitz and Kath who noticed the sharp increase in the wife and mother's consumption of alcohol, and that only because of her genetic predilection to alcoholism—not only was she of pure Irish stock, but both of her parents had died young of drink and her older brother was already become a sodden, divorced wreck of a man.

But both her husband and their surviving child had deluded themselves into the belief that the situation was only a temporary one, engendered entirely by the grief that they all shared, and that Janet would snap out of it when once she had finally adjusted to the facts and learned to live with them, soberly.

Such as the father and daughter fantasized just possibly might have occurred in fact, but ever-capricious and cruel fate had deemed otherwise, in this sad case. The agony had dragged on and on, rather than ending quickly and decently. It had been more than six weeks before the metal casket had arrived from Southeast Asia, accompanied by a young-old gunnery sergeant, bearing a manila file folder.

Sergeant Heilbrunn had been polite, but formal and taciturn, until Fitz had given him a brief rendition of his own service with the Corps. Then the young man had unwound a bit and accepted the proffered drink. No, he had not known the deceased, they had not even served in the same regiment. Heilbrunn had just been a warm body snagged on his way through headquarters after having been discharged to duty from a hospital. As he began to steel himself for the coming ordeals of wake, funeral mass and interment, Fitz thought that such impersonality was not a hallmark of the Corps in which he had served so long ago.

He had just about psyched himself up sufficiently to take it all, himself, and to provide strength for his wife and daughter, as well . . . then the mortician, Alexander Flodden, telephoned.

"Fitz? Fitz, I know you were coming down here this afternoon . . . don't."

Through clenched teeth, Fitz had replied, "Look,

Alex, I served in the Fifth Marines for the best part of three years in the Pacific, then served two more years in Korea, and I've seen . . . seen . . . Well, anyway, I'm not going to throw up or faint or anything on you is what I mean.

"Okay, he was my son, my only son, and it'll be rough, but hell, Alex, somebody has to . . . to identify the . . . him. And God knows, poor Janet and little Kath aren't either of them up to it, not now, not yet."

Flodden sighed deeply. "That's just it, Fitz, this body here is *not* your son's body. Somebody has fouled up, somewhere along the line."

"Well . . . well, of course it's my Fitz!" Fitz Senior had expostulated. "It's got to be! That Gunny, Heilbrunn, has the files and all."

"Yes, yes, Fitz," Flodden quickly interjected. "I've seen the paperwork, it's accurate, complete, but it's just that they sent the wrong body with those papers, Fitz."

Fitz had screwed his eyes tightly shut, shaking from head to foot, cold sweat oozing from his pores. If Flodden was right . . . ? If this damned, bloody, torturous business was to drag on still longer, could Janet take it without cracking completely and/or crawling so far into the bottle that she could never get out of it alive? Kath, too, was beginning to crumble a bit around the edges. And he, himself . . . ?

"But, Alex, you never saw that much of Fitz as he was growing up, so do you think you remember his face well enough to . . . ?"

Once more, the mortician interrupted in his calm, sad voice. "Ah, Fitz, ah . . . this body has very little, ah, face left to it. I, for one, would hate to have the task before me of having to restore it for an open casket . . ."

"Then, damn it," Fitz had shouted into the telephone mouthpiece, his eyes still tight-closed, but now with tears compounded of grief and frustration and fear for his wife and daughter oozing from beneath the lids to trickle down his cheeks, "just how in hell can you assume it's not my boy?"

Sensing the undertones of incipient hysteria, Flodden's voice became instantly, professionally soothing. "Fitz, my friend, it disturbs me deeply to have to add to your grief this way, please believe me. But this body is clearly not that of your brave, departed son, and there is no question about it. Fitz, this body is that of a negro—a very dark-skinned negro."

More than three months after the initial notification of his demise, the remains of Lance Corporal Fitzgilbert, Alfred O'B. III, USMC, really came home. But by that time, his father's worst fears for his mother's emotional balance had been realized in full.

Fitz had just lived with Janet and the endless problem she was become. Kath did too . . . for a while; but when the girl had had enough, she left home and, try as he might and felt he should, Fitz could in no way fault her decision, for Janet, when she was not comatose, was becoming more and more disgusting and unbearable with each passing day.

The Janet he had married after World War Two had kept an immaculate house, had been an accomplished and innovative cook and had been possessed of high standards of personal cleanliness and appearance. This new Janet, however, went long periods without bothering to either bathe or change her clothing, and the house about which she staggered in her filthy, slept-in clothes was become as unkempt and slovenly as was she, herself, acrawl with flies and roaches. Now, those few meals that Fitz took at his home were of his own preparation—mostly TV dinners, cold sandwiches or canned beans or soups.

Cursing himself for a coward, the time, he actually sought the out-of-town travels that once had been something he had accepted only when there had been no one else of his qualifications to send. But he always made arrangements before such trips for one of the sympathetic neighbors to place food outside for Tom—that and keep the back door water dish filled.

At last, when matters had progressed far beyond the beyonds, he closed Janet's checking account and signed the necessary papers to deny her any access to his own. He took every one of her credit cards from her wallet, then paid off and closed every account. When next he came into the one-time home, she railed long and obscenely at him, spat out profane crudities that he had never in all their twenty-odd years of marriage suspected she knew.

Then, a piece at a time, the sterling silver began to disappear. When he had cleared out or locked up everything of intrinsic value in the house, Janet began to steal.

It was only after he had had to leave in the midst of a very important conference to fetch Janet—a sober, very shaky and sobbingly sorry Janet—from the city police lockup, wherein she had been immured for some hours after being apprehended and booked, caught in the act of shoplifting table wine from a supermarket, that he and Father Dan Padway had been able to convince her to enter a "rest home." He had had to dip deeply into their savings to finance the steep costs of her care and treatment, but he had felt the money well-spent when she had at length emerged so very much the old, much-loved Janet.

The matted grass, weeds and woody roots of the bushes had made the digging slow with nothing but the dull, rusty spade, but nonetheless, Fitz felt that the grave was almost wide and deep enough when he struck a much harder obstruction—stone, from the way the spade rang upon it. Sighing, he tried gently pushing the edge of the tool down in first one place, then another, endeavoring to get under the rock and lever it up, out of his way.

Janet had stayed dry for almost a year, faithfully attending her AA meetings, being counselled by Father Dan, as well as by a psychiatrist recommended by the priest and by the staff of the rest home that had done the job of drying her out. They had given her back her lost dignity, too: the house was once more become a well-tended home for her and Fitz and Tom. Fitz had begun to breathe almost easily once more and was considering the best ways of finding his absent daughter.

But then, of a day, Kath appeared on the doorstep. Painfully thin she was, with sallow skin and permanently dark circles under her unnaturally bright eyes. Her once-golden hair now hung dull and matted and lifeless over the shoulders of her too-big man's shirt. The shirt and her torn jeans were crusted with layers of filth and her cheap, ankle-high boots lacked more than a trace of what had been heels and soles. There were open sores on her face and neck, her hands were broken-nailed and grubby and a nauseating stench hung about her. The girl was—although it would be a while before they were confronted with all the unpalatable facts—suffering from the combined effects of malnutrition, drug addiction, two venereal diseases and enteritis. She also was by then three months pregnant and had not even the foggiest notion as to who might have fathered her bastard.

At some time during those first weeks of discovery atop painful discovery—none of them helped by the fact that Kath had allowed her health insurance to lapse and so every one of the multitudinous medical expenses had had to come out of Fitz's shrinking financial cushion—concerning the returned wreck of their only surviving child, Janet had crawled back into the bottle for good and all. And Kath, when once she had ingested everything in the house that even looked as if it might have been a drug, joined her mother in the bottle.

Fitz had then tried to lose himself in his job, coming to the house that had once been his home as little as possible, and then only to collect the mail and feed Tom. Otherwise, he lived out of his car, staying out of town as much as he could and, when unavoidably in town, sleeping on the couch in his office and washing in the small sink of his half-bath there.

Each and every necessary visit to the house left him sadder and more haggard. None of the neighbors any longer even spoke to him as he made his way through the knee-high grass from the driveway to the front door. Unless one or both lay comatose, Janet and Kath would be screaming filth at each other, usually ignoring him except to demand money.

Upon entering, he had to gulp and breathe as shallowly as possible. The house stank, the air thick with a miasma of dirt, stale booze, rotting food, long-unwashed female flesh, excrement, urine and vomitus. The mail was always strewn the length and width of the tiles foyer, lying just as it had fallen through the door slot and been then scattered by heedless, stumbling feet. When he had stuffed it all into his briefcase, he went directly to the kitchen, now become roach paradise, where bowls and plates of unidentifiable food substances sat on the floor and on every other surface, covered with mold or alive with white, writhing maggots.

In the beginning, he had at least tried. He had scraped and bagged and canned the garbage and trash, washed the dishes enough to run them through the dishwasher, mopped the floor and scrubbed the counter tops. But in the end he gave up, just as he had given up on Janet and Kath and trying to live any sort of life in close proximity to the two of them.

From his briefcase, he would take two large cans of cat food and a one-pound box of cat kibble. He had given over leaving canned cat food at the house after he had come back to find the opened cans here and there throughout the place, the spoons still in them, like as not, clearly eaten by one of the two women after the food money had all been spent for drugs or alcohol.

Then he would go through the screened porch and down the back steps to heap the contents of both cans into Tom's licked-clean plate. He would rinse out and refill the feline's water dish, then empty the box of kibble into the weatherproof gravity feeder. After sitting for a while beneath the trees and giving the loving cat the human affection that he craved, Fitz would steel himself for another pass through the fetid house, retrieve his briefcase, get back in his car and go back to work, hating himself for having given up on his wife and daughter, but fearing for his own emotional equilibrium should he try to do other.

"Maybe," Fitz mused as he dug, widening the hole in the mound top, vainly trying to find an edge to the flat-topped stone, which looked to have the smooth regularity of worked stone, "maybe Janet's death was not really accidental. Maybe, deep down inside her, she really wanted to die. But maybe not, too. At least the Janet I knew and loved and lived with for all those years, the good years, would have never—no matter how personally suicidal she'd become—have taken her own daughter and unborn grandchild with her into death."

At last, the entire slab of stone was cleared of its covering of earth and roots and smaller pebbles and Fitz softly whistled to himself at the size of the thing. No wonder his prying spade had accomplished nothing on the first couple of stretches of edge he had found. The flat, rectangular stone was a good five feet long, nearly three feet in width and just how thick was anybody's guess. Yes, it was most definitely made work, not natural, though the master craftsman who had cut and shaped it had done it with such expertise that the fading afternoon light showed not even a single faint tool-mark on it—on it or on the stone-block framing around it.

He felt, after so much expended effort, that he had to give one more try to moving the stone before he dug a grave for Tom in another location. He jammed the jagged point of the spade straight down into the interstice between one of the shorter edges and the framing and gingerly levered, not wishing to snap either the oxidized metal or the loose handle.

Slowly . . . ever so slowly, and with a grating of stone upon stone that set his teeth edge to edge, bristled his nape hairs and raised gooseflesh on his arms and legs, the closest edge of the slab rose an inch or two, while the farther end sank an equal distance. When he had raised it still more and so wedged the spade that, hopefully, the weighty slab of stone could not slam back down on his hands, he worked his fingers down beneath the stone and crouched to put his back and his leg muscles behind the imminent effort.

But, when open it did, the massive slab came up so easily and so suddenly that Fitz almost lost his balance and pitched, face-foremost, down the flight of steep stone stairs that led down into earthy-smelling blackness.

"Now, what in God's name . . .?"

Although apparently never mortared, the stonework that he could easily see was all so smoothly and finely finished and set that he doubted he could have inserted the blade of a penknife between any of them. Seventeenth century or not, surely this construction was not, could not be the work of American Indians.

Colonial, maybe? A root cellar? Or could it be some long-lost and always secret fabrication of that enigmatic, missing Englishman, Mister Dineen? Was this why he had so promptly chased those anthropological or archaeological types off his land? Well, only one way to find out what lay down there in the darkness, and that was to go look.

Upon his return from the house, Fitz had fortified himself with some two ounces of John Jameson and he came equipped with flashlight, the old, well-worn revolver from his tackle box—thinking that such a subterranean haunt would be perfect for snakes—a length of rope, a hatchet and a piece of lumber he had quickly and roughly pointed with the dull, rusted tool. When he had driven the stake into the ground with the back of the spade, he tied one end of the rope to it, looped the rope around the now-upright slab of stone tightly, then tied it off. It would not do to have the thing suddenly close, trapping him underground, possibly.

After clipping the angle-head flashlight to his belt, Fitz cautiously commenced his descent, bracing himself with a hand on each of the cold, slimy stone walls. He quickly became glad that he had thought to don his sure-grip, canvas-and-rubber tennis shoes, for the steps not only were damp and slippery as the walls, but the treads of them were far too shallow for even his size-nine feet, appearing to have been wrought for feet no larger than those of children . . . and small children, at that.

When the bright beam of light shining from his midriff showed a flat, wetly glistening wall just ahead, he at first thought that he had come to the bottom of the underground structure, but when he reached that point, he realized that he stood on a tiny landing, with the stairs continuing downward to his right.

Fitz now doubted even Colonial construction, for no hard-working Colonial farmer would have exerted the stupendous amount of labor that had gone into making so deep an excavation—all by hand, too, in those days—plus the quarrying of the stones, transporting them here from wherever, and building this . . . whatever it was or had been.

After yet another landing and right-angle turn that sent him in the opposite direction from that at which he had set out, above, Fitz at last reached bottom. Bottom, he quickly discovered, was but a bare, stone-walled, -floored, and -ceilinged chamber. It was rectangular, some six feet high throughout and eight or nine feet long, by perhaps four feet or less in width, with the stairs debouching at the end of one of the longer sides.

The chamber was fashioned of the same fine, smooth, unmortared stonework as the rest of the edifice and it lay completely empty of anything. Recalling how the entry slab, aboveground, had pivoted, Fitz inched along the walls of the chamber, exerting pressure here and there along the edges of the stones, to no slightest avail. Finally, he gave it up. After all, it was getting on toward dark, aboveground, and he still had to bury poor old Tom.

He had ascended but three of the steps, however, when some impulse impelled him to half turn and once more sweep the light over the length of the patently empty stone chamber. At least, that had been what he meant to do. But balanced with one too-large foot on each of two of the shallow, steep and slimy steps, he lost his precarious balance as he turned about and, his arms flailing, pitched face-first toward the hard, granite stones before him!

His body tensed against the pain that was sure to be imminently inflicted upon his flesh and bone, his eyes tight-shut to hopefully protect them, Fitz instead felt his body land jarringly enough, but on a flat, *warm and relatively soft* surface. Gasping, he opened his eyes to see, bare millimeters from his face, what looked like nothing so much as sand—sand that his nostrils told him strongly emitted the clean, salt tang of the sea.

"Oh, Christ!" He relaxed his arms and sank back down to lie supine, certain now that he was hallucinating as a result of a head injury and that his broken body actually still lay crumpled against the wall of that empty stone room at the foot of those treacherous stairs. He wondered if anyone would find him before he died of exposure or thirst or shock.

"Damn, my legs are cold," he groaned to himself.

"Oh, my God, don't tell me I've broken my *back*? If I have, I hope I do die before anybody finds me!"

He would much prefer to die here, like this, alone, unseen and unheard, unshriven, even, than to be seriously injured, as little Kath had been in the terrible automobile accident that had claimed her mother's life. For all that the medical people had at last admitted to him that the girl's brain was irrevocably dead, still had they kept her mindless, wasted body there for long months, kept alive—if such could be dignified by that term—only by bottles and tubes and machines. And all the while, the horrendous costs of these doctors and bottles and tubes and machines had been taking away from Fitz every cent and possession he had acquired in thirty years. He thought as he lay there that a relatively quick, so-far painless death would be far preferable than to be subjected to such a perverse atrocity of medical science.

When the greedy doctors and the even greedier hospital had taken and absorbed the last of Fitz's medical insurance and Janet's life insurance, the house, the furniture and every valuable personal possession, the savings account in toto, the cash value of Fitz's own life insurance policies and the last sums he could borrow from the company credit union, he had gone to visit Kath, late one night and very drunk. After sitting for he never knew just how long, listening and watching while the liquids dripped from the bottles into the tubes and the hellish machines rhythmically did their unnatural tasks of giving a semblance of life to a corpse, he had arisen, wedged the door shut and given his daughter the last gift he could give her—a quick and decent death, letting her long-tortured body join her brain.

Because his personal car had been almost new and an appropriately expensive model, sale of it had brought him just about enough money to pay the lawyer whose expertise had gotten him free of all the many charges that had been filed against him. He had been adjudged not guilty by reason of temporary insanity. But that same judgment had also cost him his job, his twenty-four years of long and faithful work for the firm notwithstanding. Not fired, of course; just retired on medical disability, complete with testimonial dinner, gold watch and pension.

However, with the credit union deducting a hefty chunk of the pension each month, it had been necessary for Fitz to find another job, not an easy task for a fifty-three-year-old sales executive, he quickly discovered, especially for one just publicly tried for the highly publicized murder of his own daughter.

Employment in his old line was completely out of the question. None of his former competitors—some of whom had been endeavoring to lure him into their operations for years—would now even consider him for any position and they were quite blunt about refusing. Even the mercenary, bloodsucking placement agencies had been most cool toward him, when once they had found out just who he was. At last, in his financial desperation, he had applied to and been accepted by a door-to-door vacuum cleaner sales outfit, but on a straight-commission basis, of course.

Once he had secured a job of sorts, he had borrowed enough at an exorbitant rate of interest from a small loan company to pay two months' rent and a security deposit on the bungalow and to make a down payment on an aged coupe. He had now been selling vacuum cleaners for above two years. It was hard work and not a very dignified form of selling, but then Fitz had always been a superlative sales-

man, possessed of an intuitive ability to sense just
the proper approaches and closes in a given situation, so he was earning a fair income. But a cripple
would be unable to do the job, he knew, no matter
how good a salesman, yet another good reason to
wish for quick death now.

Something warm and wet plopped down upon his
raised cheek. His exploring fingers encountered a
thick, viscous substance and brought it to where his
eyes could see it.

"*Gaaagh!*" Hastily, he drew his fouled fingers
through the warm sand, then fumbled his bandanna
from around his neck to clean his face of what looked
like and distinctly smelled like fishy-stinking bird
lime. He looked up when his ears registered an avian
scream. There, wheeling in a blue and cloudless sky,
was the probable source of the pale-greenish dung—a
large white seagull. That bird and the stinking mess
now clotting his old, faded bandanna were, if truly
hallucinatory, the most thoroughly vivid hallucinations of which he had ever heard.

Deciding, finally, to get it over with, face facts and
see if he could determine just how serious were his
injuries, Fitz first examined his face and head, finding no single lump, bump, broken skin or even mild
pain . . . except in his hands. Scrutiny of them re-
vealed blisters on each palm, apparently broken by
contact with the abrasive sand and now stinging with
the salty sweat from his face.

But his feet and legs still felt cold. Without yet
trying to roll over and thus possibly compound any
spinal injury, he gingerly moved his legs and feet.
They felt to be moving normally, with no dearth of
sensation, though they still felt cold. So he rolled
over very slowly and . . .

His legs and feet were gone! They ended cleanly at

mid-thigh, as if they had both been thrust through roundish holes in a sheet of plywood. Beyond, where his reeling senses told him that his legs and feet should be, lay only undisturbed sand and a bleached, almost-buried log.

Suddenly, his entire body was gone cold—cold and clammy and bathed in icy sweat, while his nape hairs prickled erect. His wide, incredulous gaze fixed upon that space, that preternaturally empty space, which should have contained the feet and legs of Alfred O'Brien Fitzgilbert II, he brought up his shaking right hand to solemnly sign himself, mumbling the while half-forgotten childhood prayers.

"Oh, Holy Mother of God," he at last stuttered, "Wh . . . what's hap . . . happened to m . . . me?"

CHAPTER II

Fitz felt that he must have half-lain there for a very long time, his trembling body resting on his elbows, his confused mind roiling with half-formed thoughts and speculations. At last, mentally shaking himself out of his funk, he used one unseen foot to pry the shoe, then the sock from off the other. When he applied the bared skin to the surface beneath it, it felt like nothing so much as the cold, slimy stonework of the underground room.

Slowly, carefully, a little hesitantly, he slid through the sand on his rump, propelling himself with his fists in order to save wear and tear on his raw palms. He moved in the direction of those vanished but still felt legs and feet and, shortly, his hips too had disappeared from his sight and into limbo. Presently, he found it necessary to flex his legs as his feet seemed to have struck stone.

"Probably the first riser of those damned stairs," he muttered to himself.

Then, with absolutely no sensation of transition from the hot, sunny sand-world to the dank, dark crypt, he was sitting upon the wet stones of the floor, the beam of light from the shattered lens of his flashlight picking out his legs and his two feet—one now bare and one, shod—and the first couple of shallow stairs.

He half-turned to look back whence he had come and gasped. His right arm, beneath the clenched fist of which he still could feel the hot, gritty sand, ended a bit below the elbow as cleanly as had his legs when he had lain in that other place, seeming to be immured within one of the solid-looking, greyish stones of the wall.

"Now, wait just a damned minute!" he exclaimed aloud. "That's *behind* me, God damn it. I shouldn't be able to see it without the flashlight."

Not until he had reached out, secured the now-battered flashlight and switched it off could he recognize the source of the other, dim, diffuse light. The radiance was emitted by the very square of stonework in which he more or less sat. So very dim was it that it quickly became clear to him how he had missed noticing it at all during his earlier exploration of the room; his bright, white flashlight's beam had blinded him to the lesser light source.

Those stones that shone with light were arranged in a rectangle that began a foot or so from the nearest corner of the room. That rectangle was, he estimated roughly, about five feet high and four feet wide, its lowest point at or so close as to not matter to the floor and its highest point some foot below the stones of the ceiling. Only a child or a midget would be able to walk through it upright. Anyone else would have to at least duck his head, himself included, in order to pass through the wall.

"What the hell am I thinking about?" Fitz demanded of himself. "Here I sit, rationally considering how best and easiest to do something that is utterly impossible by every law of physics of which I ever heard. It's all completely impossible; none of it can be happening."

His mind whirled when he consciously tried to reason out the events of the last few minutes, so he resolutely shoved reason onto a back burner, for the nonce.

Now, if he could so easily and effortlessly return to the stone crypt, then why not have a better and longer look at the warm, inviting beach beyond the wall? Nothing to lose by doing so.

When he was once more fully shod, Fitz drew himself backward, into the sun-drenched sandiness again, finding that his legs and his feet came just as easily as did the rest of him. But just before his toes had fully cleared the . . . the . . . the whatever it was, he pulled the scarred flashlight from its place at his belt and jammed it down into the soft sand to mark the invisible portal. Exploring was one thing, he felt; getting lost from his world of normality was another thing, entirely.

He arose as far as his knees and looked about him to discover that he was kneeling in or near the center of a shallow depression. To his left, high dunes marched, one after another in succession, their tops grown with sea-oats, coarse grasses and what looked to be a few stunted shrubs. It was from his right that the surf sounds came, but he could actually see only the slope and low ridge of another dune, so he stood up on his feet.

In slow, gentle, curling-crested swells, white-topped surf broke upon a sloping, sandy beach. Within his vision, dozens of small birds paced on thin, stiltlike legs just beyond the constantly varying reach of the combers, their sharp-pointed, spiky bills dipping now and again to glean sustenance from sand or water. The sea or ocean or whatever it was seemed empty and endless, stretching on to misty distance where it became as one with the blue sky. There were no offshore islands in sight or any ships, only a few, very distant specks which most likely were gulls or other flying birds.

Fitz could not recall having ever in recent years seen a beach so clean. The only objects marring the smooth, natural sweep of the sand were some bright shells and, here and there, some larger and small bits of driftwood and rafts of sunbleached seaweeds —no candy wrappers, empty bottles, used condoms, grease-stained fried-chicken buckets and not one pop-top beer can or discarded, well-used, disposable diaper.

The low breakers proceeded from his left to his right and he recalled that that fact was supposed to tell him something about his geographical location, but just then he could not remember its entire significance.

"First things first," he said to himself and stepped back over to where the flashlight stuck out of the sand hard by the six- or seven-foot length of a thick, bulky, near-buried log of faded, bleached wood. Bending at the waist and resting his hands on his flexed knees, he essayed thrusting his head through the opening his senses could not detect.

Sure enough, while his body was sweating in the hot sun, while the sand crunched beneath the soles of his shoes, his head was suddenly back within the almost-darkness of the stone-walled crypt and his nose was breathing of the cool, damp, earthy-smelling underground air. And from somewhere, far above those stairs, he heard-felt what was either a sonic boom, or old Henderson illegally blasting out stumps with dynamite again.

A sudden brainstorm sent him moving haltingly to one side until his neck and shoulder encountered the clamminess of the buried masonry and then, bracing his left hand against the invisible wall, he extended his left leg backward as far as it would reach and plowed a furrow in the sand with the toe of his shoe. Working back over to his right, he repeated the process. Then, with all of him once more in what he now was thinking of as "the sand world," he squatted before the driftwood log and, using his worn pocket-knife, scribed marks precisely aligned with those furrows in the sand, plus a much larger, centered, "this way" arrow. The flashlight might become deep-buried in blowing or drifting sand or displaced by a high tide, but the huge, heavy log stood, he felt, in far less such danger.

With his way back home now as clearly marked as he could make it, Fitz felt finally safe to further explore this new-found land of his. The beach just stretched away into the far, dim distance and was as empty as the expanse of water, so far as he could determine with his unaided vision, so he turned inland, setting his feet to the incline of the nearest dune. But with the successful ascent and descent of it and the ascent of the next one beyond it, he suffered a return of the cold, prickly, uncomfortable sensation. His way back might not be, he realized, as clearly and enduringly marked as he had at first so rashly assumed.

For below him, in a deep canyon between towering dunes, lay ample proof that the gentle, now-placid sea or ocean could at times assume demonic proportions. Such force as could lift and deposit so far from the high-tide marks a wooden ship that looked to be more than a hundred feet long could displace his flimsy marker-log with consummate ease and hardly an afterthought.

But then he resolutely mastered his quick fears. He rationalized that such as the apparent shipwreck was more than likely the result of a storm or hurricane, and the sky above him just now harbored not so much as the bare wisp of a cloud, so there was almost no chance of any serious blow in the time it might take him to examine the wreck, below, at closer range.

Close up, he found the hulk to be really huge, impressive despite its sad condition. Timbers of its fabric ran from several inches to a full foot and more in thickness. But he was at first hard-put to think of a satisfactory explanation for the regularly spaced holings in the sides of the ship, extending in lines on both port and starboard and almost from one end to the other.

"Cannon?" he thought, aloud.

No, the thicknesses of the decking between the tiers of openings would have been insufficient to bear the weights and recoils of even small cannon. It was not until he had clambered up into the open waist of the hulk that he understood. The cluttered profusion of thick, broken off and splintered shafts told him the story.

"Oars! Of course, it's a galley. No, I think I recall that galleys only had one bank of oars, this one had at least two. What was that old word for a ship with two banks of oars, anyway? Trireme? No, not trireme, that meant three banks of oars. Bireme? That was it, a bireme. This is a bireme, I'm on . . . or, rather, what's left of one.

"But, good God, man, that's plain ridiculous, on the face of it. I mean, I don't think this kind of a ship has been used for a thousand years, anyway; maybe two thousands years. And this close to water, no kind of wood would've lasted that long in any recognizable shape. And even without water and rot, in that length of time wind and sand would've ground it down to nothing but dust. Hell, maybe I am just hallucinating, after all. I . . . *OWWW!*"

The renewed thought of hallucinations speedily departed his mind, for the baulk of sun-bleached timber against which his shin had just made painful contact while he had wandered, musing, was just as solid and real as anything he ever had felt before, in the other world above the stone-walled crypt.

Only the uppermost portions of the wrecked ship appeared to be in any way easily accessible, Fitz soon found. All of the low forecastle and the entire length below the deck on which he was standing seemed to be solidly packed with sand. The splintered stubs of two masts stood up out of that deck, it being the larger of them against which he had barked his shin, so oars and men's strong backs had not then been its only motive power.

At the level on which he stood, he could see that the sterncastle was pierced with two low doorways, each of them plugged with solid-looking, unwarped wooden doors, the wide planks bound and hinged and studded with rust-flaking iron. Once Fitz had, with a shrieking of long-unused metal, shouldered open the left door, he was glad that he had marked the log back there on the beach and brought the flashlight with him. The yawning cavity before him was—especially now, after his lengthy exposure to the bright sunlight, enhanced by the mirror effect of the sand—as pitch black as it could be.

A bit hesitantly, fearful of what horrors the ancient wreck might still hold within its dark, secret places,

Fitz switched on the flashlight and played its beam
about the interior of the low-ceilinged, cramped space,
only to find his fears to be utterly groundless.

Despite the closed door, fine sand had drifted in
over the space of the long years to dust the spartan
furnishings of what looked to have once been sleeping quarters for one or more men. On the top of a
tiny table built into the very fabric of the ship itself
sat a few shallow, earthenware cups and one smaller
one, of verdigrised copper; a stack of plain, uneven
earthenware bowls; and a big, rusty knife, half out of
a rusty sheet-metal case, with a throat and chape of
greened bronze or brass.

Ducking his head, Fitz stepped through the low
doorway into the cabin. He picked up the knife and
drew the full length of the blade—which, overall,
was about the size and heft of the Ka-Bar knife he
had carried in the Corps, so long ago—from out its
sheath. Rusty, it most assuredly was, but both the
lower edge and the first third of the upper edge still
were frighteningly sharp. Deep fullers ran down both
faces of the blade to a wicked point. He hefted the
sizable knife, clearly more weapon than mere tool,
then carefully resheathed it and thrust it under his
belt. Finders, keepers. The small copper cup looked
cute, so he stuck it into a pocket; his rented home
boasted few enough knickknacks.

The door on the port side seemed shut permanently and for good, barring the destructive use of a
wrecking- or crowbar, an axe or a heavy sledge, and
Fitz had all but despaired of budging the contrary
portal until he noted and finally recognized for just
what they were the two badly rusted slide bolts at
top and bottom. But, even then, the pitted, decom-
posed metal did not move in any way easily after so
long in the one place and, before he was done, he

had added to his raw palms, barked shin and bruised shoulders, two sets of skinned knuckles and an assortment of broken fingernails; also, he had dusted off and brought vehemently out some choice words and phrases that he had not used since the Korean War. But at last the stubborn door swung open, gaping wide, and he could view the interior of what seemed an appreciably larger cabin.

Strangely, inexplicably, a sense of *deja vu* swept briefly over him as he ducked to enter the low door, but it was gone almost before it had come. His flashlight beam picked out the furnishings—a low armchair of carven and inlaid wood, a brace of even lower stools, a small octagonal table centered under a large brass lamp coated with verdigris and hung from the ceiling with three equally coated brass chains. A chest or locker was built into the hull side of the cabin and atop it was a shallow trough looking a bit like a dry sink; from the rotted remnants of cloth and felt within it, Fitz assumed that it had once been a bed or bunk.

"And a damned hard bed," he muttered to himself, poking with the chape of the knife scabbard at the moldering strands and pieces of felt and wool. "But, then, nothing I've yet come across on this whole boat seems to have been designed or built with comfort or pleasure in mind—anybody's comfort or pleasure."

Three great, massive hasps of rusty, pitted iron on the front of the chest-dry sink-bed were secured by three equally massive padlocks. The leftmost and the center of these hung stiffly open but, though the rightmost still was locked, the ring-handle of a bronze or brass key jutted from the face of it. It turned very slowly and very, very stiffly under Fitz's fingers and he had to tug and work at the shank for some time before it finally quitted the body of the lock. With all three of the heavy locks on the floor at his feet, he pulled up the hasps and opened the lid of the chest with yet another scream of rusty hinges.

The interior he found to be some five and a half feet long, by about two feet wide and deep, and fitted with a hinged bar that could be swung up to prop open the lid. It contained numerous large and smaller cases of various shapes and constructions. Some were of metal-bound wood, some of tooled, dry-rotting leather; a couple of smaller ones seemed to be wrought of sheet metal, the lack of rust showing that metal to be nonferrous in nature.

The largest chest within was about the size and shape of a GI footlocker, but with a convex lid. An experimental tug at one of its metal handles told Fitz that it either was bolted to the deck beneath, or contained something extremely dense and weighty; also, it was locked with another of those iron padlocks, so he turned his attention to the smaller caskets, for the nonce.

A leather box secured by a pair of strap-and-buckle arrangements caught his eye so he lifted it out and bore it over to the octagonal table where light from the opened door spilled in. But the array of instruments, each fitted into carved openings in a wooden form, were an utter mystery to him. The largest of them did put him somewhat in mind of the ancient predecessor to the modern sextant called an astrolabe—he had once seen one in a museum and had seen others drawn in books—while yet another instrument looked vaguely like a navigators' parallel.

The second case he chose, though much smaller, was infinitely heavier. It seemed to Fitz to be about the size and general shape of a .50 caliber ammunition box, though with a slightly convex lid. But when he had gotten the box upon the table and opened, he could only gasp and gawk, open-mouthed, at so graphic and thoroughly unexpected an explanation for the bulkless dead weight. *Gold!*

After he had sunk, rubber-legged, into the inlaid chair and forced himself into a measure of composure, he dipped his still-trembling hands into the nearly brimful box and found the treasure to all be in coin—some of them rather crudely made specimens, but coin, nonetheless. They seemed to vary in size from tiny things less than half the diameter and thickness of an American dime to pieces as large as or larger than a half-dollar coin, averaging out at about the size of a quarter-dollar or, possibly, a five-cent piece. He guesstimated the total weight at thirty to forty pounds.

Thirty to forty pounds of gold! How many ounces was forty pounds? Let's see . . . sixteen times forty? No, no, precious metals used another scale, ahhh . . . troy weight, they called it, back when I was in school. Okay, twelve times forty is four hundred and eighty. How much is gold selling for, these days? Back during the war it was thirty-five dollars an ounce and some of the more morbid types in the Corps in the Pacific carried around a pair of pliers to take the gold teeth out of the jaws of dead Japs.

But I think it's gone up in price since then. Somewhere between a hundred and a hundred and fifty dollars an ounce, last I heard . . . I think. Good God Almighty damn! There's somewhere between fifty and seventy-five *thousand* dollars sitting here on this old table!

"Sweet Jesus, I thank you," he breathed fervently. "It looks like a bit of the Luck of the Irish has finally come the way of Alfred O'Brien Fitzgilbert II."

* * *

On the following morning, Fitz missed the bi-weekly sales meeting and pep rally for the first time since he had secured the job. He just phoned in that he was sick, pinching his nostrils shut to impart a nasal quality to his voice and forcing a few coughs for emphasis.

That part of his scheme accomplished, Fitz carefully dressed in his shiny-suited "best," coaxed the elderly clunker he now called his car into life, then drove to have the tank filled at the overpriced filling station of Bates' Shopping Center, which offered thirty-day credit accounts to area residents.

Two hours later, in the business section of the city he once had called his home, Fitz opened his old briefcase and laid out upon the counter of a coin dealer he knew from the American Legion and the Veterans of Foreign Wars a bit over a pound of his find in the sand world. Along with it, he spun a deliberately vague tale of a deceased, distant relative and a modest inheritance.

A short, paunchy, balding man, Gus Tolliver was about the age of letter carrier Bartlett, some five or six years Fitz's senior, with thirty years of enlisted army service and three wars behind him. He cursorily examined a brace of the coins picked out at random. All at once he whistled softly, glanced up enigmatically at Fitz, then pulled a thick book from a shelf behind him and began to riffle through it.

When he at last had found the page and article for which he had been looking, he opened a drawer beneath the display case counter and lifted out a jeweller's scale and its bronze weights, a loupe and a steel micrometer, along with a long, wide, thick pad of dense velvet. Thus supplied, he spread out the coins and, without a spoken word, commenced weighing and measuring and scrutinizing each of them with an exceeding care, referring often to the first big book, as well as to others he selected from the same shelf.

The process took some hour or more of time, while Fitz just waited and tried to not fidget and also tried to think up some more plausible tale to spin should Tolliver demand more and more detailed information concerning the genesis of the pieces of gold and his, Fitz's, acquisition of them.

At length, Tolliver shoved the loupe up onto his hairless forehead and slumped back on his high, padded stool, regarding Fitz with a narrow, very guarded expression.

"You got an asking price on these, Fitz? Understand up front, though: I couldn't buy them or sell them, not around here, not in a month of Sundays. No demand, see. But I can be your agent. I got lots of contacts through ANA, see. We can work out a commissions scale."

Fitz shrugged. "Hell, I don't know a price to ask, Gus. I never collected anything like this. What do you think they're worth?"

The bald man cleared his throat noisily. "Welll . . . and this is purely a ballpark figure, mind you: at least fifty thousand dollars, maybe a bit more—maybe even twice that. Hell, I don't really know, Fitz. A Byzantine expert would have to see them before anybody could say for sure. Yes, they're all in damn fine shape . . . maybe too fine a shape for their age. Your uncle or whatever just may've got stuck with a passel of forgeries whenever he bought them, but I don't think so, somehow.

"Now I know a man who could tell us—you and me—for certain sure, both the value and whether or not they're forgeries. We'd have to pay to fly him in and pay his expenses while he's here and . . . maybe even have to cut him in for a little piece of the action, too. But it just might be worth the cost, if you got what I think you got here, Fitz.

"But before we go that far, Fitz, didn't your uncle ever have these appraised, at least for insurance purposes?"

Fitz couldn't answer; he could breathe only with concentrated effort. He was glad that he was seated, for he was suddenly become as weak as the proverbial kitten. For the pound or so of old, crudely minted gold coins, he had expected and hoped to net as much as fifteen hundred dollars, though he would have settled for less . . . for much less. He tried several times to speak, to answer Tolliver, but though his numb lips and tongue moved, not a sound came from his constricted throat.

All that he could think was: *Fifty to a hundred thousand dollars?* Yes, fifty to a hundred thousand dollars for this paltry handful of the coins he had found in that strange world of sand and hot sun. And that leather casket back there in the cabin of that wrecked ship lying among the dunes, then, must still hold the worth of four or five *million* dollars!

Tolliver hopped from his stool and rapidly rounded the counter, a look of deep concern on his wrinkle-creased face. "Fitz? Fitz, boy, you a'right? Fitz, you want some water or somethin'?"

The cost of the crumbling rental house set Fitz back little more than the depressed value of the land on which it sat, moldering. During the next eight weeks, however, a top-flight general contractor and his horde of subcontractors and laborers converted the ramshackle cottage into a small luxury home, complete with every conceivable convenience. The ancient Ford clunker had been retired to a junkyard and the new garage housed a Mercedes 280, a Jeep Wagoneer and a powerful trail bike.

The pantry and the big new deep-freeze now both were well-stocked and Fitz was beginning to gain back some of the weight he had lost in the course of the last few hellish years of suffering and privation. He had quit his job with the vacuum cleaner company; for one reason, he no longer needed the money, for since he had paid off the credit union of his former employer in full, he now was receiving his full pension, not to even mention the thousands of dollars that kept rolling in from the sales of gold coins. But the other reason he had quit was that the time necessary had been cutting deeply into the time he felt that he needed to spend in and further explore the world beyond that underground wall below his backyard. Besides, he was getting not a few odd looks from employers, fellow salesmen and customers alike, as he had gone about selling vacuum cleaners, door to door, while driving a brand-spanking-new Mercedes sedan and dressed in expensive, custom-tailored clothing, all his visible skin surfaces deeply and evenly tanned amid his winter-pale fellow humans.

As for Gus Tolliver, he had to all intents and purposes closed down his shop to the general public, now receiving customers therein only by way of preset appointments. The bulk of his time and energy now was going toward representing Fitz as sole agent in the sales of exceedingly rare, early medieval coins to an ever-widening sphere of avid and generally well-heeled collectors.

As *Anno Domini* 1974 became *Anno Domini* 1975, and the word spread, mail, wires and telephone calls from all over the world poured into the small shop—bids, want-lists and simple inquiries. The twenty-percent commission on all sales to which Fitz had agreed was making a wealthy man of Gus Tolliver, while merely the fact that he now was noted, world wide, as a factor in the sale of a collection of rare coins had guaranteed him a bright future in the field of numismatics.

Because Fitz had been leaving his home less and less frequently, of late, Gus had begun driving out from the city on each Friday night to settle the past week's accounts, have a few drinks and just talk. He and his client had quickly become fast friends during the still-short course of their most-lucrative mutual enterprise. So close were they two now become that Gus and Fitz now held one each of the only three keys to the gate of the twelve-foot-high cyclone fence that now circumscribed the entire property.

Fitz had had the barrier erected—complete with three strands of barbed wire at the top, rigged with tripwires and pressure points and electric eyes which activated bright lights and banshee-loud alarms—after the third time he had returned from the sand world to find that his home had been entered. On the first occasion, he had called the sheriff and it had been that dignitary who had first suggested a good fence and some sophisticated locks.

"Look, Mistuh Fitzgilbert," Gomer Vaughan had said, "you got you a damn fine house in a damn crummy neighborhood. Most the folks 'round here don't even own the crackerboxes they lives in, they just rents, long's they can pay the rent, then my boys has to put them out, like as not. And the way the kind of scum 'round here thinks, they're just natcherly going to resent you and this house and all. They don't none of them have the kind of minds that might stop and think you might of worked your ass off to get whatall you got. Naw, they'll just be as jealous as old Hell 'cause you got it and they don't and prob'ly never will, neither, the most of these deadbeats.

"Folks like you got 'round here is too fuckin' lazy to work for a good life, but they sure ain't none of them I's met yet too lazy for to steal anything what ain't redhot or nailed down solid. So, I tell you, the best thing you can do—aside from setting here twenny-four hours a day with a scattergun on your lap, that is—is to get you a good locksmith or security service comp'ny and get this place hardened up good. Might not be a bad idear to get a tall, strong fence put around the house if not the whole lot, too."

The lanky man had extracted a card from his shirt pocket and given it to Fitz, adding, "Once you gets a written plan and estimate from whoever you get, you call me, there, and I'll come by and tell you whether it's worth a shit, hear? And you have any other break-ins, you call me right away, too."

That first break-in had netted the perpetrator or perpetrators, as close as Fitz could figure: something less than a hundred dollars in bills and change that had been lying around, his fishing rods and tackle and the old, worn .22 caliber revolver that had been his snake gun, some odds and ends of men's jewelry—cuff links, tie bars and tacks, some studs and an old key chain from the 1939 World's Fair, two half gallon containers of ice cream from the deep-freeze, a fifth of John Jameson Irish Whiskey from off the sideboard, two six-packs of German beer and an equal amount of bottled ginger ale.

Upon reading the list, Sheriff Vaughan had nodded. "Most likely kids, Jay Dees. Enybody older wouldn't of took that ice cream and pop and prob'ly not a bunch of cheap jewelry, neither. And I tell you, Mister Fitzgilbert, I bet I knows just which ones 'round here did it, too, not that I could prove

it, prob'ly. But them two boys, they both comes by it
natcherl. Their pa is a damn hillbilly from up in the
mountains. He's a boozing, brawling, hell-raising bastard from the word go and he's woke up more than
one time in my jail with a hangover and a new lump
or two on his damn hard head. Some damn night,
he's gonna either kill somebody or get kilt his own
self and then his pore, long-suffrin wife's gonna be a
whole lot better off. But I'm mighty feared that he's
already done bent them two boys so bad they ain't
never gonna be nothing but trouble all they lives."

But before he could get the fence up or the other
security measures installed, there had been a second
break-in, this one a much more professional job,
according to Sheriff Vaughan. The only thing that
had turned up missing, however, although the entire
house showed clear evidences of a painstakingly thorough search, had been the big, rusty knife Fitz had
found on the wrecked ship during his very first visit
to the sand world. Fitz told the sympathetic lawman
that, although he had not had it appraised, the knife
had been an antique worth roughly a couple of thousand dollars.

The third burglary had occurred, again, while he
was in the sand world, on the very night before the
wire netting was due to be installed on the already
erect and concrete-based steel posts. And since all of
the doors and windows had already been rendered as
secure as money and expertise could make them,
just how the intruders had gotten in was a question
no one could seem to answer. This time, the thorough search had been repeated, but the only object
missing was the small cup of incised copper that Fitz
had picked up on the same day he had acquired the
stolen knife.

But after that third search and theft, with the new

locks and the towering fence in place, the trespassers seemed to have been effectively barred from within his home. However, he considered the fence to be not so much a protection of the house and its contents as a way to bar any would-be interlopers from the sand world, wherein he had yet to see as much as one other human being, or even any recent trace of one. He liked it that way and he meant to keep it just so by any legal means he could employ, buy or utilize.

After two near-accidents on the slippery steps leading down to the crypt, Fitz had bought and erected over the pivoting stone slab an eight-foot by ten-foot wall-tent to keep out the rain; ground water, he knew he could not do much about. Also, the tent gave him above-ground storage and a private place to change into clothing suited to the more rigorous weather after his sojourns in the salubrious climate of the sand world. Not that his immediate neighbors were all that nosy; most of them seemed to be too busy scratching to make ends meet to pay close attention to the private affairs of others.

The wrecked warship—for such he was now certain it had been, since shifting sands had uncovered a massive, bronze-sheathed ram affixed to the prow at just about the waterline—was become a second home to Fitz, one in which he had spent so much time over the past months that he was become as brown as a Polynesian from head to foot. Nor was the ship or the beach nearby any longer the scope of his new-found world.

The trail bike in his new garage was the mate of a pair he had bought. The other he had manhandled down the steep, sharp-angled stairs and, thence, into the sand world. On it, he had travelled far up and down the seemingly endless beach.

He also had journeyed inland to discover that the dunes marched on for miles, to finally peter out onto a rolling plain of sandy soil on which grew coarse grasses, shrubs of various sorts and a few small trees. Beyond this plain, bluish with the haze of distance, lay what looked through the binoculars to be wooded hills.

But nowhere in all his travels had he spied any other sign of man than the long-wrecked ship, unless the small herds of big-headed ponies that grazed the sandy, inland plain were feral rather than just wild. Although obviously frightened of his noisy, smelly bike, he had found that they were not in any way chary of a human and that he could get pretty close to them, if afoot, the herd stallions making threat-displays whenever he overstepped his bounds, but never really attacking him . . . so far.

The biggest of the ponies he had seen to date was about fifteen hands at the withers, but most of them ran much smaller. They all were about the same color—a solid, strawberry roan, with manes, tails and a single broad stripe down the spine of a chocolate-brown. They all were heavy-barrelled, big-headed and -eared, with short, thick legs, but for all their rough, ungainly appearance, they could move very fast when the occasion so demanded.

The stern cabins of the wrecked warship Fitz had gradually cleaned up and converted into a base camp for his ever-wider-ranging explorations. The doors to both the larger and the smaller side cabins he had removed, repaired, planed, varnished, then rehung, weatherstripped and fitted with new, rust-resistant hardware and padlocks. Moreover, in the course of the interior cleaning, he had discovered that the two cabins were connected by yet a third, much larger cabin which might be entered from either and which ran from beam to beam of the stern.

This newest-discovered cabin, in addition to showing clear signs of having served as sleeping quarters for a number of men, also had housed three long, brazen tubes. Each of them was five or six inches in diameter, some six feet long and open at both slightly flared ends. The tubes were securely mounted upon small, wheeled carriages and positioned before shuttered openings let into the stern which looked like nothing so much as gun ports. But the metal of the tubes was simply far too thin for any real resemblance to cannon, nor had Fitz ever read or heard tell of any ancient cannon that was open at both ends.

Immediately after his first overnight visit to the sand world, he had bought and brought down the materials and tools to fashion screens for the three "gun ports" and screen doors for the outer portals, for the sand world, he had discovered to his pain and sorrow, harbored a full complement of huge and voracious mosquitoes, and these had been but the vanguard of a plethora of annoying flying insects, all drawn irresistibly to the white brilliance of his gasoline lanterns.

Despite the fact that he had come to simply accept the sand world, seldom thinking about the many very odd (to say the least!) facets of his discovery of and repeated entries into it, there were some things that he could not ignore. One of these was the peculiar time difference between the world into which he had been born and in which he had lived most of his life and the sand world. He had quickly found that a mere day or so in the sand world meant that he would be gone from the other world for several days and nights.

One result of this anomaly had been that he hardly ever saw his friend Bartlett anymore, since he had felt obliged to arrange with the postmaster to not any longer trouble the carrier with trying to make route delivery of his mail, but rather to drive to the post office, when and as he "got back from his frequent trips" and pick up the mail.

As the aft cabin of the wrecked bireme was wider, longer and higher than either of the other two, Fitz had there established his sand world *pied-a-terre*. With a folding canvas cot, air mattress, light sleeping bag, a chemical toilet and camp stove, in addition to the gas lanterns and the table, chair and stools dragged in from the next-largest cabin, he made it quite a comfortable home away from home.

In the largest of the two side cabins he stored his bike, along with necessary tools and parts, lubricants and gasoline for it and for the stove and lanterns. In the smaller, he stored hardware, weapons and ammunition, canned and freeze-dried foodstuffs, liquor and water. He had as yet to come across any save salty sea water in his extensive explorations of the sand world, though he felt certain that there must be some somewhere, for the ponies and birds must surely drink.

Although he often felt a bit silly lugging carbine, revolver and weighty ammo in this empty country, still a nagging, frequent sensation that he was being watched, observed by some unseen sentience led him to strap on his weapons whenever he set out on any exploratory trip.

He could not tag time or place to the first time he had felt the invisible presence, save that he was sure that it had been at some time after he had begun to actually live, off and on, in the sand world. Not that it was really a new feeling for Fitz to experience; he, along with his siblings and both his parents had all their lives had the ability—often a singularly unpleasant ability—to feel, to sense the presence of noncorporeal entities and influences in buildings and places; therefore, he knew that his sensory awareness of this something as yet unseen was of more merit than merely an active, Celtic imagination playing upon his mind in the loneliness and mystery of the sand world.

No, he *knew*! He knew that some thing—or things?—were out there trailing him, if not somehow pacing him in his journeyings, watching and observing, though careful to remain unseen, never seen, by him. While out in the vast reaches of sand on the bike, he could sometimes almost—but not quite—see a presence atop the next dune—or the one closest to left or to right . . . or on the one just behind him.

True, he could not sense anything threatening or malicious about the presence, this watcher in lonely places, even when he was become terrifyingly aware of occasional nights that the . . . whatever had somehow passed soundlessly through barred doors or bolted gun ports to share with him his very cabin. Nonetheless, he always felt a bit better for the pull of the canvas-webbing sling on his shoulder, the sagging weight of the big-bore revolver at his belt.

CHAPTER III

"*Yes*, by God, yes, I *saw* it . . . but still can't . . . don't believe it, Fitz!" Pale, sweating, tremulous, obviously shaken to the innermost core of his being, Gus Tolliver sat in one of the overstuffed leather chairs in the front room of the refurbished bungalow, clutching the liter stein of dark beer so tightly that the big knuckles stood out whitely from his scarred, liver-spotted hands.

"You can't . . . can't *nobody* just walk th'ough no hard stone walls, Fitz!" he asserted earnestly, but with a finality that was no longer quite assured, bearing a distinct undertone of a plea for reassurance that the impossibilities he had witnessed could not be and, therefore, were not, had never taken place. "Yes, I saw it . . . or thought I saw it. But Fitz, it just couldn't never ever happen, and no matter whatall you say, Sergeant Major Gus Tolliver here sure ain't going to try his own self to do it, too!"

Earlier on this Friday evening, shortly after his arrival on his regular weekly business-and-social visit, Gus had at long last pinned Fitz down on the exact origin of the hoard of golden coins, asking such shrewd, probing questions that Fitz had at last given up prevarication and subterfuge, feeling compelled to level with his friend and finally reveal the source of their wealth.

Out the back door and down the brick steps, he had led the way, a way by now well-lit by floodlights mounted on the eaves and along the high fence. They had crossed the manicured ten yards of lawn, then up the new, short flight of brick steps to the top of the low mound and so into the green canvas wall-tent.

Inside the tent, he had lit the two gas lanterns, hung one from a hook screwed into the ridgepole immediately above the rectangular slab of greyish granite, and then, from out his pocket, taken a key ring and selected the two keys that fitted the two big padlocks that secured a wide, thick strip of mild steel across the slab. After he had raised that slab and cautioned Gus to be very careful of his footing on the steep and shallow treads, he had led the way down to the crypt.

In the stone-walled chamber, Fitz had first set down the lantern and then, with a cheery, "Just follow me, Gus," he had with all the relaxed naturalness that reflected his own long, intimate experience, half-bent at his waist and passed through the portal and into the bright, sunlit and untenanted sand world.

He had stood on the marked driftwood log waiting for Gus, but Gus had never emerged from the unseen doorway that somehow existed in the empty air there. So Fitz had at last stepped back through, into the chamber and had, for a quarter hour or more, tried to persuade his stunned friend to, if not immediately pass through the section of wall, at least thrust an arm or a leg through the seemingly nonexistent opening in the stonework. Once he knew it was really there, Gus would surely follow him through it.

Tolliver, however, had stoutly and most profanely, finally, refused to even attempt the—to his mind—impossible and, when it became more than obvious to Fitz that the balding man's self-control was fast slipping away, that indeed he was teetering upon the edge of real hysteria, he had ushered his friend back up the stone stairs, through the tent and the yard, and so on back into the bungalow to his chair and his beer.

Himself ensconced in a matching chair, facing his guest across the width of a leather-topped, cherrywood table, Fitz had been still trying ever since their return aboveground to convince his shaken pal that the sudden disappearance and equally sudden reappearance had been no sleight-of-hand exercise of stage magic, that it had not been a strange hallucinatory experience, but had really happened. His efforts had been all in vain. He was become convinced that, no matter what he said or did, Tolliver would not, could not, would never allow himself to believe what he had seen that night.

Gus went through his liter in silence and was well into a second one before he again spoke. "Fitz, boy, I . . . I'm sorry. But . . . but I just can't handle things like down there in that place; nothing that weird. You know? Maybe . . . maybe if I's to think on it for a week or a month or so . . .? But look, let's us talk about something else tonight, huh?"

"You had any more prowlers or break-ins here that you knows of, Fitz?"

Fitz took a pull at his stein, wiped the flecks of amber foam from his upper lip with the back of his thumb, and shook his head. "No, Gus, not since I had the place fenced and the house hardened up and put in the lights and alarms and all, I haven't. I guess all that high-priced gadgetry and locks and chain link and barbed wire finally just discouraged the little bastards."

"You still're of the opinion it was just neighborhood kids, huh?" asked Gus.

Fitz shrugged. "Hell, Gus, I'm no detective, you know. Sheriff Vaughan seems to think it was those two hell-raising hillbilly boys from a couple of blocks up the road. He knows crime and his county a hell of a lot better than I do, so who am I to question his reasoned-out suspicions, huh?"

Fitz's blue eyes took on a hard, cold expression. "Besides, it'd really do my soul good to be able to drag that pair of little bastards into a court of law. I'm dead certain it was them who shot my cat Tom last year. Gut-shot him, Gus, and then just left the poor old thing to die of pain and shock and blood loss. So, yeah, I like Sheriff Vaughan's ideas in that regard; I like them a lot."

Gus nodded. "Yeah, I can unnerstand, Fitz. But I tell you, it sure as hell won't no kids what broke into my shop last night, though."

Fitz sat up straight, on hearing that. "Oh, hell, no, Gus! How much did they get?"

Gus just shook his near-bald head slowly, in unrepressed wonderment at what he was about to relate. "Damn it all, Fitz, that's the funny part of it . . . and I ain't the only one thinks so, neither. It was two, three thousand dollars worth of silver—cartwheels, halfs, quarters, dimes, half-dimes, World War II nickels and three-cent pieces, plus a couple dozen Mexican pesos—five peso and ten peso pieces—not to even mention the nickels and the pennies and all in the display cases. Fitz, boy, them cases won't even touched, none of them—the cash register, neither. Now, ain't that something?"

"How about your safe, Gus?" probed Fitz, while mentally picturing the tall, wide, massive ton or more of Victorian steel-laminate, with its once-colorful, now much-faded curlicues of pseudo-baroque decorations, wide, steel wheels and multiplicity of thick doors, set behind set.

"Now that had been opened." Gus grinned, slyly. "The bastards tried hard to make it look like it hadn't been . . . but it had. I knowed that right after come in to open up, this morning—knowed it first thing. But . . . but Fitz, they opened it and then didn't take one damn thing out of it. And there was *gold* in it, too, Fitz."

Fitz felt a cold chill course the length of his spine. "My gold?" he demanded.

Gus chuckled once. "Aw, naw, Fitz, boy, my mamma didn't raise up no stupid chilluns. The safe had a half a dozen Canadian Centennial sets, them an' some low-grade U.S. gold pieces and a few new-minted bullion coins, too. I keeps just enough in it so your average, run-of-the-mill burglar ain't gonna be inclined to take the time to look no further, see.

"Your stuff and all the other really valuable pieces is either in the real safe or elst stowed in my box in the bank vault, 'round the corner, on Ash Street."

With a sigh of relief, Fitz cracked a wide smile. "I never knew, never even suspected that you had more than the one safe in the shop, Gus."

"Heh, heh, heh," chuckled Tolliver. "Damn few

as does know, Fitz. Like I done said, I been around for a while. But *they* knowed it, boy, the bastards as broke into my shop last night, they knowed it, and that's for damn sure! They cut and tore up the holy living hell out of the carpets, all over the damn shop, front and back, trying to find a floor safe . . . which they didn't. Then the fuckers even chopped loose and tore down the wood panelling in my private office, looking for a wall safe, I guess. But they looked in all the wrong places and come up empty, damn motherfuckers. I checked, and the real safe hadn't been touched, much less opened."

"What do the cops have to say about it all, Gus?" inquired Fitz.

Tolliver shrugged, took a short pull at his beer, and answered, "They say it was a perfessional job, of course. But, hell, Fitz, I could of told them that much. Hadn't of been for them sliced-up rugs and tore down panelling and all, the average man wouldn't even of knowed anybody'd been in there. They won't no prints, nowhere, and they still is in the dark—and me, with them, too—about just how the damn cocksuckers got in. It won't no particle of damage to neither one of the doors or the locks on them, the bars is still set in place over the washroom window and the office window's got that big old bulky air-conditioner, you remember, mounted permanent, and not enough room for nobody to get over it, even was they to break out the reinforced glass . . . which they didn't.

"The detective, name of Hurz—and he's a pretty good old boy, I come to find out, too; he pulled him eight years in the Air Police—he don't think it was no locals broke in, he thinks they was prob'ly down from New York or New Jersey or Deetroit or Boston or like that. He was thinking and talking about maybe Mafiosos done it."

Fitz nodded. "Well, honey does attract flies . . . and other vermin. And God knows, if we've managed to attract the full attention of most of the serious coin collectors in the world, as we seen to have done, it just stands to reason we might've attracted the attention of some greedy mobster, too. God forbid! But if we have, you can bet on it that you'll be getting more nocturnal visitors of a similar stripe . . . and possibly diurnal, as well. You could well be in some danger, there in that shop alone, Gus."

Gus nodded. "Yeah, Fitz, that's what Hurz thinks, too. So I called up the A.D.T. folks this morning, while he was still there so he could talk at some other guy over there use to be in the Air Force with him. That outfit's gonna be working night and day, this weekend, 'til they gets my shop *and* my house wired up proper and all. The damn system's gonna be wired every which way from Sunday into their security office and the police station and from the shop into my house, too. It's gonna have the biggest, loud-assest alarms anybody makes, boxes and wires can't nobody get into or cut or nothing, and silent alarm buttons all over the place in both places, even in the crappers and the shower stall.

"I bought me some more guns, too, and put them around in diff'rent places easy to get to when I needs to, see. Loaded for bear, one up the fucking spout on ever one of the fuckers, office and home. It's a pure blessing I don't have no kids around, is all I got to say. My old lady, she's a better shot than a lot of men, too.

"Fitz, you might be smart to get you some more firepower, 'cause if a man didn't care how much of a racket he made, he could put a truck, even a big car, right through your fence or the gate either, you know."

"Oh, no!" Fitz shook his head vehemently and held up both hands, palms toward his friend, as if fending him off. "Oh no, Gus, no more guns for me! Hell, thanks to you, my friend, this place is already more like an arsenal than a home. In addition to all the collector guns you've conned me into buying . . ."

Tolliver looked a trifle hurt. "But Fitz, boy, them's a *investment*, a damn sound one, too."

"Yeah?" remarked Fitz, deliberately sounding skeptical. "If they are such a damned good investment, how come you didn't buy the damn things, huh?"

Gus looked and sounded a little sheepish. "Well . . . well, Fitz, it was this way, see: Sary opined that if I brought even one more old antique gun that you couldn't shoot into the house . . . Well, anyway, Fitz, she's been a dang good wife to me and I tries to keep her happy and all, but . . ."

"But, as I was saying," Fitz interjected, not caring to again hear extolled the many virtues and few but onerous failings of the widow Gus had met and wooed and won soon after his retirement from the army, "plus all those damned muzzle loaders, the Lugers— all nineteen of the things!—some hunting rifles and shotguns I've picked up on my own, the Garand and a twelve-gauge riot gun, I've got two magnum revolvers, two automatic pistols and a Ruger carbine. Oh, and not to forget that damned undernourished howitzer you brought out here two weeks ago, either. Tell me, have *you* ever fired that monstrosity, Gus?

"No? Well, I did . . . just once, on the day after you left it here. Gus, it was Monday night before I could hear normally again. And it was Wednesday before I was dead certain my shoulder and my clavicle were both still intact. You can have that booby trap back, any time, take it home with you tonight."

"Fitz, boy," Tolliver hastily expostulated, "that gun's a *real* collector's item, cased and all like it is. Holland and Holland, what made it, didn't never make no kind of cheap guns, ever. That eight-bore double rifle was custom-made, by hand, and . . ."

"And made on order for an avowed masochist, no doubt," commented Fitz, ruefully, rubbing his right shoulder in painful memory of the elephant gun's punishing recoil.

Gus ignored him and talked on: "I allowed that feller owned it only just about fifteen hundred dollars towards a bezant he was plumb dying to have. Fifteen hundred dollars, Fitz, for the rifle, the tools, the spare parts and everything in a fitted, velvet-lined, solid mahogany case, plus ten rounds of ammo for it! And hell, boy, I give you odds that gun cost that much *new*, way back when. Even the cartridges had to be custom-made for that gun, and just one of the fuckers will stop a bull elephant cold—drop him where he stands."

Fitz smiled. "Well, since I haven't seen any elephants wandering around this neighborhood, not in recent months, anyway, if you can locate a sucker . . . er, a collector, rather, who can be persuaded in any legal way to pay you what you put into that cannon, by all means grab him before his keepers find him and take him back to the State Home for the Bewildered."

Later that night, after Fitz had walked Gus out to his car and was about to go down and unlock the gate, the older man looked up at his friend and host from the driver's seat and spoke in a lowered voice, his brow crinkled, his words tinged with worry and concern.

"Another thing's been bothering me, Fitz. Feller owes me a few favors at the bank tells me there's been a whole lot of folks trying to pry into my accounts lately; yours, too, he says. Some of them, they could just flat out refuse to show the bastards anything . . . but some of the others, they had to show them anything and everything they wanted to see . . . if you gets my drift."

"*Government?*" queried Fitz incredulously. "What the hell about? I, we're not breaking any laws that I know of . . . are we?"

Gus shrugged, his meaty shoulders rising and falling under the fine wool of his coat. "Maybe, maybe not. The way the fucking laws is wrote out, it's a 'heads, they wins; tails, you loses' propersition. If the Guvamint is really out to get you, boy, they'll sure-Lawd find them a way or something to get you on, and you can make book on that, too. And, too, you can figger anytime a little man starts making money in big chunks, the prick-ears of all them I.R.S. boys is gonna perk up like a coon hound what just spotted a ringtail."

"Well, good God, Gus," Fitz burst out, louder than he had really intended, but a little angry at the thought of the intrusion of utter strangers into his personal accounts and affairs, "I've been leaving all the business end of this, the promotion and advertising and sales, to you and you alone, just as we both agreed in the very beginning of it all. You've got a lawyer, a good one, I hear tell. So, what does he say about all this government mess?"

Gus nodded. "I talked to Hamill, and he said exactly whatall I just told you, 'cept he said it better'n me, of course. He said he'd give me, you, too, all the pertection the law allows him to. But he said, too, to make damn sure we didn't have us nothing to hide, that our business was all legal and on the up and up.

"So, how 'bout it, Fitz? Have we . . . you, got something to hide? Something you couldn't tell nobody in a court, under oath?"

Suddenly, he grabbed Fitz's shirt collar and pulled his head down to his own, seated level, locking his eyes in an unwavering gaze with those of his friend.

"Tell me, Fitz! Tell me one more time that that gold ain't hot. Tell me that you come by it all legal and proper. *Tell me, mister!*"

It was not in any way, shape or form a request. The long years of command—in peace and in war, in garrison and in combat—were conveyed in that steely stare, in the suddenly unequivocal tone that demanded an answer—a thoroughly truthful answer.

"Gus," said Fitz, "you have my solemn word of honor that each and every one of the gold coins I've entrusted to you have been a part of the legacy of a man long dead that passed to me and that, so far as I know, my possession of them was and is entirely legal."

Tolliver showed every yellowed tooth in a wide grin then, and unclasped his powerful hands from Fitz's shirt. "That's all I needs to hear, Fitz, boy. Let them sticky-fingered Guvamint mammyjammers pry 'round all they wants to, then, if that's what it takes to help the frigging bastards to get their rocks off!

"G'night, Fitz."

The coin dealer had sounded more than mollified, but Fitz himself slept little and poorly the rest of that night, and on many a succeeding night. His mind churned through the hours of darkness with scores of discomfiting "What ifs?"

Were someone to really pin him down on the

identity and death date of the "uncle" from whom he supposedly had inherited the golden coins, he knew that he would be deep in the shit, for he had had no uncles . . . not so far as he knew, at least.

Although neither his mother or his father ever had even once broached upon the subject, Fitz—who always had differed in so very many ways, both physically and emotionally, from his parents and from all his siblings, as well—had for most of his life felt certain that the man and the woman who had reared him as their own, firstborn son had actually, in truth, been his adoptive parents, had both lived and died hiding that truth from him . . . for whatever reasons.

"Hell!" he muttered, savagely pounding a pillow into a shape hopefully comfortable, then sinking back upon it. "I could have, could conceivably have umpteen zillion uncles and aunts, if only I knew, could ever find a way to find out for sure just who I really am. But I've just got to face it: I started out lying to Gus Tolliver and I have no way of ever proving that falsehood true, now or ever.

"As for trying to back up, at this late date, and tell them all—Gus, his lawyer, those Government types, the folks who've bought pieces of the gold—the real, unvarnished truth . . . ? Nobody, not a one of them, would ever believe it, because, hell, I don't believe it myself, sometimes. So I'd be well advised to start getting myself a bolt hole ready for the day that will certainly come—the day that those eager-beaver, bloodsucking, Government busybodies finally run me to ground, for keeps."

But affairs proceeded very tranquilly for the next six weeks. No more break-ins were attempted or accomplished, either at his house or Gus's or the coin shop, nor did Gus's banker friend report any further government inquiries on his level. However,

Gus took the elementary precaution of moving the bulk of their profits—by now grown to quite a considerable sum—out of the United States of America, informing Fitz well after the fact.

"Switzerland?" asked Fitz.

"Aw, naw." Gus shook his head. "Fellers I talked to said the Swiss ain't too reliable no more, these days. Not for the kind of game we're having to play here, they're not. Naw, Fitz, boy, all the smart money's either going to the West Indies or to South Africa, anymore. We, you and me, got some in both places now, mostly thanks to one of our bestest customers, feller what goes by the name of Piet Bijl . . . though I got some reasons to suspect that's not the name he was christened with . . . if you get my drift."

With a raised eyebrow and a tilted head, Fitz eyed Gus Tolliver as the paunchy old soldier sat and swigged his beer. "Question, Gus: just how many of our local merchants are likely to honor a check drawn against an account in a South African bank, do you think; or a West Indian one even, for that matter?"

The older man grinned expansively, chiding, "Aw, now don't you fret yourself none, Fitz, boy. I made damn sure it was enough left in your account and at least two of mine to handle things day to day here."

But Fitz still frowned, saying hesitantly, "I still don't know. I'm still not sure that I like the idea of having so much of my money so far away. It's not as if we—you and I—were living under some kind of totalitarian dictatorship with confiscatory tax laws and tactics."

Gus lowered his voice to conspiratorial levels and leaned forward in his chair. "Fitz, most folks don't have them no idea just how damn close to broke the Guvamint of the U.S. of A. really is these days. It's a goddamn shame, too, when half or more of the other countries in the whole damn world *owes* the U.S. of A. money they ain't never even made a try at paying back, some the fuckers sincet World War One. And it seems it ain't been one frigging pres'dint or congress we's had is ever had them the guts to get up on they hind legs and get as hardnose with all these furrin deadbeats as they all of the time gets with they own hardworking, taxed to death folks here in the U.S. of A., neither.

"But, enyhow, cain't nobody—individuals or guvamints—keep living on next year's money for too long at time. If you don't b'lieve that, just look at how them dumbasses runs New York City has fucked they selfs up trying to run a fucking welfare state and tax all the businesses to death to give the money to bums that mostly won't even try to work for a living and has got so broke now they can't even pay salaries to the folks he works for them. Naw, Fitz, if you or me or enybody elst tried running their affairs like the Guvamint's been doing, off and on, for the last near-forty years, sincet Roosevelt started it all, we'd be bankrupted and most likely in jail, to boot.

"This here shit they calls 'deficit financing' has done brought a country that was the biggest and bestest and strongest and richest in this whole wide world less then twenny year ago damn near into the fucking poorhouse. So whin them Treasury boys sees a way they can maybe lean down hard on some little feller, who ain't incorporated and wifh a whole damn pisspot full of high-priced lawyers hired on just to keep guys like the I.R.S. off of him, well then, they just gets as hard and horny as a quarn'tined stud bull. Their hot little hands gets to itching and their sticky fingers gets to twitching, and they swallers whole bottles full of nasty pills three times a day, too.

"And whin that time comes for you and me, Fitz— and I got me this here feeling that it's damn close to that time for us!—unless you's made up some way to pertect what's really yours and not really theirs or the frigging Guvamint's to take, all you can do is just lay down and spread your legs whin the legal-robbers tells you to, because eny way you turn, your ass is gonna be grass and the I.R.S. is gonna be the fucking lawn mower, see. If it's enything that crew really hates and despises, Fitz, it's folks that is self-employed and don't work for somebody elst what will take chunks out their pay ever month and send it off to Washin'ton to keep the fat-cat politicians and all the perfessional leeches they calls bewreaucrats stocked up on plenty of French cheese and wine and Russian caviar and all." The coin dealer sounded exceedingly bitter.

He drained off the last of his liter of dark beer and demanded, "You got you a passport, Fitz, a current one?" At a nodded silent answer, he went on, "Well, you keep her on you all the time, hear? What money is left in this country, aside from the penny-ante local funds, I've done got spread out in four diff'rent banks—one in New York, one in Frisco, one in Illinois and one more in Texas—that ought to keep the bloodsuckers busy long enough for you and me to get out and away, when it comes down to that, see. Oh, and keep a suitcase packed up, too. Chances is good that whin you has to move, you gonna have to move some kind of damn fast, for sure."

After Gus had departed for the drive back to the city, Fitz fretted and tossed and turned for some hours on his bed before he finally gave over trying to sleep. He arose, showered, dressed, burdened himself with another weighty, bulky load and made his way into the sand world. In the relatively commodius, rearmost cabin-cum-bedroom-cum-workshop, he spent the next couple of sand world hours in first assembling, then in fitting onto the bigger, more powerful, faster, more rugged and longer-ranging trail bike he had bought and brought in three weeks before, the steel and fiberglass cargo sidecar he had had custommade for it. *Then*, exhausted, he got some sleep.

A half day was required to reach the near edge of the coarse-grassed, sandy-soiled plain. To cross it and continue on inland would necessitate an overnight trip and probably several days, was he to even approach a full exploration of those dark, mysterious, but ever beckoning hills beyond.

He had discovered in a hard, painful way that a full pack, a sleeping bag, air mattress and weapons not only made his bike top-heavy, but dangerously hampered his general agility on it . . . and a broken leg or worse, here in the sand world, could only presage a certain death by way of loss of blood, shock, thirst or all three in a deadly combination.

Not until he had sufficiently mastered the attachment and disattachment procedures to quickly accomplish both blindfolded, on the bike and off, did he finally disassemble the arrangement and stow it all away in the side cabin.

Bone-weary by then, he sacked out on the cot and drifted quickly into sleep, despite a very strong return of that tingly sense of some unseen presence, some something there in the cabin with him, regarding him.

At some time during that night, Fitz thought he awoke and opened his eyes. Silvery moonbeams, slanting down through a break in the high, surrounding dunes, thence through the centermost of the trio of stern openings, made the cabin of the ancient, beached warship almost as bright as would one of the now-extinguished gas lanterns, though the moonlight was softer, easier on the eyes.

The sensation of a warm, once-familiar weight and of a soft, also once-familiar sound brought his wandering, sleepy gaze from the wooden beams that supported the deck above, down to his own supine body as it lay on the folding cot. There, on his chest and abdomen, lay a very large, grey, domestic cat. The cat's broad head rested on his big forepaws, around which paws and his chin was wrapped the last few inches of his thick tail. His notched and somewhat tattered ears were cocked forward and his eyes regarded Fitz's face, returning his startled look with an unwinking, but obviously nonmalignant stare.

"*Tom?*" Fitz thought that he then croaked, aloud. But then he thought that he thought, "But . . . but Tom is *dead*. I know, I buried him.

"Puss . . .? Good puss."

But just how the hell had a cat gotten into the cabin, anyway? A quick, sidelong glance showed him that the wire-mesh screen across the stern ports were all intact and screwed solidly in place. Both of the inner doors were locked and barred, as too were the outer doors and the trapdoor in the ceiling that let onto the quarter-deck, above.

At the sound of his voice, his spoken words, the cat's deep-throated purring became louder and, lifting his head and twitching aside his tail, he extended his left, black-padded forepaw to lightly stroke Fitz's bristly chin, then let the paw just rest on the cleft of the chin, while he slowly extended and retracted the claws in obvious contentment.

And Fitz felt a cold prickling along his spine, felt gooseflesh rising on his forearms. Of all the many cats with whom he had shared his life and his fortunes over the years, only Tom—old, now dead and months-buried Tom—had had that particular, very peculiar habit of displaying his affection for his human companions. Fitz had accepted, more or less blindly, many a certain and patent impossibility from the very beginning, from the first time he ever had entered—rather, had quite literally fallen into—this sand world, but this last, now, here, tonight—this was just too much. This was the one impossible thing that he simply could not credit, could not blind himself into believing. His cat, Tom, was dead, dead and buried and moldering in the black earth of the old mound, high above this place, and that was that.

Or was it . . .? If it was, then how . . .? A dream, that was it. That had to be it, was he to retain any shred of his sanity. It was all just an especially vivid, real-seeming dream.

He raised one trembling hand and very hesitantly touched the warm, furry feline head just behind the ragged-edged ears, his fingertips feeling the bumps and hard ridges of scar tissue that lay thickly all over that head under the covering fur. And, arching up to meet the petting hand, just as old Tom always had done, the strange but familiar blue-grey cat pushed its head up into Fitz's cold-sweaty palm.

Then, for a long while, Fitz just lay there and stroked the cat's head and back, feeling beneath the short, but dense and velvety fur the bumpy line of vertebrae and the twin banks of hard muscle flanking the spine, feeling the movements of the highly mobile scapulae as the big cat treaded in a transport of feline pleasure.

Nor was the cat the only one enjoying the contact. To Fitz, it felt so very, very good to once more stroke a warm, gentle, loving and furry creature. In the months since Tom's murder, he had forgotten until now, consciously, at least, just how soothing and relaxing and deeply satisfying it was to him just to lie or sit and stroke a cat.

"Such a good dream," thought Fitz, aloud. "Such a pleasant dream."

Pushing farther up onto the man's chest, the big cat, careful to keep his claws sheathed, placed one big paw low on either cheek and began to lave the stubbly chin with his wide, deep-pink tongue.

"*Tom!*" croaked Fitz from a throat suddenly constricted tight. "Oh, Tom, good old Tom, boy. God, how I've missed you, Tom."

And then . . . and then, he knew for certain that he was only dreaming. He knew because then the cat, always much loved, but still only a dumb beast for all of that, because then the cat *spoke to him.*

"And I have missed you, too, my good old friend. I often have been very lonely without you, missing the loving touch of your hands upon me. Why do you not leave this hot, dry, shadeless place and come to where I now live, among wooded hills and cool valleys and sparkling little streams of fresh, cold water, all filled with tasty fish and frogs?"

Fitz sat up then, violently, with a strangled scream bubbling from between his cold, numb lips. The moon was long since set, the first rays of the rising sun were illuming this strange world and his body was sticky, tacky with the sweat of . . . of fear? No, he could never fear old Tom, alive or dead. No, fear that he might be losing his sanity, more likely. Might be going mad, as the woman he had known as "mother" had, shortly before her death.

Preoccupied with his chaotic jumble of thoughts and half-thoughts and suppositions, he did not take out either of the bikes to bear him down to the sea for his regular morning swim, but simply walked, barefoot and naked, over the dunes and down the beach to where the gentle surf broke lazily upon the shore. He did not really fully awaken until he felt the shock of the night-chilled water. Then he swam about for as long as he could tolerate the cold, at which point he allowed the roller to bear him with it and deposit him in a place shallow enough to stand with the returning sea water swirling and tugging at his legs, even while the ever-constant, warm, dry beach breeze began to dry his body. It was while he stood there, some mile up the coast from the spot at which he had entered the water, that he noticed the strange large tracks leading from the surf-line mark off inland, toward the nearer range of dunes.

They were not bird tracks; even at the distance he could tell that immediately, or if they were, he had no faintest desire to meet the bird that had impressed them so deeply in the damp sand. Nor did they look at all like the tracks or trails of the occasional pinnipeds of various species or the huge sea turtles that came ashore on rarer visits.

No, the beast that had made these particular tracks had feet like wide, long, five-fingered hands with no discernible thumbs and marks that looked to have been left by long, broad nails or claws out beyond each "fingertip." There looked to be the marks of two pairs of the handlike feet and a scuffing between the digits that could have been left by webbing. There also was a wide, rather deep furrow inscribed between the right and the left sets of tracks. He faintly recalled having, at some time and place in his past, seen tracks very much akin to these, though he remembered those as being quite a good bit smaller.

Most sagaciously, as it later transpired, he resisted his initial impulse to trail the thing, whatever it was, on foot. He returned, rather, to the ship at a fast trot. There he dressed, got out the old, lighter, short-range bike, and armed himself with the carbine and the heavy-caliber revolver. Nor did he have the slightest cause to regret the elapsed time when, from the crest of a dune, he spotted just what a monster he had been blithely trailing.

Half at the least as long as the wrecked ship looked the thick-bodied, armor-plated, dragon-like beast, which had earlier scooped out a hole in the sand between the dunes and now was depositing in it a profusion of slimy-looking, yellow-brown eggs, each as big as the egg of a turkey, but more round than truly oval in shape.

It was then, as he sat the bike on the crest of that seaward dune, scrutinizing this newcomer to the stretch of coast he was already beginning to consider his, that he finally recalled where and when he had seen similar tracks. It had been on a beach on one of the Solomon Islands, early in World War Two. The tracks had been those of what were called estaurine or saltwater crocodiles.

Superficially, the leviathan he was studying through his binoculars did resemble to a large extent an alligator or a crocodile of his other world, but Fitz knew that he had never before seen or even heard of a crocodilian of that other world that was—at a very conservative estimate—between thirty and forty feet in overall length, stood between four and five feet at the shoulders and mounted four parallel rows of two-to-three-inch, yellow-white teeth in the ten-foot jaws of a head that had to be at least twelve feet long.

All at once, one of the vertically slitted, moss-green eyes detected the watching man atop the low dune and, with a loud explosion of sound that was half roar and half hiss, it began what appeared at first to be a lumbering shuffle in his direction. But the creature's progress was deceptive. She abruptly raised her weighty body up onto legs that were much longer than they had seemed to be when she had been crouched, laying her eggs, and in fleeting moments was at the very foot of the dune—close enough for Fitz to whiff her rank, fetid, squamous stench as she started up the inland face of the dune, headed directly for him and hissing like the safety valve of an overheated steam boiler.

Briefly, very briefly indeed, Fitz considered unslinging his carbine, drawing his magnum revolver, but quickly thought better of such notions. For unless he were lucky enough to hit an eye, the nightmarish beast would most likely absorb the entire magazine and cylinder of cartridges and never even slow down. So he wheeled the light bike about . . . and then, the stuttering little engine died.

CHAPTER IV

"Oh, shit!" breathed Fitz, heartfeltly. Forcing himself to move slowly, calmly, carefully, he went through all the correct, by-the-book procedures and, sure enough, with a real-life dragon by then breathing down his neck, the engine roared back to life.

The crocodilian chased him at a good clip for so big a beast, but only for about four hundred yards along the level beach. Then, she just suddenly stopped and flopped down on her belly in the sand. Yes, she could be very fast, Fitz thought, but she had no staying power. So the best protection would be to studiously avoid close proximity to her or any others of her dangerous kind that might happen along. She was the first such reptile he had seen and he fervently prayed that she represented a true rarity in this world. But . . . just in case there might be more of them, maybe it would be a good idea to bring down that elephant gun, perhaps even have a gunsmith or somebody make some more ammunition for it, too, then keep it all at the ship. It was either that or try to track down someone who would sell him a bazooka or a recoilless rifle, he felt.

He did bring down the cased Holland and Holland express rifle and he did obtain—at a truly horrendous price—twenty more brand-new, custom-made and -loaded rounds for the piece. But that was not all he bought or brought down to the sand world in the wake of his near miss with becoming a snack for an outsize monster.

A friend of Gus Tolliver, in the city, sold him in a transaction that he swore was completely legal and aboveboard a thirty-odd-year-old antitank rifle—designed by Lahti, in Finland, manufactured by Sweden and used, so the dealer attested, by Germans on the Russian Front during World War Two, before the invention and introduction of the German version of the antitank rocket launcher, the *Panzerfaust*.

The gold coins were selling most briskly just about then, and it was a good thing, for the one hundred or so pounds of anti-tank rifle and about twice that weight again in related equipment and two boxes of the 20mm ammunition for it cost Fitz more than ten dollars the pound, including sales taxes. Fortunately, the manual that came with the old piece was illustrated with pictures and diagrams, for Fitz could not speak, write or read the German language and, in order to get the long, heavy weapon down the stone stairs, he found it necessary to strip it down to component parts, carry it down a little at a time and reassemble it on the beach.

Once on the beach and back together, however, it was less of a problem than were the cases of parts and ammunition. The foot-long skids on the bipod which had been designed for snow worked equally well, he quickly discovered, to his delight, on sand, so he just towed it to the wrecked ship behind his bike, with all of the other cases and similar paraphernalia stowed in the cargo sidecar.

With the piece set up on the quarterdeck above the cabins, tightly shrouded against the seeping, abrasive sand and the corrosive sea air by its original canvas-and-leather case and some plastic film to reinforce it, Fitz felt about as safe from giant, reptilian predators as he could be.

The Lahti was semiautomatic, took a twenty-round box magazine, and would spew out one 20mm solid-steel round after another just as fast as a man could aim and squeeze the trigger, or so he had learned from some familiarization shooting of the piece. The sights were calibrated out to fifteen hundred meters, though the range of the inch-thick, cylindrical, sharp-pointed steel slugs must be considerably more than just that, the maximum range, the calibrations probably denoting only the effective accurate range. The Lahti and its old breed might have been superseded on the battlefields by new generations of more powerful weapons for use against more thickly armored tanks, but no way was one of those steel bullets likely to bounce off the scales or scutes of a damned crocodile, no matter how big and fast and vicious said beast might be.

Fitz had been back in his bungalow for less than an hour when the telephone jangled.

"Fitz?" said Tolliver's voice, sounding agitated. "Fitz, where the hell you been? I been trying to get your ass for two weeks now. Naw, don't you talk yet, just listen, *then* talk, tell me you ain't been lying to me all along.

"Fitz, way things has turned out, I don't think now

it was real mob what broke into my place; yours neither, prob'ly. You know what Interpol is? Well, two of them and some Customs Service fellers come to call on me more'n two weeks back. They're all some kinda mad, too. They say you been illegally importing into the U.S. antiquities what was stole from either Turkish or Greek or Eyetalian or Syrian tombs and then smuggled out of wherever.

"When I told them whatall you've done told me, boy, they said it just won't wash because, for one thing, your pa, he didn't have no brothers and for another thing, it was more what they called artifacts than just the gold coins involved here. So what do you say to that?"

Fitz nodded grimly. "I say, to begin, that now I know who broke in here to take only a big, rusty old knife and a little copper cup, both of which came to me with the coins."

"And where did the whole lot come to you from, Fitz? For the love of God, boy, tell me the truth, huh?" pled Tolliver.

Hating himself for having to be so evasive with his friend, Fitz said, "For one thing, Gus, no, my father didn't have any brothers, but I had a mother, too, you know. As for the coins, the knife and the cup, hell, I didn't even know they were Byzantine, Greek and Italian until you told me so. Remember? I brought the first batch in to you to sell just for the gold content, remember that, too. Exactly where they came from, or when or how they were imported, I have no foggiest sort of an idea, though I do recall some talk of a shipwreck many years ago on some beach somewhere."

"Fitz, boy, I wants to believe you, you don't know just how bad I wants to. But Fitz, one the fellers was in here—the big, nasty one, the Greek, I think it was—he said them there artifacts was a good thousand years old, maybe more. He said the both of them done been analyzed by experts and it ain't no question they's the real McCoy, not just cheap copies of old ones. So, what you got to say now, Fitz?"

He sighed. "Gus, I can say nothing I've not already said. Either you and those types believe me or you and they don't. That's it."

There was a pause, then Gus asked, "You got anymore of those so-called artifacts, Fitz? Like the knife or the cup, I mean?"

"Why, yes, come to think of it, Gus. I've got a copper bowl. It was soaking in a mop bucket that I guess they never thought to look in the last time they 'visited' my home. But I've got all the verdigris off now and I'm using it for an ashtray," Fitz answered, then asked, now a bit suspicious but concealing it, "Why do you ask, my friend?"

"Oh, no pertic'ler reason, Fitz," replied Gus, too nonchalantly to suit Fitz.

"I'll tell you what, Gus." Fitz spurted out the fruits of a sudden brainstorm. "When you come out here Friday night, I'll give you that bowl and you can give it to your friends there. Okay?"

Fitz had had the old bowl of hammererd-out sheet copper since his post-war college days and had, indeed, used it for an ashtray back when he still had smoked. He took it off his bureau as soon as he hung up from talking to Gus and whoever else had been on the line with the coin dealer.

After treating the thing with a copper cleaner, Fitz dug out a steel scriber and an English-Greek/Greek-English dictionary which had once been the property of his dead son. By the time that Friday rolled around, the bowl had been inscribed with shaky Greek alphabetical characters all the way around it, then sufficiently buffed to remove the sharp edges and impart a look of long handling and use.

Gus Tolliver rolled up to the gate about an hour earlier than usual and, when he had been admitted and had wheeled his sedan around so that he could drive rather than back out, he took his underarm case and trailed Fitz into the bungalow, with only a mumbled word or two of bare greeting.

Once inside, he hurriedly drew the drapes over the big front window and said, "Fitz, where the hell were you gone off to for so long, boy?" But then, when Fitz opened his mouth to speak, the old soldier shook his head forcefully from side to side, stuck a forefinger up to his own lips and, with the other hand, beckoned his host to come closer. When Fitz was less than arm's length away, Gus took both his wrists and placed the hands upon his own chest, that Fitz might himself feel the trails of wiring and the lumps and bumps to which they were connected.

Then he said, "Naw, boy, never mind the beer, just tell me where you went off to for two weeks? Not Vegas again, I hope."

Fitz caught on fast. "No, not Vegas. This time I went to Reno to try their tables."

Gus sighed. "You win or lose this time?"

"About broke even, for a change," Fitz replied. "Now, you ready for a beer?"

Gus nodded. "A gallon of it, boy. This has been a rough fucking two weeks for me, I tell you!"

It was Wednesday of the following week before Fitz again heard from Gus. The loud traffic noises at once announced that the paunchy man was not phoning from either his shop or his home. Though still with a note of agitation in his voice, he sounded more like the old, friendly Gus.

"Fitz, boy, I cain't talk long, I'm on a pay phone

on the corner of the bank. All I can say is, you got all them fuckers mad enough to chew up twenny-penny nails and spit out carpet tacks, is all. They says that copper bowl ain't no artifact at all, ain't more'n forty years old, if that, and that what them squiggles says is dirty and plumb insulting. Did you do it?"

Fitz chuckled. "Damn right I did, Gus. Insulting, it may be, but it's not dirty. It says 'Go copulate yourself' in Modern Greek; I copied the words out of a dictionary I have. As for it upsetting the fuckers, it was intended to do just that. I'm overjoyed that it succeeded. I don't like being accused of theft, and that's just what this business all boils down to, you know.

"And another thing, Gus. How come the bastards are just leaning on you? Why haven't they come to me?"

"They say they've tried and ain't never been able to catch you at home," replied Tolliver.

"I guess they don't believe in burglary anymore, huh?" snapped Fitz.

Gus chuckled. "I hear tell they tried that once, after you put ever thing in and they damn near got to see the inside of the county jail out there, afore they could get on the horn to somebody in Washin'ton to haul their little asses outen the fire your county sheriff was toasting 'em with. Then, too, they seem to think you got you a hardsite out there, a fucking fort, with heavy machine guns and everything. What'd you get, anyway? Browning fifties? They're the best, allus was."

Fitz sighed. "Gus, I do not own *any* machine gun, heavy, light or sub. The last time I even fired a full-auto weapon was in Korea, some twenty-odd years ago. Somebody probably saw me bringing a

Lahti anti-tank rifle into the house. But it's not here now. All I've got is the guns you know about, many of which can't even be fired.

"I'll tell you, Gus, give them a message for me. Tell them that I will be willing to meet with them, one at a time, here, by appointment. But you can also tell them that the next time somebody breaks into my home . . . or even tries to do it, I'm going to start installing some very nasty, deadly burglar traps, legal or not, and maybe scattering a few land mines between the house and the fence, and not because I have anything to hide, either; simply because I get furious at the thought of a bunch of strangers pawing through my effects whenever the mood strikes them to do it."

"I'll sure to God do 'er!" Gus assured him fervently, then said, "And Fitz, boy, whinever you get ready to put in mines, you let me know, hear? I know a feller's got him two, three cases of U.S. Army anti-personnel mines, M-8s, with primers and fuses and everything you needs. And how 'bout grenades, Fitz? You and me, we could rig up some grenades in place of some them trip flares you got 'round of your perimeter out there and . . ."

Now it was Fitz's turn to chuckle. "What do you want to help me do, Gus, start a full-scale war out here? And all along, I'd thought you were just a coin dealer, not a gun runner. Or are you a secret stockholder in Interarms Corporation, on the side?"

"Naw, Fitz, boy, I just knows some folks, some of 'em old friends from the Army and all. Fitz, I gotta cut this all short, but let me just say this: you be damn careful who you talks to and what you says on a telephone, 'less it's a pay phone, like this one here. And if you talks to me at the shop or my house, either one, don't say one fucking thing you don't want somebody elst to hear, hear? They done got my lines all bugged twenny ways from Sunday . . . for all you knows, yours is too, see."

"Well, all I can say, Gus, is that this bunch behave more like mobsters than anything else. Are you certain they're who they say they are?"

"Yeah." Gus sighed gustily. "I checked up on the fuckers, the U.S. ones, leastways, and they're legit, so I guess them furrin Interpol bastards is, too, and it's three of them now. One Turk, one Greek—and you look out for him, he's big and mean and ornery as hell; he ain't got no use for no Americans and he don't give a fuck who knows it, neither—and one Eye-talian. Him and the Turk don't seem to be too bad fellers, as cops of eny kind goes, though neither one them two talks as good English as the Greek geek.

"Look, Fitz, I really gotta go now, 'fore them fuckers comes looking for me, hear?"

Immediately the line went dead, Fitz took another load into the sand world, bringing back a couple of the cracked, chipped earthenware bowls from off the wrecked ship. He had not earlier brought up any of them because, partially, they were not very esthetically pleasing—being wrought roughly of thick clay with an uneven, blackish glaze and no decorations or even lettering of any kind—and partially because he didn't know what he would use the ugly things for in his home. They most resembled handleless teacups that the potter had all at once decided to flatten slightly, giving less depth and more width. But now he thought he might have a use for them. If he could actually catch those bastards in the very fucking act of a completely illegal burglary, then maybe they'd crawl down off poor old Gus's back. He also, therefore, brought back one of the rust-pitted, wrought-iron bolts he had removed from one of the cabin doors when he had refurbished it, and a finger ring of bronze or some similar alloy he had found while cleaning up the sternmost cabin.

The telephone rang about an hour after his return from the sand world. He gave it three full rings, then picked it up. "Fitzgilbert speaking."

The voice on the other end bore the slightly nasal quality, the clipped speech patterns of the northeastern United States. "Mister Fitzgilbert, my name is G. Rowland Biscuitt, I represent the U.S. Customs Service, and it is most urgent that I talk with you immediately, concerning certain antiquities from the Eastern Mediterranean area. We have a legal right to know if they were legally acquired by you, Mister Fitzgilbert. If they were, if you can prove to my satisfaction that they were, why, then, you will have nothing to worry about, sir. When may we come to call upon you, Mister Fitzgilbert? We have Mister Tolliver with us."

The Ford sedan that drove up to the gate had a driver and four other passengers in it. But Fitz adamantly stood close by his original terms and refused to so much as crack the gate until they had sorted out amongst themselves just which two—and two only—would come onto the property with Gus Tolliver. When once this had been accomplished, with no little bad grace and acrimony and hard, mean looks at him, he proceeded to anger them even more.

"And leave your guns in the car, both of you. Otherwise, you can just sit out there until hell freezes over solid . . . or you manage to come up with a legal search warrant. Come on, I'm not stupid, you know. You're both armed and I know it."

The Customs man, Biscuitt, shrugged and, reaching under his suit jacket, withdrew a hammerless .38 caliber revolver and passed it into the car. The other man, however, just stood there, glaring at Fitz, a near snarl showing some of his teeth.

Fitz returned the glare with an icy stare of his own, then slouched against one of the steel fence posts and began to affect to contemplate the conditions of his fingernails, while a heated conversation couched in some foreign language took place between the snarly man and two of the men still within the car.

After a few minutes of this, the man—with a full-fledged snarl of frustration and some grated-out words whose language Fitz did not need to understand in order to identify them as utter crudities, probably very profane—flung open his coat, pulled from its shoulder holster a big Browning P35 automatic and passed it through the open window to one of the other men.

At this point, Gus said, "Fitz, he's got anothern, in a ankle holster, and a knife on his right leg and another knife on his left arm, just above of the wrist. And it's something damn funny 'bout one his so-called pens, too; it either shoots a bullet or throws gas, I think. Mister Biscuitt, he's got one in *his* pocket, too, 'long with a flat blackjack in his right hip pocket."

By the time that the two visitors had been persuaded to relinquish the totalities of their extensive personal arsenals, Fitz could almost see steam arising from the big, black-haired foreigner, whose dark-olive complexion was also become a good bit darker. Nor did Gus's short, mock-sympathetic comments, chuckles and grins seem to be helping to smooth down the man's very ruffled feathers.

Comfortable for two, the small parlor was less so

for four. Fitz and Gus took their accustomed over-stuffed leather arm chairs, leaving the visitors to choose between standing and occupying a short leather couch backed against the wide window. On the table between the two chairs, Fitz had carefully arranged a stack of assorted mail held down with the big wrought-iron bolt and with the two ugly little bowls on either side of a cigarette box. The bronze ring was on his right thumb, having proven itself to be too big for any of his fingers, and he had already noticed both of the visitors staring at it.

Biscuitt started the interrogation; although polite, it could be nothing else, in truth. "Mister Fitzgilbert, I never got the chance outside to introduce my associate. This is Doctor Lekos Vitenelis. He is from Athens, Greece, and he works for Interpol and he holds his doctorate in Byzantine Art. He represents both Interpol and the Greek Government in this affair.

"Mister Fitzgilbert, where did you obtain the artifacts your agent, Mister Tolliver here, has been selling? Please, don't try to spin me the same fable you spun for him; we have had you investigated, you see, and we know that you had no paternal uncles, and that both of your maternal uncles are still living—one in Saint Paul, Minnesota, and one in Ann Arbor, Michigan. So tell us the truth, where did you get the gold and the other items, and when, and how?"

Fitz had rehearsed assorted answers for whenever this time came, as he had known it would come, either soon or late, and now he began to trot them out. "I never told Gus or anyone else that it was *my* uncle, sir; I only said *an* uncle. Right, Gus?"

Tolliver nodded. "That's right, Fitz, boy."

"Actually," Fitz lied on, warming to his prevarications, beginning to enjoy what he was doing, making certain that the bronze ring stayed always in plain sight of the two strangers, especially of the big, glowering, hostile Greek, "it was a great-uncle of mine, one of my grandpa's brothers who never came over here to this country."

The two men exchanged a brief glance. Then Biscuitt demanded, "And where did he live, and die, this great-uncle? What was his name and how long has he been dead? Answer me those questions, please, Mister Fitzgilbert, and I'm warning you, you'd best be fully candid with me."

"Don't threaten me, Biscuitt," said Fitz, calmly, "don't even think about it, hear? There's something not quite kosher about you and your bunch of supposed Interpol agents. If you were all completely on the up and up, by now you'd have called in the local police, the state police, the FBI, the IRS, the BATF and, probably, the CIA, for good measure. You'd have gotten search warrants and come in here legally, when I was home, not broken in like sneak thieves to paw through my possessions and rob me of the things you wanted."

Another exchanged glance, then, "Those are very serious accusations, Mister Fitzgilbert. If you cannot prove them, I would strongly advise you to cooperate fully with us and answer all of our questions truthfully. I doubt that you would like any of the alternatives.

"Now, where did this great-uncle live? Where did he die, and when? What was his name?"

"His name was Robert Emmett Dempsey. He lived and died in Dublin. When? Hell, I don't remember, exactly. Some time in the nineteen twenties, during the Irish Civil War, while I was just a toddler. I never knew him, never even met the man. He was one of my grandpa's horde of step-brothers. I never knew he'd left anything to anybody 'til that box was delivered to me, last year," declared Fitz.

"Who sent it to you, Mister Fitzgilbert?" Biscuitt demanded immediately. "Where was it sent from? Did it come via mail or express?"

Fitz shrugged, convincingly . . . he hoped. "It was mailed from Dublin, Republic of Eire. I couldn't read the return address or the signature on the note that only said that this was a bequest from my great-uncle, Robert E. Dempsey, originally meant to go to my father, sent finally to me because it had been discovered that he had died. And before you ask me, no, I can't find that note; I suppose I just threw it out with the box and the wrapping papers. So, now, what else do you want to know?"

"He is lying," said the Greek in good, if rather accented, British English. "You are a liar, Mister Fitzgilbert. You accuse us of theft, but you are the thief, you and your accomplices, who have and probably are still looting the antiquities of my country, or of Turkey, Italy or Syria. Such robbery of sites of archeological value is thoroughly despicable, a crime in every country of the civilized world. Your evil greed cannot be, will not be tolerated longer. Do you hear me? You decadent Americans sicken me. You all seem to think you own all the world. But you do not and if you do not immediately tell us just who are your European accomplices, where they can presently be found and where are located the sites they are despoiling, you will be made very sorry that you did not cooperate.

"Have you ever seen a Turkish or a Syrian prison, Mister Fitzgilbert? Have ever you been into one, perhaps? They are not at all like the overly luxurious prison facilities of the United States of America. They, and we Greeks, too, know what criminals are and how to deal with them. Soft, effete Americans placed in those prisons quite often never live long enough to come to trial, you know. Those who are not murdered by other prisoners, or beaten to death by guards when they have the effrontery to disobey orders, very often kill themselves or go mad, unable to live with the thought of the things that have been done to them in the processes of interrogation and imprisonment."

"Are you admitting that you Greeks torture prisoners, then?" asked Fitz bluntly. "That you use physical torture to obtain 'confessions'?"

"Of course not!" snapped the Interpol man. "Unlike Turkey and Syria, Greece is a civilized country, Mister Fitzgilbert. All of Western art and culture, philosophy, democracy and civilization itself is owed to Greece. You arrogant Americans should remember these debts owed my country far more than you do. The Golden Age of Greece . . ."

"Has been gone one hell of a long time, Mister Vitalis," said Gus coldly. "What the hell have you fuckers done recent, huh? You done had you two . . . or is it three? . . . civil wars sincet the end of World War Two alone. If it won't for American loans and the Marshall Plan and American tourists to Greece, you'd all be so fucking broke you'd be eating dog turds for breakfast!"

Turning on Gus, the Greek said icily, "You would be well advised to hold your tongue, you fat, hairless, uncouth cretin. You are already in serious trouble. Do not further compound your difficulties."

Old Gus Tolliver was not fazed by the threatening words or manner. "Listen here to me, you fucking, over-eddicated Greek prick, you, I got me connections don't none of you know about, and I done a'ready put some feelers out on the bunch of you bastards. Fitz is righter then he knows, I think. You bunch might've started out working for your guvamints, is what I think, but I think when you'all come to realize just how much gold and money was involved here, I think it was all of you got really greedy, real sudden-like. Now, you trying to scare Fitz into telling you things so's you *won't* have to bring any other bunches in on this here, so's you can all divvy it up between the five of you."

While the old soldier had been talking, Fitz had been watching the two men. Biscuitt had become a greenish pale and was repeatedly gulping. The Greek had darkened to lividity; both of his big fists were tight-clenched and knots of muscle stood up at the hinges of his jaws. Fitz was dead certain that Gus had hit the nail precisely on the head.

To Fitz, Gus said, "Maybe I shouldn't ought to of said all this out here tonight, but I just couldn't take no more of that damn Greek sod and all his anti-American commie crap, is all. Way things is now, maybe I better sleep out here tonight and take one your cars to drive back in the morning, huh? Someway, I don't think it would be too healthy for to get back in that car with these fuckers tonight."

Biscuitt regained a usable quantity of aplomb first. "Mister Tolliver, to . . . to just whom did you speak of . . . of these wild, utterly groundless suspicions of me and my colleagues, may I ask?"

Gus grinned. "Sure, you can ask . . . but I ain't gonna tell you. I will say this, though, the guys I talked to a'ready done tol' me that the guys *they* talked to was all damn int'rested and said they meant to get on it right away, too. So, was I you bunch, I wouldn't go making no long-term plans."

"These persons with whom you spoke are, I would assume, connected with some Federal agency, Mister Tolliver, so tell me this: are they aware that you have been, via most circuitous channels, some of which are less than legal, shipping large sums of money out of this country?" asked G. Rowland Biscuitt, adding, "As you—neither of you—are not without sins of your own, you would assuredly have been better off to not have thrown stones at others.

"But throw them you did, I'm sure. Therefore, since time is now very important, I would suggest that we all make an even distribution of the remaining gold. Then we can go our separate ways rapidly. Now, we know that there is very little of the ancient gold in the smaller, most cleverly disguised safe in Mister Tolliver's shop, although there is a bit more in his bank box. Is that all not sold? Or is there more . . . perhaps in a hidden recess of that stone root cellar or whatever it is in the backyard here?"

Fitz drew from under the cushion of his chair a M1911A1 .45 caliber service pistol. In one smooth movement, he pointed it at the two on the couch and palmed back the slide. Within the confines of the room, the metallic sounds rang loud and ugly. Biscuitt regained every bit of his earlier greenish pallor and, this time, even the Greek—staring down the black, nearly half-inch bore that was being steadily held only some seven feet from him—lost color in his face.

Between spasmodic gulps, Biscuitt gasped, "What does th . . . this mean? I am a . . . federal employ . . . ee in performance of . . . his duties . . . and—"

"It means, my crooked friend," grated Fitz, "that this interview is at an end. Unless one or both of you wants to make it a very final end, I'd advise you to get up and leave my house and my property while you can still do so under your own steam.

"The gold is mine, all mine, and I came by it and

the other things completely legally. If there are any crooks about . . . and there are!—it's you and your cohorts, Biscuitt.

"Gus, go get the Garand. You know where I keep it. It's loaded. I want some backup when I let these two out the gate. There's a bandolier hanging on the barrel, armor-piercing and ball, three clips of each."

"Damn right!" The short man hustled down the hall, his beer belly flopping, to come back with the military rifle.

At the car, Fitz and Gus warily watched the others have to physically restrain the big Greek. They finally had to pinch a nerve to get the Browning away from him. Then they all piled in and drove off at speed.

"I still think I should oughta stay out here tonight, Fitz," said Gus stubbornly from the driver's seat of Fitz's Jeep wagon. The big, familiar service pistol now was jammed under his belt and his jacket side pockets were weighed down with spare loaded magazines of the fat cartridges for it. "It ain't that I'm scared for myself, driving back; in fact, I just hope that pack of fuckers *does* try something with me, so I can show them furriners what kinda shooting the U.S. Army useta teach us.

"But, boy, it's five them fuckers and if they comes back, with you here all by your lonesome . . ."

"Gus, you've got to go back, and the faster the better. I'm okay here. I'm well armed and not afraid to shoot, if I have to. Nobody can get over that fence, or even touch it, without lights going on and alarms and trip flares going off all over my whole perimeter, you know that. But Gus, those hoods are just mad enough now, and mean enough and frantic enough to go after your wife and try to use her to shake loose the rest of the gold from us. She needs you there; I'm okay out here. So you get the hell going and phone me when you get there."

"Okay, okay, Superman." Gus put the wagon into gear smoothly. "You can go th'ough solid-stone walls, but can you jump over tall buildings with a single bound, too? Okay, yeah, I'll call you up when I gets back."

It was something under an hour and a half when the telephone rang and Gus's voice said, "Okay, Fitz, boy, I'm here and everything's okay. I think I set a new land-speed record for a Jeep and I kept looking for them bastards, too, but I never seen hide nor hair of them, all the way back. Sary, she's okay. I told her mosta everthing and we both is loaded for bear here. You seen the fuckers, boy?"

Fitz hung up the phone and went back to his loading. He loaded each and every weapon that would shoot and for which he had the requisite ammunition. He thoroughly checked the fences and every window and door. Then he just waited, the house darkened. Like Gus, he too was dead sure that the gold-hungry pack would return. And since they now knew from Gus that they shortly would find themselves very deep in the shit if they were so unwise as to hang around and be apprehended for their misuses of their authority and resources, they would almost certainly make their return visit tonight or tomorrow, latest.

Fitz brewed a pot of strong coffee, dragged his chair around so that it faced the window of the smaller of the two bedrooms—which, due to its location, gave a good view of the entire front of the lot and the street beyond—and then just sat there in the darkened room, sipping coffee and thinking. The .44 magnum revolver rode in a holster at his side and the Garand leaned against the wall beside the window, easy to hand, as too was the twelve-gauge riot gun on the other side. He was as ready as he was ever going to be, he figured.

"Why?" he thought, sitting there. "Why did I choose this particular house, on this particular lot, on this particular street, in this particular, run-down neighborhood? Was it all God's plan? Did He think I'd finally suffered enough? If so, then why did He have to let poor old Tom die, too? Was it just necessary that I lose everything, every single tie with the happy life that once had been? If that *was* it, then why?

"I can't think of any reasonable explanation for the sand world or how I got there and still get there. I can't conceive of any explanation for the weird time differences between that world and this one, either. Are there human beings in that world? There must be . . . somewhere, because that ship certainly wasn't built by birds and seals and sea turtles and ponies, or even by crocodiles.

"What is the sand world, for that matter, and where is it? If it's an island, it's sure as hell a damned big one. Those hills beyond that plain look to be a damned long ways away, and I never have been able to get to either end of that beach; it just seems to go on and on in both directions forever. Too bad Gus got shocked so bad that night and wouldn't go through to the sand world with me; he's travelled a whole hell of a lot more than I have and he just might've been able to tell where it is. It's bound to be somewhere in the tropics of damned near to them, because it never gets very cold, even on rainy nights, when the wind picks up.

"It can't be in the West Indies; otherwise, those beaches would be swarming with tourists. Same thing for any of the seacoasts of this country or any other western hemisphere country I can think of. So, what's left? Australia? See above. Hawaii? Ditto. It looks to be too damn big to be any of the South Pacific islands. How about New Guinea, then? Possible, I guess. Or maybe somewhere in Indonesia or the Philippine Islands? Could be. But until I find people there, I won't know anything for sure.

"But all of that aside for now. What about this merry pickle I'm in—and have dragged Gus into with me—now? Even if we drive this bunch of international predators off, get the bastards all sacked or jailed, there'll surely be others, but legal ones, just as anxious to prove Gus and I are crooked somehow, so they can legally rob us blind. And I know damned good and well that no-fucking-body is going to believe a word if I try to back up at this late date and tell them how and where I really came by that gold. I sure as hell wouldn't if somebody told me such a fantastic yarn. So I guess that means that Gus and I are going to either have to leave the country or go directly to jail and not collect two hundred dollars, either.

"And, goddamn it, that's just not fair, no matter how you cut it. I love my country, America. I fought to protect her in two fucking wars, Gus in three, for God's sake. And Gus is right on the money, it's been getting worse for years and I never even noticed it, living smack-dab in the middle of it all.

"The fuckers in D.C. have gerrymandered everything around until the productive citizens are being robbed blind to keep the nonproductive, nonproductive. The middle class, who made this country the great and powerful republic it used to be, are being eroded, ground down, and if it goes on for much longer, there won't be any middle-class people left to rob, only the very rich and the great masses of the poor . . . and then America will be ripe for the Reds to take over. And maybe, just maybe, that's exactly what the fuckers who are doing it to us want to see: a Soviet Socialist Republic of America."

Despite the black, bitter coffee, he must have dozed off, for how long he didn't know. The bass grumbling of a powerful truck engine awakened him—that and an odd squeaking-creaking noise that seemed to be coming either from the front yard or the street beyond.

Slowly, carefully, he eased the soap-lubricated window up and could then hear whispered conversation in some foreign language. That was when he pulled the string lying across the windowsill. There was a loud *pop* from out on the lawn near the fence, something streaked up into the night sky, whitely flashed with a louder noise, then a parachute flare began its slow, drifting descent back to earth, bathing house and yard and street in bright white light.

Just beyond the high front fence sat what looked like a power company truck, mounting a cherry picker on a long, multi-jointed arm. This contrivance was in use, having just deposited the Greek—now momentarily frozen where he stood, staring stupidly up at the flare, his mouth open in surprise—on the front lawn, with another smaller, but equally olive-skinned man about to clamber out of the cup and hop down to join him.

CHAPTER V

But the Greek was clearly a man of action; his reflexes were quick and he stood frozen for only split seconds. He had shed his suit coat and vest already, so he only needed to drop his armful of tools to rapidly draw his big Browning autoloader. It was more than that, Fitz soon found out, as the man sprayed a three-round burst through the dark front window, then another through the front-facing bedroom window with a crashing of broken glass. There was only one window left unperforated and Fitz threw himself out of the chair and onto the floor beneath it barely in time to escape the three sizzling 9mm rounds that came whizzing through it.

Then he was up on his knees, returning fire with the huge, booming magnum. He did not hit the Greek, but he did hit the cup of the cherry picker and, apparently, a truck tire, to judge by the sudden loud hiss of escaping air. Someone, somewhere shouted something and the Greek shouted back, in angry-sounding tones. The other somebody shouted once more and there was a grinding sound as the truck was wrestled into gear by someone obviously inexperienced at driving the model.

The cherry picker began to rise jerkily and the smaller man shouted something at the Greek. Throwing back something harsh, the big man let off another wild, three-round burst from his pistol, then jammed it back into his shoulder holster and leaped high to grasp the lip of the still-rising cup. The smaller man leaned from the cup and took a grip on the bigger man's belt, trying to tug him up into the cup with him.

But just as he did, just as the rising and sidewise moving cup's bottom came to a point a little higher than the top of the fence, Fitz decided that they were not proceeding fast enough and, after firing off the last three .44s, took up the Garand and began to pump steel-jacket, armor-piercing rounds into various parts of the truck. Seemingly heedless of the fact that the cherry picker had not been fully recovered and ignoring the now-frantic shouts of the Greek and the smaller man, the driver of the truck began to accelerate.

The Greek began to scream then, as his dangling legs and loins were dragged relentlessly up the twenty-five-foot length of three cruel strands of barbed wire. Fitz cringed; he had heard men scream in just that way before, long ago, in wars, and he had hoped, had prayed, that he never would hear the like of them again.

Every light and alarm had come to full, glaring, blaring life by the time the dead flare came to earth and the wobbling, swaying, swerving truck reached and turned a corner of the bumpy, potholed, ill-lit street.

Fitz dialed the private number that Sheriff Vaughan had left him, and the sheriff himself answered on the first ring. "Mister Fitzgilbert, what the everlovin' hell is goin' on out there? You fightin' off Injuns or suthin'? I done got three calls so far, my own se'f, and the other number's ringin' off the hook. They says it sounds like a fuckin' war out there."

One of the deputies found the Browning near the corner of the fence, in the grass between it and the street. He brought it to Vaughan, who stood sipping some of Fitz's coffee in the driveway.

"What in tarnation you use this stuff for, Mister Fitzgilbert, battery acid, mebbe. You got a mile of guts, though, that's all I can say. If you was so damn sure they was comin' back, you should oughta give me a call, that's part my job, you know.

"What is it, huh? What you turn up, Colley?"

"Watch it, Sheriff!" Fitz said just a little too late to do any good. The three rounds of 9mm ripped out of the barrel and, fortunately, found lodging in Fitz's manicured front lawn.

"Keerist on a fuckin' crutch!" the startled lawman exclaimed, now gingerly holding the pistol by the butt, between thumb and forefinger, keeping well away from the trigger. "Thishere thing is illegal as all hell, it's a fuckin' machine pistol, is what it is! You mean it was really them four guys from U.S. Customs and Interpol used this thing for to shoot up your house tonight? You know, I dint like them from the word 'go,' 'specially that one furriner, the Vitinellis or whatever his name was. And that feller, Biscuitt, he was just as slick as dog shit, I could of told you he was a wrong 'un. I knowed it. But then, I gotta be able to peg folks for what they is, quick-like, it's part my perfession, you know."

Vaughan's repeated telephone calls and visits filled Fitz in on all that followed that hellish night. The truck had been stolen from the lot of a power company branch office. It was found, abandoned, on a narrow dirt road that led down to the river, dusty, rather battered, riddled with bullet holes and covered with drops and smears and splashes of dried blood. One of the rear axles had suffered severe damage because the truck had been driven at speed over bad roads with two flat tires, and Vaughan averred that the power company was looking for more and fresher blood than had been found on their wrecked truck.

The Interpol agent, Lekos Vitenelis, had been dumped at the door of the emergency room of the county hospital, in shock and nearly bled dry. Vaughan, himself, had not yet been allowed to question the man, but he had learned as much as he could from the medical staff.

He shook his head and shuddered as he told of his learnings. "I tell you, Mister Fitzgilbert, whatever he done, whatall happen to that pore fucker shouldn' ought to of happened to a fuckin' dog, is all I can say. The way his damn legs was tore up was bad enough, but I just hope he's got a unnerstandin' wife back at home and a whole lot of kids already, 'cause he ain't never gonna get no more babies on nobody, they says over to the hospital.

"That damn wire got 'tween his legs, somewheres along the way, too. And heavy as he was and fast as the truck must've been goin', thet bobwire came damn close to slicin' his whole body right up the fuckin' middle, they tells me. The doc, he thinks they can save one his balls, but thet won't do him much good, 'cause of how bad his pecker was tore up. All I can think about is what the Good Book says, 'Vengeance is mine, saith the Lawd. I will repay.' God save us all from His awful vengeance, Mister Fitzgilbert, God save us all."

A few weeks later, both Fitz and Gus were much relieved to hear the news that G. Rowland Biscuitt and company had been caught and turned over to the appropriate authorities. All, that is, save the Greek agent; upon being apprised of the nature and the full extent of his grievous injuries, the big man had waited until night, then managed to open an important artery and bleed to death before the next shift checked in on him.

Fitz had breathed a silent prayer for the repose of the suicide's soul. Gus had just snorted, "That so? Well, now he's another *good* damn commie, it should oughta be a whole lots more just thet good, too!"

Near the end of the month, Fitz returned from town with a heavily loaded Jeep Wagoneer to find a car bearing government plates parked on the shoulder of the street just beyond his gate. Clearly recalling the last automobile that had been outside his gate with similar plates—a certain black Ford sedan—and in no mood to trifle or be trifled with by anyone, he handled the short-barrelled .357 magnum he now wore in a cross-draw, belly holster underneath his jacket.

As he slid out and unlocked the gates and swung them wide enough for the Jeep to pass easily through, he heard car doors open and close and footsteps behind him. Making certain that he was standing with both feet on his property, he spun around and drew his revolver all in one movement, although he did not point the piece directly at the two men now slowly approaching . . . not yet.

The younger man, trailing a little behind and to the left side of the other, slowed perceptibly at sight of the threatening gesture, but the older man, in the lead, just kept pacing forward, carrying a briefcase in one hand, the other holding his suit coat gaped wide to show an empty clamshell holster, a hesitant smile on his face. That face looked to be about Fitz's own age, though the man's hair showed quite a bit more grey than did his and he walked with a slight limp.

Fitz said, courteously but very coldly, "If you want to talk to me, sir, please get back into your car, the both of you, until I've gotten my Jeep inside the gate. I'd hate to have to use this thing so early in the day . . . but I can and I will, and that's no bullshit, gentlemen."

"Why, of course we will, Mister Fitzgilbert," said the older man, adding, "and please believe me, I quite understand and sympathize with the reasons for your understandable trepidations. Come on, Agent Irby, we're not here to make the man nervous or provoke any more incidents."

Not until he had parked the Jeep in the garage beside the Mercedes did Fitz walk back toward the gate, his revolver once more out and ready. The two men had once more quitted their car, but they both stood at the corner of the open gate, having made no move to enter it uninvited. Two points for this pair, thought Fitz.

"Mister Fitzgilbert," said the older man with the briefcase, "I am Lester Harland, representing the

Customs Service of the United States. If I may reach inside the pocket of my coat, I'll show you my identification."

Fitz nodded and lowered the revolver's muzzle a few millimeters, then bent closer to scrutinize the leather folder, with its badge and laminated I.D. card. "All right, that says you're who and what you say you are. Now, what do you want with me?"

Despite his cool brusqueness, Harland did not evidence any resentment or loss of self-assurance. "Mister Fitzgilbert, you have been made to suffer grievously at the hands of miscreants representing the Customs Agency. I am here to offer the Agency's profuse apologies for the wrongs done against you in its name and to do whatever can be done to rectify those wrongs."

Grinning, Fitz said, "Some fat cats up in D.C. are smelling 'lawsuit' and are crawfishing around to get out from under, right? Well, tell them not to worry, I consider the incident will be closed as soon as I get back the antique knife and cup that were stolen from my home by Agent Biscuitt and his pack of thieves."

"Mister Fitzgilbert," said Harland, smoothly, soothingly, "your attitude is completely understandable and your forbearance most commendable. But please, I wonder if we might continue this chat in your house, where we can all sit down?"

"Sure thing," Fitz shrugged, "that is, if you two don't mind doing your chatting over this loaded revolver I intend to keep holding. Oh, and let me see an empty holster on your partner, too, first."

When Agent Irby had reluctantly passed Fitz his revolver—almost a twin to Fitz's own new one, save that the government issue was blued, rather than nickeled—he ushered the two into his home and waved them to the couch, where they must constantly look at the three bullet holes in the wall. Born to and reared in the Catholic Church, Fitz owned full understanding of the uses of guilt in intimidating human beings, having seen it practiced by the clergy for so many years.

Clutching the briefcase on his knees, Agent Harland stared for a long moment at the scarred wall, then asked, "Those . . . ahh, those holes, Mister Fitzgilbert, they are from . . . ahh, that night?"

"Oh, no, not a bit of it, mister," said Fitz, broadly sarcastic, "we have gunfights around here every day and twice on Sundays." Then, sobering, he nodded. "Yes, those represent the first burst fired from the machine pistol that Biscuitt's Greek buddy was packing. He was sure some sweet character. Are all Interpol agents that nasty?"

Harland looked and sounded a bit embarrassed. "Mister Fitzgilbert, the late Doctor Vitenelis, although then working for Interpol, was not and had never been an agent for that organization. He was simply an expert on loan from the Greek government and, as such, he should not have been carrying a firearm of any sort. Agent Biscuitt should have seen to that . . . But that's all now in the past; the doctor is dead and Agents Biscuitt and Grossman are both incarcerated and awaiting trial in federal court.

"Agents Biscuitt and Grossman and the two Interpol agents, Brazzi and Levrek, have been thoroughly, exhaustively debriefed on all their activities, both the legal and the many onerous illegal. Biscuitt swears that he was tempted and led astray by Doctor Vitenelis, while Grossman swears that his temptor was Biscuitt. Neither of the others, either the Turkish agent or the newer come Italian agent, seemed to have been aware that anything of an irregular nature was going on until that power company truck was hot-wired and stolen that night; they had been given to understand by their superiors that Agent Biscuitt was in charge of the operation and they, being good agents, simply followed his instructions."

He opened the briefcase and laid out on the leather top of the cocktail table two items sealed in clear plastic bags and labelled with combinations of numbers and letters. One of the bags contained the big rusty knife, while the other held the small copper cup and the doctored copper ashtray, which latter was now badly dented on one edge, looking as if it had possibly been thrown hard against something solid.

"These are your property, Mister Fitzgilbert, and before we leave I would greatly appreciate it if you sign a receipt for them. The Service deeply regrets the manner in which they were . . . ahh, seized from you, of course. The longish delay in their return was necessitated by the fact that the Service had to seek out experts to confirm the suspect findings of the late Doctor Vitenelis."

"And these experts of yours said?" prompted Fitz, curiously.

"They said that, whatever else he might have been, the late doctor did know his period of specialty in great detail. The small cup was crafted on the island of Cyprus at some time between 800 A.D. and 1050 A.D., more likely earlier than later. The style of the knife blade is Thracian, but it appears to have been hilted elsewhere, probably in Byzantium. Although the case fits it well enough, it was not made for the knife, but rather for another with a blade of slightly different shape and thickness. They are not in complete agreement on the place the case was made, but the current consensus is that it was fashioned somewhere on the northern coast of Asia Minor. Its bronze fittings, however, are of well-known Celtic patterns and far predate case, knife or even cup, probably approaching an age of twelve to thirteen centuries before us. These items are, of course, of quite some value—priceless, indeed, in many ways—and I know that several museums intend to bid on them, once your legal ownership is firmly established."

Oh, boy, thought Fitz, here we go again!

"We have investigated in the Republic of Ireland the information you gave to Agent Biscuitt, earlier on the night of this . . . ahh, most regrettable incident." He waved at the bullet-pocked wall, then took a small notebook from out the briefcase, opened, riffled and then began to read.

"Robert Emmett Dempsey seems to have been a well-to-do man for the times and the place, having been a master brick- and stonemason and also done some contracting of a general nature. However, during the Insurrection of 1916, he was detained by one of the units of the British Army who were just then maintaining order in Dublin and found to be carrying a revolver and two hand grenades. He was tried by a military court and sentenced to death; however, that sentence was never carried out and he was released after nineteen months in prison.

"From that time until his death, he continued to work off and on at his original trades, as well as at demolishing buildings damaged during the 1916 Insurrection . . ."

Fitz interrupted, finally, "It was not called an insurrection . . . except, maybe, by the damned British. It's known to history as the Easter Rebellion, Agent Harland."

"Yes . . . well," Harland went on, "Robert Emmett Dempsey was shot and killed on the afternoon of the eighteenth of July, 1921, on O'Connell Street, in Dublin, by person or persons unknown. Although his wife and seven children died during 1917 of influenza, he seemingly had many relatives and friends, for the Dublin newspapers of the period note that his funeral services and interment were quite heavily attended.

"Persons who knew him—and there are not too many of them left, after all this time, more than fifty years—all seem to recall that he kept in his home many strange and curious and often valuable things that he had found while demolishing old houses, which may very well be where he acquired these artifacts and the gold coins. And who, at this late date, could decide whether or not his acquisitions were strictly legal? We still, however, are endeavoring to discover just who sent you the carton containing them, but I do not know how successful we will be in that search, for two rather elderly, distant relatives of yours have died since the date you think you received it—one, one of Dempsey's sisters, and one, the widow of one of his brothers.

"All things considered, Mister Fitzgilbert, I tend to believe your story—it sounds just implausible enough to be truth, strange truth, but still truth— and I know that most of my superiors agree, so unless we find someone in Ireland who is willing to swear that a man now dead for nearly fifty-four years never in fact owned the treasure and the artifacts, then I think that we all can agree that they are yours in both senses—*de facto* and *de jure*. So I doubt highly that you will be seeing agents of my service again, although you may be subpoenaed to give testimony at the trials of former agents Biscuitt and Grossman.

"Now, if you would be so good as to sign this receipt for your artifacts . . .?"

Fitz could hardly believe it, any of it. Dead certain that he was sure to be found out in his web of lies, possibly prosecuted and jailed for a plethora of crimes, including that of making false statements to federal agents, he was stunned that investigation had sufficiently corroborated his fables to get him out of a very sticky situation. He had, actually, known damn all of his long-dead half-great-uncle, he had simply pulled the name out of his dim memories as a way to slow down the Biscuitt Bunch. Fitz had not been quite a year old when Robert Emmett Dempsey had been murdered; who would ever have thought that the fiery patriot of Irish freedom he had always been pictured to Fitz would turn out to be a man who squirreled away and kept odd things he had found in the course of tearing down old edifices?

Just as they reached the gate, Harland smote his forehead and exclaimed, "Mister Fitzgilbert, I almost forgot, here." He fished a long government envelope from an inside pocket and proffered it. "I was asked to give you this by a chap from another agency, there in the Federal Building, when I happened to mention that I was driving out here today."

The envelope was rumpled and did not seem, when Fitz accepted it, to contain very much. When he opened it, after the Customs agents had driven off, he found that it held only an oversized card, noting that he had an appointment at the Federal Building in the city with a Henry Fowler Blutegel, of the Internal Revenue Service.

Mounted on the bigger, longer-range bike, carrying spare fuel, water, sleeping bag and supplies in the sidecar, Fitz rode days and many miles up and down the sandy plain that lay beyond the dunes, finding that the plain seemed to be just as endless as the beach on the other side of those dunes. By following the tracks of some of the small herds of wild ponies, he found three spring-fed pools of fresh water, a salt lick and one good-sized fresh-water lake, all of these located near the inland edge of the plain, however—half a day's journey at the top speed he considered to be safe over the rough surface in which holes and irregularities often were concealed by the stands of grasses until he was too close to avoid them.

More than just ponies dwelt on or beneath that plain, he quickly discovered. There were hordes of lizards of a dozen or more varieties, rodentlike, burrowing beasts ranging upward from the size of meadow mice and voles to animals which were the size of and maintained mounded "towns" of burrows like prairie dogs. There were what he soon began to call "flying rabbits"—creatures that launched themselves with the long, muscular hind legs of a Western jackrabbit, then spread wide membranes grown between fore- and hind legs to prolong the distance covered by gliding through the air.

There were a plethora of insects—flying, crawling and hopping—hairy, huge, burrowing spiders, scorpions of varying sizes, and some of the largest, longest centipedes Fitz had ever seen. There was a profusion of birds of every size, shape, color and habits he could imagine. There were also some very singular flyers about and he could not decide whether they were bird or beast or reptile, as they bore at least some resemblance to all three.

Another peculiar case was that of the flocks of what he called, for want of a better name, "rat-tailed ostriches." They looked about as big as an ostrich, most of them, they walked or ran at speed on two legs like an ostrich, true enough, but they had no feathers or plumes like an ostrich, rather a growth of fluffy, fuzzy, very fine hair. They also grew tails—thick, up near the body, but tapering along a scaly length of six or seven feet to a point.

With such an assortment of prey animals about, he was certain that there had to be a number of predator species, as well, but thus far the only ones he had seen had been a few weasel-sized and -shaped creatures, some snakes and a hefty beast that had looked, through the binoculars, a lot like a badger. There were raptorial birds, of course, but none of these avian predators spotted to date looked of a size or a lifting capacity to pose a threat to anything larger than a good-sized rat or an underweight prairie dog or one of the smaller of the flying rabbits.

Several times, he had seen impressed in the damp banks of the spring-fed pool and on the shores of the fresh-water lake spoor that looked to his inexperienced eyes a lot like much-oversized house cat pads, but he had never seen any actual cats of any size or description on the sandy plain, so he assumed that either they did not den on the plain or that they were, like most felines, nocturnal hunters.

He could hear the telephone ringing from the moment he closed the stone slab and began to dress for the cold, damp, inclement weather outside the wall-tent, and it just continued to ring, on and on, incessantly, as he finished dressing and made his way across his backyard, onto the back porch through the back door and into the kitchen of the house, where he finally was able to make the annoying sound cease by picking up the receiver of the wall phone. There was no reply to his repeated hellos, so he hung up. But he had only had time to get back to his bedroom before it rang again.

"Mister Fitzgilbert? Mister Alfred O'Brien Fitzgilbert?" asked a woman's voice.

"Yes," said Fitz. "This is Alfred Fitzgilbert speaking. Who's calling me?"

But she failed to identify herself, only saying, "Please hold for Mister Blutegel."

Fitz still could not recall the name when a man's voice came on the line, a raspy voice that sounded angry and exasperated. "*Mister* Fitzgilbert, where have you been these past weeks? You had an appointment with me, here at my office. Why didn't you keep it or telephone me to reset it? Don't you know better than to try trifling with the Internal Revenue Service?"

Then Fitz remembered the name and the card in the government envelope that the Customs man, Harland, had given him on the day before he had left for the sand world.

"Mister Blutegel," he said politely, "I did not make any appointment with you, at your office or anywhere else. You or someone scribbled on one of your cards that I had an appointment with you, but when I got that card, I already had other plans and . . ."

"Then why didn't you telephone me, immediately, tell me where you were going and when you would return, Fitzgilbert?" It was not so much a question as an unequivocal demand, and it, plus the grating voice and the supercilious manner began to irk Fitz. "Because, Mister Blutegel, I'm a private citizen, have been for many years, and where I go and what I do is my own business, not yours or anybody else's. What did you want to talk to me about, anyway? My taxes are prepared by . . ."

"Now, don't you get snotty with *me*, Fitzgilbert," the raspy voice broke in to say, "unless you think you'd like living in a federal penitentiary. "I *know* who prepares your tax returns, if such pieces of arrant, nonsensical fiction can be rightly justified with the name of tax returns. Like most of your class of criminal, you obviously think we of this service all are morons."

Fitz took a deep breath while the arrogant man was speaking, then another. "Just who do you think you're calling a criminal, Blutegel? I think that such a charge delivered over an open telephone line is considered slanderous. Maybe I need an attorney."

"It is *Mister* Blutegel to you, Fitzgilbert," grated the voice. "Yes, you do need an attorney. You'd better get the best one you can find, too. You are already in a great deal of trouble, in case you don't know it, Fitzgilbert, both with my service and with the state taxation department, with whose Mister Schabe I was just conferring yesterday, concerning you and some other notable tax cheats. If you know what's good for you, you'll be in my office at three today."

"Impossible!" snapped Fitz.

"Why?" demanded the voice.

"Because I say so," Fitz replied. "I am not some subordinate under your jurisdiction and I need give you no other answer. And not tomorrow, either. I'll see you . . ." he glanced down at the calendar on his bureau, "on next Tuesday morning at eleven."

"You have been and are being uncooperative,

Fitzgilbert, most uncooperative indeed. I *might* be inclined to be more lenient with you if you come in to see me today or tomorrow. Otherwise . . . well, do you think you will look good in grey denim, Fitzgilbert?" rasped the voice ominously.

"I don't know who or what you presume yourself to be, Blutegel. No, don't bother to correct me again. It's this way—you don't grant me the dignity of a title before my last name, you don't get granted one by me," Fitz stated coldly. "I am getting a lawyer, and that, damned fast. I also intend to contact certain people up in D.C. and make a determination of what right, if any, you have to call me such things as 'criminal' and 'tax cheat' or to threaten me with federal prison. This entire conversation is on tape, you see; all of my conversations from my home phones are.

"Goodbye, Blutegel. Don't ring me up again. I'll see you Tuesday."

After he had heard the tape, Gus Tolliver shook his head slowly. "Yeah, Fitz, boy, they after your ass, the pack of the bloodsuckers. At least this here pair is got them the names for it."

"What do you mean?" asked Fitz.

"Oh, that's right, you don't talk no German, do you?" Gus nodded. "Well, Blutegel is the German word for a leech, and Schabe means a cockaroach. They's both of them good names for bastards is in that line of work, too. I tell you, you come on into town today and I'll take you over for to see my lawyer, Pedro Goldfarb. Bring along that tape and I'll get this feller up the street from the shop to copy 'er, two, three copies, enyhow. I think you right, see, I don't think that fucker's got no kinda right to threaten you and call you names like he done. With that there tape, you just may have him by the balls, so you oughta have you more than just the one, see.

"You really know some guys in D.C.?"

"No," replied Fitz, "but Blutegel doesn't know I don't."

"Well, I *do*," said Gus. "And while you driving in, I'm gonna call two, three fellers I knows up there. It's fuckers like that Blutegel, use to make good Gestapo men for the Nazis. In Russia, they have 'em working for the KGB. Over here, they gets their rocks off finding them some poor fucker screwed up trying to do his own taxes and they drags him th'ough a fucking wringer by his cock. Maybe I can get his Kraut ass dragged acrost the coals a few times, ain't no sense in not at least trying."

But at his office, they were told that Pedro Goldfarb was in court and was not expected back before closing time of the law firm.

"Well, then, how 'bout Miz Dardrey, is she in?"

While the receptionist busied herself with the intercom, Gus said to Fitz, "I got a feeling we better do some legal-type talking today, see. And Pedro, he tells me this pertic'ler partner of his is just as smart as a fu . . ." he screeched to a halt in mid-word and glanced at the receptionist with a brief, guilty look before continuing, "smart as a whip. He says she's helped pull him out the sh . . ." another fast pause and another guilt-ridden glance, "out the soup, more than once. She's a real looker, too. She's 'bout forty, I'd say with a body and legs that won't quit. Looking at her makes me wish *I* was forty again, I tell you!"

"If you were forty, Mister Tolliver," a warm, smooth, female voice spoke from behind them with overtones of amusement, "you'd be too young for me . . . but I do thank you for the compliments."

The two men turned to see a slender, very fair-skinned woman, her heart-shaped face framed by cascades of red-brown hair, regarding them with blue-green eyes which reflected the fleeting smile on her full, red lips. Despite her tailored suit, there could clearly never be any hiding her lush, thoroughly female figure.

Striding forward, she held out her hand, saying, "I'm Dannon Dardrey, Mister Tolliver. How can I help you?"

When Fitz took her cool hand in his own, he felt an immediate and a very strong sense of . . . of what he suddenly realized was *kinship* with the attorney. The feeling was stronger than any he had ever before sensed with any other relative—parents, brothers, sisters, even his own children. It was uncanny.

Apparently, this weird sense was shared, for the handsome woman suddenly wrinkled her brows and tilted her head to one side as she looked up at his face quizzically. "I am very pleased to meet you, Mister Fitzgilbert, but . . . haven't we two met before . . . somewhere, sometime? It seems that I know you."

In her comfortable office, she heard them both out and listened to the tape, then leaned back in her big chair and began to fill a small meerschaum pipe from a canister of dark, spicy-smelling tobacco while she spoke her thoughts on the matter.

"I don't know, Mister Fitzgilbert, but what that Pedro or one of our other associates might better represent you in this matter, unless we can get your case switched over to another person, down at the local offices of the I.R.S. I have had to deal with Mister Blutegel before, on behalf of other clients, and there is a definite lack of rapport where we two are concerned, principally due to the fact that he feels women should not be in the professions or in business—you know, the old *'Kinder, Kirche, Kuche'* mind-set. You were most unlucky to have had your file land on his desk, for he is a very unpleasant man; thank God he is atypical of your usual I.R.S. person.

"I'll still be here tonight, when Pedro gets back. I'll cover this matter with him, all right? Should there be any questions, Mister Fitzgilbert, give me a number at which I can reach you tonight. Unless you should hear differently from either Pedro or me, be at this office at nine o'clock on Tuesday morning and one of us, maybe both, will go with you to the Federal Building.

"Please let me keep these files and copies of your tax returns. Oh, and this tape recording, too. I can't be sure yet, of course, but *Herr* Blutegel just may have overstepped even his overblown concepts of his God-given authority, this time around.

"Schabe's much easier to deal with. There is a lot of politics at work in his department, state politics. Members of this firm did a good bit of work for and contributed some fair sums of money to the successful campaign of the current governor . . . and Schabe intimidates quite easily, so we may be able to handle the state's business with you entirely by phone and mail. But here again, I'll have to confer with Pedro on this."

Again, that powerful sense of kinship as he shook her hand, returned her firm grip, felt the hidden strength, thick velvet over tempered steel. Their eyes locked for a fleeting moment and he saw hers filled with wonderment and . . . with something else, something that he could not just then define. His own feelings were jumbled, chaotic. He knew that he and Gus must leave now, their meeting with the woman concluded, but. . . but he did not want to leave her, did not want even to release her hand.

But, of course, he did.

He and Gus conducted their accounting session in the shop, then had dinner in the fine restaurant of the businessmen's club of which Gus was a member. It was an early dinner and Fitz was back at home by nine. It was by then too late to drive in to pick up his mail from the local post office branch, so he showered and went to bed, to there experience the strangest, most vivid dream he ever had had . . . in this world.

CHAPTER VI

The springless pony cart bounced and swayed along the bumpy, deep-rutted road, or what passed for one. It was a very uncomfortable ride in the damp, misty, drizzly weather, and the sights frequently espied along the way were even less pleasant. It might have been an easier journey at a slower, more careful pace, but the old, bearded man on the tall horse led the two draught ponies at the best speed of which they were capable, heedless alike of rocks and ruts and other impedimenta to the forward progress of them and the cart to which they were yoked.

The bodies of two men hung by their necks from a tree near where the road traveled by the cart and another road intersected. The feet of the bodies were only a foot off the ground and their twisted faces, with protruding eyes and swollen, purplish tongues told of a hard, slow death of strangulation. Beneath their feet lay the almost-naked corpses of two women.

119

Their throats had been cut with such force as to almost sever the heads from the bodies, and the bellies of both had been slashed open from crotch to breastbone. Their breasts had been sliced from off their chests and hideous savageries had been done upon their faces and heads with sharp knives. They looked white as swans, lying there in the last hours of the grey day, their bodies all drained of blood and washed as for burial by the cold, drizzling rain.

The old, long-bearded man muttered something too low to be clearly heard as he and the cart passed the terrible tableau, then tried to urge still more speed out of the ponies.

Fitz knew that he was in the cart, nor was he alone. Of course he was not alone. *She* was with him, naturally: his sister, who would one day be his bride and the queen who would rule with him.

She was crying now, crouching low against the side of the cart, hiding her head and face in her cloak. She was terrified that the Dark Ones would catch them and do to her what they had done to so many others, like that fair child they had seen earlier on this terrible journey through mist and rain and cold, the child whose small body had been impaled on a lance shaft.

Fitz was terrified, too, but he meant to be a warrior-king and so he steeled himself not to cry or show fear. Nonetheless he was very fearful. His kind were being mutilated and butchered from one end to the other of this land that had been all theirs only a very short time ago. The Dark Ones were inciting and abetting and even joining in the orgy of rapine and murder in the names of gods and goddesses alien to this ancient land.

The bruising ride seemed to go on forever. But at last, with the ponies exhausted, stumbling, nearly foundered, the old, long-bearded man let the pair halt, to stand with their big heads hung low, their dripping roan flanks heaving like smith's bellows, their heated breaths rising in white clouds from their distended nostrils.

Wordlessly, he leaned down from the war saddle of his tall horse and gathered the two young children from the cart-bed up, into his sinewy arms. Then he turned the horse about and rode on, up the steep hill, on a path that would have been impossible for the ponies and the cart, where even the horse stumbled now and again on loose rocks.

At last, it became too steep and precipitous for even the sure-footed horse and the old man dismounted and proceeded on up, bearing both Fitz and his sister in his arms. Pushing through high, dense brush, among the thick trunks of ancient trees, he finally came to a boulder higher than his head, on which were carvings so weatherworn as to be unidentifiable.

Setting down the two children at his feet, the aged man took from beneath his cloak a wand of peeled willow wood, raised it, and began to speak. The rapid spate of words were couched in the Old Speech, but were so fast and slurred that Fitz could only understand snatches of the formula.

From far down below, on the lower slope of the hill, there came sounds dim with distance—the thudding of many hooves, the shouts of men, the winding of a horn, then the agonized scream of a pony.

Fitz, looking up, saw the old man grip the hilt of his fine bronze sword in its enameled sheath so tightly that the knuckles stood out from the hand like snow-white pebbles, but he calmly continued the formula, his willow wand never wavering.

Then, all within the space of an eyeblink, the

center of the huge old boulder ceased to exist, leaving in its place an oval opening some six feet high and four feet broad. Light and warmth poured out from the opening, along with the good smells of something savory cooking with herbs and onions and garlic.

Just as he swept the two children back up into his arms and made to step through the opening, the war-trained destrier down below them screamed out his challenge, another horse screamed with pain and there rose up, much closer than before, renewed shouting of men. But when they were through the opening, having taken but a step or two, the noises were become so muted that Fitz had to strain to detect them and, after a few more steps by the old man, he could not hear anything at all, save the clumps of boots on stone and the ritual greeting words of a woman.

"It finally came to open battle, just as I said it would," stated the old man without preamble. "We lost that battle, for the arts of the Dark Ones are powerful, so the ownership and rule of the outer land is passed to them, though I doubt their strengths sufficient to penetrate this lower land, as well.

"What became of the king is just now unclear. Some say he died on the field of battle; some say that he went under a hill; others, that he was transported to The Isle of the Blest. I've had not the time to scry out the truth.

"The queen is dead, raped and murdered before she and certain others could get under the hill. The Strangers are doing the like to every one of us they can catch aboveground—men, women and children, it makes no difference to the brutal Strangers and the Dark Ones."

"You knew that this would happen, didn't you?"

asked the woman. "You knew and tried to tell the king and queen, your nephew and niece, but they would not heed you in their pity for the Strangers."

"Yes," the old man nodded, his dripping grey beard waggling wetly, steam arising from his sodden cloak in the warm chamber, "I knew. I sensed over the long centuries what was to be, what had to be. But my nephew was only two hundred years king, then. He and my niece would take in orphaned beasts, and they took in the Strangers in the same way, out of the same emotions. Now they and too many of us are repaid for their misguided charity done so long ago.

"But we may not have long. The power of the Dark Ones might seek out and find and let them enter here. I have brought the prince and princess of our kind. They *must* be kept from harm, kept from out the cruel, deadly clutches of those we befriended, now become bitter enemies. Will your doorway go to an under the hill anywhere, or to The Isle?"

"No," she sighed, "not without a lengthy period of resettings. It now goes only to the The World That Is To Be."

"Well, then," said the old man, "that is where we will have to take these precious ones. We will take them both back to infancy, first, though. That done, we will exchange them for other infants in that other world, as has been done before. What chances with them there will be in the lap of the Highest, but we will know and cause others to know where and how they may be found when our world once more needs them and is become safer for them."

Fitz awoke to the sound of the gate bell. He jumped up, drew on his robe and pushed his feet into his slippers, then padded into his office and thumbed on his newly installed intercom. "Yes, yes. Who is it, please?"

That so-well-remembered voice came through the wires to warm him and his chilly office. "Mister Fitzgilbert? I . . . it's Dannon Dardrey. I know it's late, but . . . Mister Fitzgilbert, I just drove down from the city, I *must* speak with you. *Please.*"

"Okay." Fitz pressed the button that now unlocked the gate. "Drive your car inside, don't leave it parked out there. Some of my neighbors . . . well, some of the kids hereabouts don't like me very well and are light-fingered, to boot."

The Dannon he let into his front door looked not one whit so calm and self-assured as had the attorney with whom he had spoken only a few hours earlier. She looked worried, harried, more than a little confused.

"That's a long drive," he said. "You could've phoned me, you know, you didn't have to come clear out here at almost midnight. Am I in more trouble than you thought?"

"You may well be," she answered enigmatically, adding, "and me, too."

"Well, then," he waved at one of the leather chairs, "sit down and fill your pipe while I get some clothes on. Would you like a drink?"

"No, damn it!" she almost shouted. "I don't want a drink, I want *you*! I don't even know why I want you, but . . . but it's like you're a . . . a part of me that has been missing forever and . . . and now I want it back, I've *got* to have it back. Do . . . do I make any sense to you? I don't to myself. I'm a perfectly respectable, fifty-five-year-old widow and I rank high in my chosen profession, if I say so myself. I just don't do mad, impulsive, immoral things like this, Mister Fitzgilbert. But there's . . . I don't know, there's . . . *something* about *you*, hell, maybe it's *me*, maybe I'm having a nervous breakdown or something. Do you understand any of this, Mist . . . oh, hell, if I'm going to have sex with you, and I *am*, I might as well call you Fitz. Please tell me there's a sound, logical reason for the way I feel about you, a man I never saw before today. Please tell me that, Fitz."

Gravely, Fitz said, "From the first moment that I touched your hand this afternoon, I've felt strongly and very strangely drawn to you. The immediate feeling that I had then was what I thought was a feeling of kinship, but a much stronger feeling of kinship than I ever have felt for any real relatives in the past. I felt as if you were the other half of me, long ago sundered, and that I had to have you back, no matter what it took to get you. When the time came for Gus and me to leave, it was all that I could do to make myself tell you goodbye and then turn and walk out of that office. Leaving the proximity of you was like tearing off a piece of my body, Dannon."

Her eyes became misty, and she nodded slowly, "Yes, I know, Fitz, I could hardly bear to part from you, either, this afternoon. I suppose that I knew, even then, that I'd drive out here tonight. That's why I fought it so hard and for so long. And my name is Danna, it was once Mary Diana Flaherty. My late husband's name was Dardrey. I passed the state bar as M. Danna Dardrey,, but some clerical error made the middle name into Dannon and I've kept it ever since."

"All right," said Fitz, "now, do you want a drink?"

She shook her head. "No, I want directions to your loo. I'm going to take a shower, if you don't mind. Maybe that will give me back enough sanity to leave here before I commit mortal sin with you."

* * *

Much, much later, as they lay very close on his rumpled bed, her red-brown hair lying in disorder over his arm as it pillowed her head, she gasped out a long, shuddering sigh and said, "I pray God that it was as good for you as it was for me. I loved my young husband, Kevin, Fitz, I loved him with all my heart and soul, and I took inordinate pleasure from pleasing him as he pleased me. But now I know that that long-ago lovemaking was but a pale, almost-invisible shadow of the real article. It hurts me terribly to have to so speak of that poor, brave young man, but it's all truth and it must be spoken, regardless."

"You never had other lovers, Danna?" he asked.

"No, Fitz, since Kevin, there has never been another . . . until you, my own. We had been married for almost two years when the Japanese bombed Pearl Harbor. I tried my damnedest, along with his folks and mine, to persuade Kevin to hold off his passion to enter the military for only six months, until he had his degree and could go in as an officer, but he had to disregard us all and enlist, leaving me with our year-old son, Kevin, Junior. I saw him three whole times after that, before he was killed in North Africa, at the Kasserine Pass, never having been allowed to get even as close as ten thousand miles to the Japanese he had joined the army to fight. Four months after he had died, I gave birth to our younger son, Richard.

"Kevin had had both GI and civilian insurance and his mom and pop were relatively well-off for those days. With Kevin dead, I just kept on living with them and invested most of the money, saving out only enough to go to college and learn enough to become a legal secretary. That was the work I did

*   *   *

ad spent much time in bed over
t not all that much of that time in
uickly drifted off to sleep on Sunday
ad phoned to let him know that she
y at her apartment. Then, sometime
, he found himself experiencing yet
e vivid, incredibly real and utterly
ms. As he lay there, he knew not
s truly awake or still asleep, but in
knew without even opening his eyes
alone in the big bed.

?" he breathed, reaching out toward
of the bed. But his hand found not
, delicate skin or silky hair. Instead,
uched, sank into dense, plushy fur,
oking a deep bass purring noise.
d and dear friend," he suddenly heard
at he recalled from another fantastic
yment of one's mate is very pleasant,
other, even more important things that
eeded hand and powers, while you daw-
urney much of the length and all of the
Pony Land, innocently unaware of the
gers that dwell there, the horrible and
creatures that stalk its flatnesses in search
ere, make use of your paw and its so-
sions, and scratch my belly."

thought that he opened his eyes to see
cat, Tom, whose body he knew lay buried
yard, nearly a year dead, lying sprawled
. Even as he watched, the big, blue-grey
onto his back and lay with his hind legs
ayed and his forelegs folded down upon
s on either side of his chest.
what are you waiting for? Scratch," said the

until the boys were both old enough to fend for
themselves, then I quit work and went back to college, taking my law degree in 1957, just prior to my
own thirty-seventh birthday."

Fitz raised his head so he could better see her
face. "You were born in 1920? Damn, so was I. You
sure as hell don't look like any fifty-five, Danna. Or do
you dye your hair and go in for face lifts?"

"I've never had a need for hair dye or even rinses,
Fitz, and my face is just the way God made it, thank
you. But you don't look to be your actual age either.
Fitz. Until I got into your records, I had taken you to
be no older than your early forties, if that," she said
bluntly.

"How did you pick up the name Danna, Danna?"
he inquired. "It's an odd one. I don't think I've ever
heard or even seen it before."

She laughed throatily. "My mother's name was
Mary, too, so I was called Diana, the middle name on
my baptismal record. My eldest brother—I was the
firstborn child in the Flaherty household—when he
was very young couldn't say Diana, so he called me
Danna and the name just stuck from then on. I've
already told you where and how I came by the
Dannon name; I keep it because it confuses the hell
out of your average, staid, stodgy, chauvinistic busi-
nessman or attorney who telephones or comes to the
office to see M. Dannon Dardrey. I freely admit that
I derive a sadistic thrill from hearing or watching
them squirm."

"What do your sons think of having a top-flight tax
lawyer and an admitted sadist for a mother?" he
chuckled, then wished he'd said anything else but
those words when he saw the infinite sadness that
came upon her face.

In a low, grief-laden voice, she said, "They were

very proud of me when they were still alive, Fitz, and I of them. Kevin, Junior, went to West Point, he graduated in 1962, and his brother and three of his grandparents and I were all there to see it. So was the sweet, dear girl who became his bride within weeks of his graduation. By 1970, he was a captain of infantry in Vietnam, with medals for his inherited bravery, others for his competence in his profession and still more for his combat wounds. Then, one night while he was sleeping, some soldier—a disgruntled troublemaker Kevin had had disciplined, I've been told—threw a hand grenade into the place and killed my boy and severely wounded another officer. The murderer was almost immediately shot and killed by yet a third officer . . . but that couldn't bring back my Kevin.

"Dicky always had to be different from his older brother, it was like an obsession with him, so when Kevin was accepted for West Point, he set about trying to get an appointment to Annapolis. Failing at that, he went to a college that had a naval cadet program and did so well in it that he was awarded a regular Navy commission upon his graduation. Not quite a year after his older brother was murdered, Dicky was stung by a scorpion fish while skin diving for pleasure and died before he could be gotten to medical attention.

"Kevin and Barbara, for some reason, never were able to have any children, so I was denied even the small solace of grandchildren. I'm very much alone . . . rather, I was alone until today, until you.

"But you, you're a widower, aren't you? Care to talk about your life?"

He told her. He told her all of it, from beginning to tragic end. And she cried for him, for his long years of suffering, and what could he do but comfort

her. Comfor
kisses and m
exploring the
They they ma
and yet again.

They awoke
slats of the blin
saluting the new
other and of thei
wholesome whole

That weekend
ing period of time
with anyone in all
her eight-year-old
let her out the gat
did not feel lonely,
Danna was still the
she had touched or
invisible, welcome p
she had used, lay st
two had experienced
other. Best and most
with him, in him, trul
that now nothing—no
even grim death, itself
one from the other, as
years before these last
reuniting two parts into
and the unbridled joy he
have been, more comple

His mood was one of u
trundled down load on lo
world, knowing that he n
his other half, Danna. He
her of, then introduce he
freedom of this world of s
stars that he now considere

He and Danna
the weekend, b
sleeping, so he
night, after she
had arrived safe
during the nigh
another of thos
impossible dre
whether he wa
either case, he
that he was no

"Danna . . .
the other half
smooth, warm
the fingers t
their touch ev

"Yes, my o
in a voice th
dream, "enjo
but there are
await your ne
dle here or j
breadth of
terrible dan
most deadly
of meat. H
useful exten

Fitz then
his old pet
in the back
on the bed
cat rolled
widely sp
themselve
"Well,

dead-alive cat. "Be helpful to me, at least, before
you go down the gullet of Teeth and Legs, as you
soon or late will, if you spend overmuch time on that
fearsome plain."

"Tom," asked Fitz in bewilderment, "are . . . are
you really *talking* to me?"

"No, not really," came the cat's caustic reply. "Actually, one of the chipmunks burrowed under this
house is a ventriloquist. Of course I'm talking to
you. I'm saying, 'Scratch my belly with your short,
flat, blunt claws.' "

"I've seen nothing of a nature or size to threaten
me on that plain," argued Fitz, while dutifully scratching the warm, living, furry belly of the cat he knew
to be dead and moldering in a grass-grown grave
marked by the statue of a sleeping cat carven from
grey limestone. "Only the tracks of some beast that
was, to judge by those tracks, the size of a leopard or
a jaguar or, maybe, a puma."

"Those pad prints at the ponds at the verges of the
lake were not those of any leopard or jaguar or
puma, friend, they were mine. I have been watching
you as you move about on that noisy, smelly, three-
wheeled thing that you brought from this world.
Someone has to try to keep you out of trouble until
you come to the full knowledge of just who and what
you are and to full realization of your inherent powers. But that will never happen if old Teeth and Legs
eats you first, so cross that plain as fast as you can
and come to the hills and forests, where you are
needed, where your destiny awaits you."

Fitz left off scratching the cat now purring contin-
uously, even as he somehow spoke words. The man
took a forepaw between thumb and forefinger and
eyed it, critically. "Yes, you're big enough, Tom.
You weighed over twenty pounds. But whatever cat

left those prints by the water there, in the sand world, would dwarf a mere twenty-pound tomcat. Why, those prints were about as broad as my palm and so deep as to make me think that the owner of those feet weighed as much as ten times twenty pounds."

"You stopped scratching," the cat admonished. "Please start again. But yes, those tracks were mine. Your eyes see the Tom you remember, see me in the body that was mine in this world. But in that world, I am not so small and puny, though my color and my mind are unchanged."

"Your mind was as it now is in all the time before you . . . you died?" demanded Fitz. "Then why did you never talk to me like you now are doing?"

"Oh, but I did, and often," replied the purring cat. "It was just that then, before my old body died, you had had none of the experiences that resulted in the first dim beginnings of the reawakening of your mind and the vast powers it holds, so you could not hear my words, only the beast-noises that the power-less and savage strangers hear.

"You were overlong in awakening, my good old friend, for long and long, even in The Isle, where everything is conducive to the uses of powers, much time elapsed before you had gained—rather, re-gained—the abilities of seeing me, hearing me, even only as I was, as simple Strangers saw me in this world.

"But now, finally, your powers are beginning to manifest themselves. They are still slowed, however, slowed and stunted because you spend so much time in this world which is inimical to powers. You must be more in The Isle to become that which you can be, that which you must be, are you to fulfill your destiny. Stay as little as three moons in The Isle and

you will have it all back—your powers and, with them, the memories of all that was before, all that is now and all that is to be, with the help of you, the one you call Danna and others.

"But do not linger on the plain, old friend, else it is but a matter of time before a pair of Teeth and Legs finds you and deprives you of life and all those who depend upon you and your powers of a future. Come you, rather, directly to the hills and forests, where the Teeth and Legs never trespass."

Thinking of the toothiest beast he had seen in the sand world, Fitz asked. "This or these you call Teeth and Legs, are they like the huge crocodile that came after me on the beach?"

The cat's voice indicated a gentle amusement. "Old Kassandra? Of course not, she only eats sea creatures, like all her kind. It was just that she does not see too clearly, especially not on land. She took you at first for some robber after her eggs, but when I explained to her who and what you were, you notice, she stopped chasing you.

"No, the Teeth and Legs are much like you, in general shape, but much, much larger, covered in coarse hair and with long, wide, strong jaws filled with many big, long, sharp teeth. There are not and have never been many of them, else there would be no life at all upon the plain, and since they will feed upon anything that walks, swims, flies, hops or crawls, even others of their own kind, they seldom are seen in numbers, mostly alone. You will smell them, hopefully, before you see them. But beware, even ponies and the long-legs you think of as rat-tailed ostriches are hard-pressed to outrun one and I think that one might even outpace your noisy thing with three wheels. So cross the plain and come to the hills, where you will be safe from them. Much and many

depend upon you, so you must take care to preserve yourself for us."

When he arrived at the law offices in the city on Tuesday morning, just before the specified time of nine o'clock, a secretary came out and led him into the back of the suite, but not to Danna's office, rather to a much larger one, wherein stood a man about his own age, height and build, though he had silver-stippled black hair, vandyke and guardsman moustache.

The office itself looked much like a set from the movie *El Cid*—dark, heavy, intricately carved Spanish furnishings, Moorish rugs over highly polished hardwood flooring, drapes that resembled tapestries, arrangements of real-looking, medieval weapons and shields bedecking the walls, even a full suit of armor in one corner, its articulated gauntlets resting atop the pommel of a bastard-sword. Had Charlton Heston suddenly burst into the room through one of the side doors, his dusty armor clanking, grasping a blood-streaked mate to that long, wide battle-brand, thought Fitz, he would not have looked in the least out of place or anachronistic.

The greying man, who rounded an oversized, dark-oaken desk and strode to meet him with outstretched hand, however, wore no period clothing and not one single piece of armor. He was dressed in an expensively tailored, very conservative three-piece suit, pin stripes of grey on a ground color of a blue so dark as to be almost black. His shirt was of a blue a few shades lighter than the suit, but still dark, and the tie alternated stripes of blue and burgundy. His gleaming black ankle boots were beautifully tooled and obviously of foreign cut and manufacture.

His grip was firm, though well-controlled as his

baritone voice. "Mister Fitzgilbert, I'm Pedro Goldfarb. You are most welcome, sir. Please come in and be seated, won't you. Danna Dardrey will be in shortly. It's a bit early in the day for me to take spirits, but if you would care to indulge, there's plenty here." He chuckled. "You name it, and I've most likely got it somewhere in this suite. Or would you rather join me in a cup of coffee?"

Fitz immediately liked the man, so he frowned and asked, "You're no bigger than me, true, but do you think we both could fit comfortably into just one cup?"

Goldfarb looked at him blankly for a split second, then he chuckled, and then he began to laugh and continued to do so until his dark-blue eyes were brimming with tears and his face had darkened until it almost matched the burgundy stripes of his tie. When he had wiped his eyes and stuffed the dark-blue linen handkerchief back in his pocket, he said, "Sorry, I wasn't ready for a *bon mot* that good so early. With your kind permission, I'll remember that one and use it. There's a judge I have in mind . . .

"But back to you. May I call you Fitz? Fine, you call me Pedro. Fitz, both Gus Tolliver and our own Danna told me that I'd like you and I do, no two ways about it. Besides," he grinned slyly, "I know up front you can afford our services, that we won't have to have your legs broken before we can collect our outrageous fees from you, and that last always warms the cockles of a hard-working ambulance chaser's heart toward a new client.

"Fitz, if I hadn't been so anxious to not put off meeting you, I'd have had you called and told to stay home today. For some strange reason," merriment twinkled from his eyes as he made a show of feigning complete innocence of any meaning behind his words,

"Mister Blutegel, his immediate supervisor and that man's supervisor, as well, were all summoned to the regional I.R.S. office this morning—some kind of consultation, one would assume—and the man in temporary charge of the local office is of the opinion that we should await the return of those three before we make the attempt to set up another appointment time, which suits my own, somewhat-crowded schedule much better, I must say.

"I've looked over your files, accounts and tax returns, and I also had conversations yesterday with both Blutegel and Schabe. Yes, they can cause you trouble, Fitz. They most likely *will* cause you trouble and some amount of expense, barring a miracle from on high—and those seem to get rarer and rarer, in this old world of ours—but it's not anywhere nearly as bad as Blutegel and Schabe would have liked you to think it to be. Blutegel believes in and operates along the lines of pure terror tactics, figuring that a scared taxpayer will be a pliable taxpayer, far easier to manipulate and bamboozle with his normal thinking processes clouded by fear of notoriety and prison time. And the real sin of it all is that it often works, as well as that he and others like him have been allowed to get away with using Gestapo tactics in a supposedly free country."

He fell silent and opened an inlaid wooden box on his desk, then paused and asked, "You don't smoke at all? That's what I'm told."

"I used to," Fitz answered, "but I had to quit during a period when my circumstances were somewhat straitened, and I've never started it up again. But you feel free, if you wish, it doesn't bother me in the least, Pedro."

The attorney selected from out the box a medium-brown cheroot as long as a new pencil and just as thin, removed one end with a clip from the box, then spent a few moments carefully lighting it with a golden lighter.

Twin streams of light-bluish smoke coming from the nostrils of his thin, high-bridged nose, he said, "I ask again, Fitz, do you want some hot coffee?"

Only moments after he had called on the intercom, the silver and fine-china coffee service was wheeled in on a serving cart by a young woman Fitz had not seen before, who wordlessly placed the tray atop the attorney's desk and wordlessly departed with the serving cart.

Savoring the fragrant steam arising from his cup, Fitz smiled and said, "You go first cabin all the way, don't you, Pedro? I'm beginning to wonder whether or not I really can afford your services."

The attorney laughed. "Oh, you can, you can, never fear. Remember, I'm Gus Tolliver's attorney, too, so I knew quite a good deal about you and your affairs, and especially your finances, long before you first set foot in this suite of offices, Fitz.

"But concerning your affairs, your finances, my new friend and client, it has been my sad experience with bureaucrats of any rank, stature or agency, that they do not take at all well being called to task by superiors when in the wrong; most especially, when in the wrong. For that reason, I think it might be wise if all of your dealings with these local bloodsuckers be through me or through Danna, for a while; otherwise, they will likely do everything within their scope to make you and keep you thoroughly miserable and very harried in pure retaliation for causing trouble for some of their staff."

Fitz shrugged. "Okay by me, Pedro, but I doubt I'll have much control over them; after all, they know my number and where I live, so if they decide

to harass me, there's damn-all I can do to stop them.
Is there?"

"There certainly is," Goldfarb assured him confidently. "You can get beyond their reach for a while.
Go on a trip—the farther, the better. You have holdings in South African gold, I recall, why not go there?
It's beautiful country, you know. You could go on a
safari, a long safari, come back with some zebra skins
and stuffed antelope heads. Leave me or Danna power
of attorney to handle your affairs and get going before they think to try to restrain your movements
. . . which those bastards do have the power to do, if
they feel strongly enough to invoke it."

"Couldn't they seize my bank accounts and everything else I own if I'm not around to protect it,
Pedro?"

The attorney shrugged, then, "Sure, they could
freeze or seize the paltry sums you'll leave in your
bank accounts, any safety deposit boxes that are held
in your name, any of your money or property that
Gus happens to be holding for you, your cars maybe,
your house. But what kind of losses would those be?
And besides, when your case gets to the tax courts, I
am convinced that they'll have to give you most or all
of it back."

"Hell, I don't give a shit about the money and the
cars, Pedro," declared Fitz, "'but believe it or not,
that property and the little house on it means more
to me than you could imagine. If I deed it to somebody else, could they still seize it?"

Goldfarb frowned. "If you're thinking of Gus
Tolliver, all I can say is: I wouldn't. After all, he's
your agent for your gold coins, so you can bet they'll
be after him with hammer and tongs, once they
find you're not around to punish for the heinous
crime of not only objecting to Blutegel's emotional

rubber hosing, but actually doing something to get his knuckles rapped."

"You don't think the summons to the regional office means that he'll be chewed out, maybe demoted then, Pedro?" asked Fitz.

"Oh, hell no," said Goldfarb. "Not him. He'll get his wrists slapped a bit, his superiors, too, but not because of what he did or tried to do to you, just because he did it in such a way, this time, that his chosen victim was able to raise a stink over their heads. No, he's effective in squeezing money out of people, and that's the bottom line, Fitz, that's all the I.R.S. honchos care about; *how* it's done, the methods the field personnel use to do it, couldn't matter less to them.

"But back to hanging on to your house and land . . . hmmm. I'll tell you what, deed it all—real property, motor vehicles, furniture, personal possessions, lock boxes and anything else you want to keep their sticky fingers and greedy hands off of—to Danna. I'll have Shirl draw up the proper documents, she's a notary, too. They'll say that you've transferred title to everything to Mrs. M. Dannon Dardrey for services rendered and to be rendered while you're out of the country. Then, let's see the bastards try to seize something.

"Of course," he smiled, "you're going to have to trust Danna one hell of a lot . . . me, too. Do you think you can trust us that far, Fitz?"

"I'd trust Danna with my life," stated Fitz, slowly and soberly, then he grinned. "You, I'll trust simply because I know where and how to find you and I think I could stomp you with no trouble . . . well, not much trouble."

Goldfarb matched the grin. "Oh, really? Be careful, Fitz, I was a Marine, too, a Fleet Marine."

Fitz laughed. "Well then, Mister Fancy Pants, we ought to be an even-money bout."

The drive back home was especially slow and tedious that afternoon, with heavy truck traffic clogging the two- and three- and sometimes four-lane secondary roads leading out, northeast, from the city. As he drove, stuck in no-passing areas in lines of cars and smaller trucks behind lumbering, gear-grinding, diesel-smoke-belching behemoths, at speeds that were frankly ridiculous for his powerful Mercedes, he had time to think through the happenings of the day and try to sort them out, lay firm plans for his foreign sojourn and grieve for the length of time said sojourn would keep him away from Danna, so new-found and already so dear to him.

No doubt the widely travelled Pedro Goldfarb knew whereof he spoke and the Union of South Africa was a lovely country, indeed, but still, Fitz had no desire to go there . . . not unless Danna could go along with him. But in order for the carefully worked out scheme to keep the minions of the I.R.S. off him until Pedro felt the time right to move in his defense, Danna *had* to remain here. Nor had he any faintest desire to ride or tramp about the countryside of South Africa or any other place shooting zebras, lions, elephants, buffalos or antelopes; to his way of thinking, there were only three reasonable excuses for killing any other living creature—for food, in self-protection or to put it down when it was incurable and suffering, which last was how he had been able to kill Kath, his daughter. His opinion of people who just ran around with firearms or any other weapon shooting anything that moved was that they should be disarmed in whatever way was easiest and then confined straitly in rooms with soft walls for the rest of their lives.

Pedro was insistent that he drop out of sight and out of reach of Blutegel and the rest for a few months, however; where he went did not seem to matter to the attorney. South Africa had been just a suggestion, a for instance, that had been made clear to him. So where could he go that he would not spend most of his waking hours missing Danna? Where, in all this world?

With a long, constant blaring of a held-down horn button, a middle-aged Cadillac whose driver either was in more of a hurry than Fitz and the rest or just plain of a suicidal bent, pulled out from somewhere far back in the creeping line of vehicles and sped up the inbound lane, solid double lines in the road center, be-damned.

"Dumbass bastard!" muttered Fitz aloud. "Must've learned to drive in New Jersey . . . or Florida."

So, where? Where in the world? Well, why *this* world, at all? Why not the sand world? Well, Fitz, why not? You want to cross the plain and explore those forested hills, don't you? Of course you do. That's why your subconscious keeps making you have those weird dreams about a dead cat talking to you. You know that, don't you? Do I? It seems so damned real . . .

Wait a minute, now. If I do go to the sand world, I don't have to stay there the entire time, do I? Of course not. I could set up some sort of schedule or signalling system so that Danna could be at the house and I could come back through the doorway in the sand world and be with her a few days and nights at a time, and no one the wiser. It's her house now, after all, so why shouldn't she spend some time in it whenever the mood strikes her? That sounds like a better bet to me than the trouble and expense and loneliness of some less than delightful months in some foreign country does.

Another thing, too: with this weird time distortion, it won't seem like so long . . . well, not to me, at least. The closest I've ever been able to figure it, two and a half days in the sand world works out to a bit over seven and a half days here. Therefore, if I spend forty or fifty days in the sand world, that'll work out to four or five months I'll be gone from this one, just about the amount of time Pedro wants me to be out of sight and reach.

But first I'll have to get in touch with Danna and get her to come out so I can explain it to her . . . well, so I can explain as much as I think she's ready for, right now. Pedro's probably right that I'd better stop saying anything I don't want heard and recorded by some stranger over my telephone, or writing and mailing anything I don't want opened and read by Blutegel. He says the I.R.S. and the USPOD are thick as thieves; stands to reason, I guess, since they both are composed of very uncivil servants—many of them; too many of them—of the same government.

So I'll drive into town, pick up the mail, and drop by the gun shop and the hardware store and the pay phone between them, before I go home. I might stop by the Yamaha place, too, and see if they have any new accessories that might prove helpful on a long, possibly rugged go in those hills beyond the plain.

Fitz could hear the loud, incessant fence alarms braying long before he reached his street or proximity of his house and, when his property came in sight around the curve of the street, it was seen to be the scene of a good bit of activity. Two sheriff's sedans were parked on the street in front and, as he drove up, a county rescue squad meat wagon was slowly negotiating its way through throngs of neighbors of all ages and both sexes standing singly, in pairs and in bunches of varying sizes on the street and the neighboring lawns, shouting to make themselves heard above the cacophony of the alarms. Closer, he saw that a county pumper truck had driven up onto a lot to the left of his and was parked close to the fence, the behatted and booted and slickered firemen now draining and folding hoses and repacking them on the truck.

Fitz parked as close as he could to the chaos, pushed through the throng to his gate, unlocked it and his garage and flicked off the lights and the deafening alarms, before going back beyond the gate to seek out the sheriff or the deputy in charge and find out just what had happened now. One crisis after another, anymore, it seemed.

The roadside ditch was brimful of running, muddy water and he had to jump its width, his cordovan brogues sinking deeply enough into the soggy ground on the other side to give him a shoe full of water and a consequent squelching sound as he walked back along the fence line toward the fire truck and the knot of deputies and civilians just behind it.

He got a look at his backyard, early on. Where the green wall tent had stood was now the center of a bare area of blackened grass, some burst gas cans and other bits and pieces of fire-scarred debris. The strip of steel that had secured the stone slab had been pried up at one end and the slab itself stood up in the open position. The area of the entire mound was soaked, running water still, and those large weeds and shrubs that had not been charred completely away had all been either broken off or uprooted by the force of the streams from the fire hoses.

A tall, lanky, raw-boned man dressed in filthy, well-muddied jeans, a faded, also filthy denim shirt with the left arm of it torn and bloodstained, and a pair of—of all things—new-looking, high-topped, cheap basketball shoes, stood beside Sheriff Vaughan, looking sullen. But immediately he spotted Fitz, the ill-kempt man pushed his way out of the knot of men and half-trotted to meet him.

"You gawdam richass bastid, you!" he shouted when still ten feet away. "My pore li'l boy, he's got a busted arm and nose, too, on account of you and yore gawdam fences and all! I'm gonna purely beat the shit out'n you, mistuh!"

But Vaughan and two of the deputies were on the man's very heels and before he could attempt to make good on his threat, he was on his knees on the wet ground, whining and sobbing in pain, his right arm twisted behind his back by one of the burly deputies.

"What the bloody hell has been going on here?" Fitz demanded of the sheriff. "Who the fuck burned down my wall tent?"

"The way it looks, Mister Fitzgilbert, sir," Vaughan replied, "it was that little JD, Calvin Mathews, as done it. Prob'ly, I'd say, his brother Bubba was in on it, too. Ain't no meanness the one of them gets into, the othern ain't just as deep into. But Calvin, he's the one we found down at the bottom of your fence when we got here. He's got a arm broke in three places and a broke nose and a concussion, prob'ly, too. Looks like he got scairt by the fire he set and tried to go back over the fence too fast and careless and fell off the top of it, is what I figger happened. His brother must of just run off and left him, 'cause we found him at home caterwaulin' about his brother being dead. While we was c'lecting him, his paw, Yancy, here, come rolling up in his pick-up.

"But Mister Fitzgilbert, sir, it may not've just been the boys, see. When we first seen Yancy, he had his shirtsleeve all tore up and his arm, too, it was bleeding like hell, afore the rescue squad bandaged it up. He had a pair of big wire cutters in his back pocket, too. Looky up there, and you'll see somebody done cut two strands of your bob-wire and the other'n is got a piece of what looks a lot to me like old blue denim stuck to it.

"What's that you got under your yard, there, anyhow, a fallout shelter?"

Fitz seized upon the subterfuge so generously and innocently offered him. "Yes, Sheriff, but it's nowhere near complete inside."

"Yeah, that's what I figgered it was. Well, it's chock fulla water now, but the way the wind was blowing in spurts when the firemen got out here, the chief, he was scared the fire might get to your house. But he said they could lend you a big sump pump if you want's to bail it out fast, like. He's a nice feller, he was a Gyrene, too, in Korea, like you and me. I'll interduce you to him in a few minutes.

"But back to your fallout shelter and the fire and all, I don't see how just no two kids could of bent up that steel strap and tore the hardware clean outen the masonry, like was done. It looks to me like Yancy Mathews, he was in on it, too. I means to send that crowbar we found in your yard and some other stuff to the State Police lab and see if the prints on that bar and some other things is Yancy Mathews' prints and if they is, I'm gonna see his bony ass racked like it ain't never been racked before in his life.

"Don't you worry none 'bout having to pr'fer charges or nothing, neither, Mister Fitzgilbert, sir. Whin thet fire was set, it passed plumb smack-dab into county jurisdiction, no particle of a private matter no more. Hell, wind been right, they could of burnt down half the damn neighborhood, the dumbbells, the house they rents, too!"

CHAPTER VII

As he unloaded the last batch of supplies and equipment at the foot of the gangplank he had built and attached to the gunwale of the wrecked ship in order to save clambering up the hard way each time he wanted to go aboard, Fitz thought back to his last few hours in that other world.

Danna had arrived while the gasoline-powered sump pump was spewing up spurt after spurt of water from the stone crypt—which had been filled, initially, to above the highest landing of the stairs, although Fitz, for the life of him, could not imagine why it had not simply poured through onto the beach of the sand world—to stream down the side of the grassy mound and pool in the yard. Since she now had a key, she had simply opened the gate, driven in, then let herself into the house. Seeing her in the back door, he had left the chugging machine to squelch his way through the miniature bog to the house.

147

After they had made love and gotten dressed again, they had taken the Jeep and driven into the town for a new wall tent and replacement supplies and clothing for those lost in the fire and ruined in the flooding of the underground storage area. It was while two of Herbert Bates's grandsons were loading his purchases into the back of the Wagoneer that Sheriff Vaughan drove by, screeched to a halt, backed up his cruiser and greeted Fitz.

Eyeing Danna appreciatively, the lawman said, "Mister Fitzgilbert, sir, just thought you might like to know. We got us a free-will confession outen Yancy Mathews a'ready, so we won't have to go th'ough all of the other, sending stuff to the State Police lab, and all that. You know, I knowed he'd been in on it all right from the start, too; he claimed when he drove up he'd just then got off work, but I knowed he's lying, see. If he'd been working—he does construction work—he'd of been wearing clodhoppers, not a brand-spanking-new pair of burglar shoes.

"Then, too, I knows that outfit he's working for just now and if he'd really tore his arm up on the job, they'd of at least of put a bandage and some merthi'late on it, if they hadn't of run him over to the county hospital 'mergency room. Besides of, it was clear as spring water to a ol' country boy like me bob-wire had tore his arm and shirt and all up. But he says he didn' have nothing to do with setting yore tent and all on fire, and I b'lieves him on thet one."

"But who's this purty young lady, Mister Fitzgilbert, sir? I don't b'lieve I've had the pleasure of making her acquaintance . . . .?"

"Sheriff Vaughan, this is my fiancee, Mrs. Mary Danna Dardrey. Danna, meet Gomer Vaughan, our county sheriff. Sheriff, I'm going to have to be away for a while. The house and property and the cars are now Mrs. Dardrey's, legally, and she'll be living out here for a few days at the time, now and then, while I'm gone."

Vaughan had taken Danna's hand as gingerly as if it had been a tiny, fledgling bird that he feared he might crush, and spoken softly, with a natural, rural gentility and grace, "Miz Dardrey, ma'am, I'm purely honored for to meet you. It's gonna be real nice for to have a fine lady like you a-living in my county, and enything whatsoever me or any my depitties can do for you, enytime, you just let me know. You hear?"

"Thank you, Sheriff Vaughan, I will. But back to this business of this confession: did the man say why he had broken into Fitz's shelter?"

Vaughan sighed and shook his head disgustedly. "He did, ma'am. Seems like he thought Mister Fitzgilbert is a big-time dope dealer and figgered he kept a big stash of dope in that shelter. When he'd busted in and found out he was wrong, he stole some small odds and ends of what he had found and took off, leaving the boys, Calvin and Bubba, there to steal whatever they wanted and could get over the fence.

"Coming over into the yard, he'd cut the two top strands of the bob-wire, but going back out, he tore up his arm and his shirt on the one he hadn't bothered for to cut, see. He got in his truck and drove over to a feller he thought would give him beer money for what he'd stole and then went and got him some brews.

"The boy, Bubba, says the two of them—him and Calvin—had got real mad on account of they could find shells but no guns to shoot them in, so they just poured gas all over the tent and set it on fire out of pure spite and meanness. Them boys is like that, ma'am, the both of them. Calvin, he set the fire, while Bubba was climbing out over the fence. But when Calvin made for to climb out, he got up to the top, a'right, but then he snagged his dungarees on the bob-wire and slipped and fell. It knocked him cold as a cucumber and Bubba thought he's dead and run home, a-bawling, to tell their maw."

"But what . . . ? Why in the world would this man have thought Fitz a dope dealer, big time or otherwise?" queried Danna.

Another shake of the head, another deep sigh on the part of Sheriff Vaughan. "Because, ma'am, whin the good Lord was a-passing out brains, Yancy Mathews had gone out for a pi . . . uhh, a beer, is why. *I* knows Mister Fitzgilbert's money comes from investments and selling collector's coins, but the onliest thing Yancy Mathews has ever invested in was cases of beer whinever Bates's likker store has had a holiday sale. He couldn't get it th'ough his beer-pickled head how Mister Fitzgilbert could make money without going out to work ever morning and, too, he thought that shoot-out, out there, whin them crooked Customs guys tried to kill Mister Fitzgilbert, was a bunch of racketeers like he sees on the 1930s movies on the late show on the teevee, so he figgered Mister Fitzgilbert, he had to be one too, and he figgered he could either steal him enough dope to sell to keep him in beer money for a long time, or he could let onto Mister Fitzgilbert he knowed about the dope and make him pay big bucks for to keep his mouth shut."

It then was Fitz who shook his head. "The man must be a cretin, Sheriff Vaughan. Does he have any idea what a real mob dope dealer would have done to him, and probably all his family too, had he tried to steal dope or extort money like that?"

"Like I done said, Mister Fitzgilbert, sir, Yancy Mathews is as dumb as the day is long. He's a beeraholic, his word don't mean sh . . . ahh, nothing to nobody, he beats his wife all the time and whales all his kids so bad they hafta do their school lessons standing up a lot the time—not that his two boys don't need it, mostly—he's just as mean as a cotton-mouth moccasin and is all the time out picking fights in ever beer joint and honky-tonk in the county that'll still let him inside the door, and out in the parking lots of those what won't, but a dog tick is got more brains than Yancy Mathews does. Naw, I know all he was thinking about was beer and getting the money to buy more of it with any way he could get it.

"Well, it's gonna be a long, dry spell for Yancy Mathews, this time 'round. County prosecuter, he says he's gonna ask for Yancy to get at least a year, mebbe two, on the county farm. We gonna turn Bubba, and Calvin too whinever he get outen the hospital, over to the state juvenile folks. Mebbe they can do something with the two of them . . . but I got my doubts 'bout thet, they's both bent twigs, I'm a-feared. It's a shame, too, 'cause their maw's of a decent old farm fambly up to White Creek, church-going folks; her paw was a deacon of the White Creek Baptis' Church 'til the day he died."

In the Jeep on the way back home, Danna said, "What's all this about a fallout shelter, Fitz? You're not *that* paranoid . . . I don't think. Are you?"

"It's not a fallout shelter, Danna, but it's difficult to go into trying to explain something that even you don't fully understand, especially to a man like our sheriff. He saw it and decided it was a fallout shelter and I just agreed with him that that's what it is. When we get back, I'm hoping all the water will be out, then I can show you what's down there. Prepare yourself for a real shock, though," was the reply she got.

As he began to lead her down the steep, shallow, and now very wet stone stairs, both of them wearing crepe-soled shoes and miner's headlamps, he cautioned, "Be very careful on these steps, Danna; they just weren't cut big enough for normal-sized, adult feet for some reason. I had an arrangement of safety ropes and wiring and lights at the landings and down below, too, but either that ignorant ridgerunner and his brats cut them down or the fire took them out, but you might try grasping the masonry spikes, at least they're still in place."

In the chamber at the bottom, Fitz found water still dripping down the walls from the stones of the ceiling and so he moved the hose of the sump pump to the far end of the crypt where there still was a few inches' depth of water for it to suck up and out.

Danna still stood at the foot of the stairs, looking around, letting the beam of her light play on the walls, floor, ceiling and the water-soaked remnants of what had been stacked supplies. "But Fitz, what in the world is this for? You didn't have it built, did you? It looks old, very old, I can't see any joint that looks like it has ever been mortared. How old is it?"

"I don't know about this crypt," he told her, "but that mound up there appears on county maps from the late seventeenth century. It's possible that this crypt was built by or for some Englishman who owned an estate that included this land back from the last couple of decades of the nineteenth century up to the late thirties of this one. But I don't guess anybody will ever know for sure.

"But look, we're pressed for time. Give me your hand, step down here to my side, close your eyes and bend at your waist, then just walk beside me."

She looked at him wonderingly, but did as he directed.

"Okay, Danna, straighten up and open your eyes. Hold it, don't trip over that log, there," he told her on the beach of the sand world.

After a trip across the dunes by trail bike, Fitz sat in the stern-cabin of the wrecked ship and told Danna as much as he knew of this new world and of how he had originally gotten there. Then, going into the now-crowded and cluttered larger of the side-cabins, he gaped open the built-in locker, took out the leather box and opened it to show her the couple of inches' depth of ancient golden coins remaining.

"This world, this ship, this locker, this box, Danna, is where all the gold Gus has sold for me . . . for us, now, came from. But who would believe it if I told or tried to tell the truth about it? Hell, there are times when I still have difficulty in believing parts of it my own self."

She shook her head. "Then this business of an inheritance from a long-deceased, Irish great-uncle was . . . is a complete fabrication? You lied to me and to Pedro, from the very beginning, Fitz? How could you? Don't you know how stupid it is to not be fully candid with your attorney, especially in tax matters? I'm sorry, Fitz, I credited you to be more intelligent than that." She sounded deeply hurt and it tore at him that his actions had so injured her.

He regarded her soberly and asked, "And had I told you the full truth of the matter on that first day that Gus Tolliver brought me up to your offices, what would your reaction have been? No, don't answer me at once, think about it, Danna, what would you have thought of me, said to me? Think."

After a moment, the barest hint of a smile crept into her eyes. "You're right, of course, Fitz. How could I have doubted your proven judgment. I'd either have gently ushered you out and put you down as just another crackpot or, had you seemed dangerous, had you held until some of the city's finest could have come and taken you away to one of the paper doll academies.

"But Fitz, this means that all this trouble of an inheritance tax . . . No, *they* wouldn't believe this, either, and if you brought one of them here, they'd probably claim it for the government and then want all the gold back, or the best part of it, them or the state or both. And I do agree with you about this bright, beautiful place, whatever it is, wherever it is. The last thing needed here is a heaping helping of our world to utterly ruin it forever, the way we and our parents and theirs have let crass, commercial interests overpopulate and ruin our own world.

"So, this is where you mean to spend three or four months, eh? I envy you, my own."

"I'd like it one hell of a lot better if you were here with me . . .?" he said, a bit wistfully, then added, "but I understand, Pedro made it all clear enough to me, I have to go away and stay away alone, but that still doesn't mean that I have to like the concept . . . and I don't, not one little bit, Danna," he said, embracing her where she stood, among the clutter of supplies and plastic jugs of drinking water.

From the haven of his arms, she spoke up against his cheek, "Were it not for the time thing, I'd like living here, only going back to that other world when I absolutely had to. Things are getting all but unbearable in that world, I just wasn't cut out to live that way. You possibly don't know exactly what I mean, living out in the distant suburbs as you do, but that city—and it's far and away worse in the larger cities, too, Fitz—is swiftly becoming a combination jungle-madhouse. Civility is a thing of the past and it often seems that our entire culture is dying, that ours is becoming a dirty, smelly, very unhealthy place, full of danger and constant fear, in which only the strong and the cruel have any hope of survival and no one can expect a happy life any more.

"Fitz, human beings may be primates, but they also are much like two of the other species of omnivores—rats and pigs—and if you put too many of either of those in a confined area, they start to kill and eat each other. And that's just what is happening now in our world, I'm afraid. There're way too many people, forced by circumstances beyond their control to live far too close to each other, so they're, in effect, killing and eating each other. And I want out of it all, Fitz, I'm just not cut out to live that way.

"This place is marvelous. I haven't heard any noises except the surf breaking and the wind blowing and bird cries. No sirens, no crying children, no shouts or screams, no screeching tires or blowing horns or crashes of car against car. I'd like living here; I feel safe, utterly unthreatened by anyone or anything. So blissful it is here, heaven must be like this."

Atop the last really tall dune before the descent to the sandy plain, they sat the trail bike and surveyed the forested hills far away, beyond the grassy flatnesses.

"That's where I'll be, somewhere in those hills and valleys, Danna. Tell Gus or Pedro to get you a Very pistol and a large assortment of flares for it, about two dozen each of red and green triple stars. Then, whenever you get to this world, stay aboard the ship and fire alternate red and green signals every three hours, night and day, for twenty-four hours. Wait a few minutes after each time you do it and watch the sky in this direction. If you see another star of the same color you fired, I'll be there as soon as I can— two, three days, however long it takes. But if you see a star of the other color, go back into the other world and try again in a couple of weeks, it'll mean I'm too far away to get back in a short time. There's just a limit to the amount of speed you can get out of these machines, especially over rough, unfamiliar terrain."

Upon their return to what Danna had commenced to call their "sand yacht," they rode down to the beach, stripped and frolicked in the sand and gentle seas until the sun was low in the western sky. Tired but happy, they hurriedly redressed, for the wind had picked up some force as it always did about sunset and their wet bodies were beginning to chill to less than comfort.

As they crested the seaward dune above the ship, Danna tensed and cried, "My God, Fitz, what . . . what's *that*?"

Stopping the bike, he looked in the direction she had pointed to see a long, massive, grey-green shape leaving the sea and heading inland at an angle away from them. He unsnapped the cased binoculars and handed them to her. "It's a crocodile, at least thirty feet long, if not more. A female, she's got a hole full of eggs in the dunes up there. Keep well away from that part of the beach, please, she's very protective. She chased me once when I got too close."

They found the cot entirely too narrow and shaky-flimsy, so ended up making love on the boards of the cabin's deck, but then they went back through the crypt and so into the other world, where dawn was just breaking beyond the rusting bulk of the county water tower. So, while Fitz showered, Danna called her service and left word for Pedro that she would not be in that coming day. By the time she had done with her own shower, Fitz had prepared a sumptuous breakfast. They ate it, then tumbled into the big bed for sleep, lovemaking, sleep, more lovemaking and, finally, more sleep. When at last they again awakened, it was night, stars faintly glittering through the light of a newly arisen moon.

"Fitz . . ." said Danna, in a hushed voice that was filled with uncertainty and doubt. "Fitz, I don't understand it, not any of it, it goes against all measure of reason and . . . and logic. How can you, I, anyone, just walk through stone walls or . . . or spaces in the empty air? It . . . it's pure lunacy to even imagine doing things like that . . . and yet, and yet you've done it how many times? And I . . . I did it, too, twice, yesterday. It's completely impossible by every law of physics of which I ever heard. But you and I, we did it, so what does that mean we are? What kind of humans are we, you and I? Are we even human? If not, what are we? Fitz, it . . . it's scary, damned scary. I'm frankly terrified, oh, please hold me, hold me tightly."

He did. "Danna, I'm no mental giant, never was, and I know only as much of the sciences as any business administration major was ever taught and absorbed . . . and that was almost thirty years ago, too. I've been over the possibilities and all the impossibilities of this thing of the sand world in my mind times without number. Finally, unable to come up with any kind of logical explanation for most of it, I've just started accepting it. It exists for me . . . and now, for you, too, and therefore, it *is*—be it logical, rational, possible or not. It was the only way to live with it all and stay sane, I guess. You're going to have to work out something along those same lines with yourself, too, but you and you alone can do that, I can't help you. Do you understand, Danna?"

She sighed. "I guess, Fitz, as much as I understand anything of all this, these utterly impossible facts, these things that could not ever be, yet unmistakably are.

"Fitz . . .? Fitz," she pushed against his body until she was far enough out to see his moonlit face. "Fitz, I think Pedro should be made aware of all of . . . of everything, the crypt and the doorway and the sand world, all of it.

"No, don't argue with me, not yet." She placed her hand over his lips, and went on, earnestly, "Fitz, Pedro is really no older than we—you and I—are, yet . . . yet, sometimes, the way he does things, says things, the way he thinks, make him seem infinitely older, wiser than me or anyone else. I know, I don't explain it very well, even I can sense that much, but . . . but Fitz, I really believe that he would be . . . he would completely understand, maybe, understand things that you and I do not, cannot. So, I think he should know, Fitz. You've trusted him with so much else, why not with this, too?"

He shook his head slowly. "Look, let me think on it, Danna. Hold off a while yet. Maybe he should know, I don't know one way or the other, though, right now. For the next few months, though, let him and everybody else think I'm just out of the country, in Africa or in the Caribbean or somewhere. Get the Very pistol from Gus. He won't ask a lot of questions, he'll just get it and the flares for you. Also, get him to take you to the range and teach you how to handle pistols, rifles and shotguns. The sand world just may not be as safe as you feel it to be now. I often feel as if I'm being watched there, by something that doesn't, itself, want to be seen by me. There're plenty of guns and ammo in the cabin, more here in the house. Gus spent thirty years of his life using firearms and teaching others to use them properly, he'll make you a good instructor.

"But as concerns Pedro Goldfarb . . . Look, when I get back from my trip into those hills, I'll give you a definite answer, a yes or a no. Let's let it go at that, for now."

When he had carried up and stowed the last of the supplies, Fitz ran the bike up the planks onto the main deck of the sand yacht, disattached the sidecar, then stowed both before going back to the stern cabin and preparing to pack and set aside gear and supplies for the trip. Thanks to his discoveries of ample, potable water sources on the other side of the sandy plain, at least he was not going to have to take up a lot of the limited space by packing along gallons of drinking water; a quart canteen or two should be more than ample to his needs and there were certain to be more springs and streams in those hills, else they would not be so heavily forested.

After carefully cleaning and lubricating the carbine, he filled the under-barrel tube with ten big rounds of .44 magnum, then he inserted the weapon in the custom-made, padded-leather scabbard. He might never need it or the revolver; probably, he would not, but still he felt it was better to have them and not need them than to need them and not have them. That could be fatal. He uncased, lubricated and assembled the lightweight drilling gun, then shoved a shell of number four shot into the left barrel, a shell of number six shot into the right, completing the loading with a .22 magnum cartridge in the third barrel. This would be his pot-hunting gun, carried in the sidecar along with its pouch of shells and cartridges, fit for the taking of birds or small game of any kind. Living off the country, or mostly off the country, would mean that he could travel lighter, supplies-wise, and thus pack along more fuel to extend his range on each trip, for the hilly country looked extensive and there was no way he could cover it all at once, not unless he could tow along a tanker of gasoline—that, or somehow alter the engine so that it would run on pure water or air. Or maybe—he grinned at the thought as he carefully tucked the air mattress in its place, then tightly rolled the trail sleeping bag—in this land of impossibilities, I could turn this bag into a flying carpet substitute and fly wherever I want to go. He chuckled at his own silliness, then grimaced as he drew the straps as tightly as he could and added the rolled bag, mattress and weatherproof cover to the growing pile of gear.

When he had done all he could, all but the last-minute things, he mixed an iceless highball, drank it in four gulps, then turned out all the lanterns save one, turning it very low, that he might not trip over scattered bits of gear in the dim light of dawn. Then he extended himself on the cot and drifted off to sleep.

And, all at once, Tom was there on his chest and belly, his eyes reflecting the dim glow of the gas lantern. Tiredly, exhausted and needing sleep, Fitz said a little brusquely, "All right, I'm headed for the hills tomorrow. What do you want me to do, roll out of this cot and saddle up tonight? If so, forget it, I'm tired and sleepy."

"And very irritable," added the cat, or so Fitz thought . . . or dreamed he thought. "While it might be better if you crossed the Pony Plain at night, since the Teeth and Legs lack the proper vision to hunt on all save the brightest of moonlit nights, it might be more dangerous for you to try a crossing tonight, tired as you are, your reflexes slowed. No, cross tomorrow, but cross fast and bc your most wary, for I have found fresh spoor of a big Teeth and Legs in the very area you must go across in the shortest line from here. Don't be so foolish as to try to outrun it, though. If it finds you, not even your three-wheeled thing is so fast; no, use your noise-fire-pain thing to kill it—kill it, or it will assuredly kill and eat you.

"Once you have knowledge of your full powers, of course, even the Teeth and Legs will pose no danger to you. Then, you will have no need of your noise-fire-pain things, ever again, or of your three-wheeled thing, either. You will be free, master of all, in this world and in the other, as well. But ere that happen, you must go deeply into the hills and meet the Dagda. He will set all aright with you, with her who is yours and with the other, the keeper, as well."

"What the hell are you babbling about now?" muttered Fitz. "What's a Dagda? A keeper, keeper of what?"

But all that the cat replied was, "Sleep, my good old friend."

Fitz did. Immediately.

And suddenly, once more, he was atop that rocky crag that the tall old man with the long, grey beard had climbed, bearing Fitz and another child in his arms; tight-pressed, he had held them under his cloak, against his fine bronze armor. All hacked and scarred had that armor been, though, Fitz remembered, its enamel decorations chipped away in places and the glittering stones gone, many of them, from the places wherein they had been set.

Then Fitz was within the warm, brightly lit chamber that lay within the huge boulder that the old man had caused to open with a peeled wand of willow wood and a formula couched in the Old Language. The old man now stood naked in that room, stripped of cloak, armor, sword, clothing, everything. Despite the age that showed upon his face, his body was still that of a warrior, a vital man. The naked old man was talking to an old woman, the same old woman who had welcomed them into the chamber from the cold mountainside beyond the boulder.

"But if you render me, too, a babe, and exchange me on that future world as you and I did the young prince and princess, that will leave you alone here to face the Strangers when the Dark Ones finally have penetrated this fastness. You are one of the wisest of us all; I cannot see you sacrificed for me."

She shook her almost-white-haired head. "Never you fear, Keeper, you have done your duty well, so far. Are you to continue so, you must live and be near to your assigned charges. This way, my way, you will live and will be near to them . . . well, at least in the same world and time. As for me, I have ways to protect myself that not even the power of the Dark Ones can penetrate."

"But if I am to be rendered a helpless babe again, even as were my charges, how can I protect them . . . or even find them in that weird world so filled with Strangers and oddities that we just visited?" the naked old man protested. "And who will there be to tell their father, if still he lives, where they and I, too, have gone?"

"Their father will be informed, soon or late," she replied. "As regards the finding them and the care of them that you owe, think you: you are a man-grown, full of your great powers, so although made a babe once more, through my different powers, you will come to the full memory and use of your powers very soon after your new body is become that of a full man.

"The little prince and princess, on the other hand, were not that much more than mere babes when once more they so became. They will require long years to remember, if ever they do, indeed, without help. You will need to seek them out, find them by their auras, and then guide them as well as you can, prompting them until they start to remember how to realize their full powers and make use of them. I was a Keeper, too, once, long ago, you may recall; so I, too, will go into that other world if I can and I'll be of as much help as I can to both you and them.

"Now the Strangers are at my gate, they are bringing up a poor, sad prisoner, one of our kind, to try to make her open the stone, so let me render you, quickly, and take you into that other world."

The warm, comfortable chamber faded away and Fitz found himself outside, on the mountaintop, before the huge boulder all carven with symbols so old and weathered as to be barely perceptible as other than mere natural disfigurements of its grey surface.

A knot of men stood before him, obviously unable to see him as he could see and hear . . . and *smell* them. They were a scruffy lot, Fitz thought, but still possessed of a look of dangerous, violent, brutal men. A couple wore byrnies of mail that reached from shoulder to knee, but most had as body armor only rough jerkins of hide, strips of horn and bone sewn onto them here and there for added protection. A few showed the blood and tattered, filthy bandages of relatively fresh wounds. They were armed with steel swords, mostly, axes, spears and long knives, though one had as weapon nothing save a wooden club, the bark still on part of it.

The clothing beneath the protective items was

mostly of poor quality and as long unwashed as their stinking bodies, ragged, hopping and acrawl with vermin. But each and every one of the mangy pack wore a silvery amulet hung on his chest from a chain. In addition, they sported such outré' items as golden torques clasped about dirty necks, arm rings and finger rings of gold, electrum, copper, bronze and gems, brooches of brightly enameled bronze and copper, strings of pearls, pins and ear-bobs set with brilliant stones. A single look at the contrasts spelled but one word to the observing Fitz—loot.

One of the men in a byrnie, his head and neck covered by a bronze helmet of splendid construction and decoration, banged a few times on the face of the boulder with the pommel of his sword. Then he showed rotting, yellow-brown teeth in a grimace.

"This is where the he-witch went, sure enough. See, the tracks lead right up to it. But mere steel doesn't work on it. Where's a priest?"

The other man in a byrnie answered, "Not caught up to us yet, I'd imagine. He and the others have only cold-bred mounts, rounseys and worse, most of them."

"Then bring the blonde witch-woman up here," snarled the first. "She'll either open it or I'll have her evil head off, on this spot."

Presently, the man with the club half-dragged a near-naked blonde woman of, Fitz estimated, about twenty years, up the trail onto the top of the mountain, to shove her before the rock and the two men in byrnies. Her hands, feet and parts of her face were blue with cold, her fair-skinned body showed the clear evidences of cruel use and abuse—whipweals on her shoulders, back, buttocks and legs still fitfully oozing blood and serum, both her breasts showing savage tooth marks and one nipple torn raggedly off, dangling by only a thread of flesh. She stood before the two mail-shirted men with her head of dull, matted hair hung low, the look in her eyes dull and apathetic.

"Here, witch-woman," rasped the first man, "open this rock and let us all into the under the hill and you'll be given your freedom."

Raising her battered head, one eye swollen almost shut, she gazed upon the face of the rock for a moment, then said, "This is a gate, but not a gate to the under the hill, Master. There is most likely only a cave behind it, the home of one of the Old Ones. I might have been able to open it . . . once, but after all that you and the other Strangers have done to me, after the burning water that the Dark Ones poured upon me, I no longer have the power to do such."

With a roar of pure rage, the first man grabbed a handful of the dirty, matted blonde hair, whirled his sharp steel sword on high, then swung it hard, driving it completely through the slender neck of the woman, so that he still held the head with its staring blue eyes and its open mouth, while her body—spouting high-soaring jets of ropy-red blood from the neck, legs and arms jerking—was beginning to collapse at his feet.

Tossing the severed head away to go rolling and bouncing down the rocky slope of the mountainside, the murderer bent to tear the last shreds of tattered clothing from the headless body and used it to wipe clean his precious steel sword-blade. Then he snapped to one of the other men, "Go down there and mount and ride, take my horse, too, but find that priest and bring him back as fast as horseflesh will travel. Go!"

The men stamped and paced back and forth and

blew upon their cold hands for a while. Finally, two of them gathered such wood as they could find on the mountainsides below, then brought it up to where the second man in a byrnie had kindled a tiny blaze with tinder and stray, windblown twigs and dry leaves. After it had begun to blaze, the first two squatted beside it and the others gathered as close around the two leaders as they dared.

Fitz felt neither the cold winds that ruffled and jerked at the ragged clothing of the men, the slow, misty rain that continued to drizzle slowly down out of the leaden skies, or the fitful warmth of the small fire. He knew, without really knowing, that he was not on that mountaintop, not really; only his mind and his senses were there.

The fire still was sputtering its way through additional, damper wood, when there came a staccato clatter of hooves from below, down the mountain trail. In a few minutes, the man who had been sent out came panting up the steep slope, followed at a few yards' distance by a big, burly man clad in a long, black, woolen robe, the hood of it thrown back to reveal a plain steel cap and a red, sweaty face. The chain about his neck was heavier and the amulet on his breast was much larger than those of the others, but he wore at his side a cross-hilted sword of steel and helped his progress up the trail with a shepherd's crook of some very dark wood, shod with a wide band of steel near its butt. The shaft of the crook showed nicks and splintery dents all along its length, as if it might have recently been used as a weapon.

To Fitz, the man looked cleaner and more civilized than those he was climbing up to join, but as he neared, the watcher could see in his eyes a blazing fire of fanaticism that was awful to observe. This man might not be a brutal, savage barbarian by nature, but he could be every bit as cruel as the worst of them; this Fitz knew without really knowing.

Not so much as glancing at the pitiful, naked, headless body or at the humbler men, he strode to stand before the two byrnie-clad men, who had arisen from their squats at sight of him.

"Why have you sent for me in such haste, my son?" he asked of the first man, in a tone of equal speaking to equal, but with a bare tinge of condescension, too.

The first man waved an arm at the boulder. "Yonder's a gate, Father. The tracks of the he-witch we were chasing went right up to it and stopped. Her," he pointed his bearded chin at the white, drained body lying grotesquely sprawled, "we brought up here and she affirmed it to be a true gate, but said she couldn't open it, so I slew her, the damned witch.

"But it must be gaped, Father, are we to catch that he-witch and wipe out the breed of the witches for good and all and make the world safe for the worship of Our Gentle Lord, Jesus Christ, Savior of all mankind."

A grim, purposeful look on his hard face, the man in black nodded. "You did well to send for me, my son. Yonder portal of evil will be opened, never you fear. The power of Our Lord will gape it even in the very face of the damnable evil that assuredly lieth within."

The black-robed man strode over to stand before the boulder's face. Standing with his bare, round-muscled legs spread wide apart, he took the shepherd's crook in both his big, hairy hands and held his arms high, then began to chant some words in a language that Fitz could not understand, though he nonetheless thought it not to be the Old Language, such as the old bearded man had used with his willow-wood wand to open the stone.

The stone did finally open, suddenly, but not gently, invitingly, as it had earlier. With a thunderlike clap of noise, the face of the boulder split down its entire face and chunks of it burst away to roll, crashingly, down the mountainside to either side of it.

Armed with bared weapons and grasping blazing brands from the fire, the men filed into the narrow, jagged-walled cleft in the rock to find only a cave chamber, but slightly wider and higher than the passage through which they just had entered. The cold, musty place in no way resembled the warm, well-lit chamber that had been there so short a time before. There were no lamps, no carpets, no other comforts of any nature, only a tick of straw in a corner, a circle of sooty stones surrounding a pile of long-cold ashes, and some bundles of dry, crackly herbs hung from twigs driven into small cracks in the walls. No living thing, other than the intruders, was within that cave, and the only thing at all familiar that Fitz could see was the very faint glow of a single section of one wall of the place.

Although he could see it, obviously the black-robed man and the barbaric warriors could not. After searching every nook and cranny, jerking down and scattering the dried herbs, tearing apart the tick of moldy straw and kicking the fire stones out of their places, they all departed, cursing.

Just before he—whatever there was of him—was no longer there, Fitz thought he saw the green-eyed face of the old woman protruding from the stone wall of the then-empty cave room, the face appearing near the center of the glowing rectangle.

*   *   *

Fitz could hear Tom purring loudly before he opened his eyes. But when open them he did, the cat was not lying upon him, although he still could hear the purring. He thought he sat up then, swung his legs over the side of the cot and looked around the cabin. Then he sat frozen for a moment.

Lying in typical feline posture on a stretch of floor only bare feet from him was a something that, save for its solid-grey color, he would have taken for a leopard, a very large leopard. Just as he sat up and looked at the creature, it yawned, showing a fearsome number of big, sharp-pointed cuspids and a full complement of carnassials and molars, all white and gleaming against the background of red-pink gums and tongue.

Since first he had had that eerie feeling of being watched, here in the sand world, Fitz had slept with one of his three big magnum revolvers hung from a corner of the cot. Now, moving very slowly, he recovered from his momentary shock at sight of this obviously dangerous visitor and began to ease his hand toward the holstered gun.

He had just gripped the butt and was unsnapping the strap with his thumb, when this cat, too, spoke, *in Tom's voice.*

"Don't do that, old friend. I've been shot once, that was enough and more than enough for me, thank you; you wouldn't believe how much the metal pellets from those noise-fire things hurt before finally you die and stop hurting. Being crushed to death by one of the huge four-wheeled things is much easier to bear, believe me, I know."

"*Tom* . . . ?" gasped Fitz. "What . . . ? How?"

The huge feline used the inches-wide tongue to lick a massive paw and begin to wash its face, remarking the while, "Rather an inept name to keep using, since it denotes a male cat and I now am a female cat, but we'll let that pass, for the nonce. If you will recall, I told you when I visited you last that you saw me in that other world, then, as I always had looked to you when I was alive there. I thought that, as you will be coming to the hills, it was better that you see me once as I now look, lest you not know me and thus fear me.

"Yes, it is me, the one you call Tom. Still the same cat, only bigger and better. Now that you've seen me, I'm going to leave and get across the Pony Plain while still it's dark. You go back to sleep, old friend."

CHAPTER VIII

His alarm clock awakened him just at moonset. Having belatedly recalled a few small items he wanted or would need from the other world, he took the lighter bike down the gangplank and rode to the portal. In the house, he took the opportunity to treat himself to a long, hot shower and a hearty breakfast—for all that it was still fully, very dark night there—then he collected those things for which he had returned, dashed off a quick note to Danna, and went back down the steep stone stairs to find the sun beginning to peek over the eastern horizon in the sand world.

Back aboard the wrecked ship, he connected the cargo sidecar to the heavier, long-range bike and wheeled the resultant unit down the gangplank, then made trip after trip from stern-cabin to bike, loading the necessaries for the journey into the hills beyond the sandy plain. Then, with the last things stowed away or strapped on, he closed and bolted both the inner and the outer shutters over the stern-ports, locked all save one of the outer doors and secured in place sheets of plastic film that would, hopefully, prevent sand sifting into his home during his absence.

With everything locked or bolted or secured, he shoved the heavy planks over the gunwales into the waist of the ship, mounted the now-warmed bike and put it into gear, then began to negotiate the miles of dunes that lay between the ship and the plain that separated dunes and the forested hills and valleys of the interior, these latter, his destination.

As he drove up and down the dunes under a rising, warming sun, Fitz tried in vain to sort out the—events? dreams?—of the preceding night. It would have immeasurably comforted him to have been able to confidently assure himself that everything concerning the repeated nocturnal visits of his long-dead cat had been nothing save dreams, but he could no longer so assure himself with anything approaching confidence, for so very many completely impossible things had recently taken place in his life that he now lacked the confident assurance to name anything, any circumstances as impossible, ever again.

"All right, then," he thought to himself, while the vibration of the bike's sizable engine permeated his body, "let's say that Tom—or what used to be Tom, in that other world—was really there, in a locked and barred chamber that not even a house cat-sized beast could have really entered, much less a two-hundred-odd-pound feline. No, forget for the moment the imposs . . . no, improbabilities of it all and concentrate on the premise that it really happened. Right? Right!

"Okay, Tom was there, not only last night but all those other nights, too. He says he lives in the hills and he wants me to come there, also. That much is understandable, at least, he was always a sociable cat and I don't doubt that he longs for the companionship of a proven friendly human being. It's this other business of which he spoke, though, that really throws me; this business of some powers I'm supposed to regain or develop in those hills, this personage or thing called 'Dagda' I'm supposed to meet.

"And what am I to think of this bugaboo, this thing Tom calls Teeth and Legs. He says that it, they, are shaped like a man, but with the jaws and teeth of a true predator, can run as fast as my bike can travel at top speed—which sounds a bit imposs . . . unlikely— and that not even the biggest pony-stallion can stand against one of the creatures. And there's supposed to be one or more right now, on the very section of plain that I have to cross to get to the hills from here, the shortest route.

"Am I to believe that Tom was really there last night, then I guess I have to believe in this Teeth and Legs, too, so I'd better keep my eyes peeled and my weapons ready; if I can't outrun it, then I'll just have to be prepared to kill it, like it or not."

From the crest of the last high dune, Fitz could see no animals on the plain, unless a cloud of dusty sand far and far to the westward represented a herd of ponies. It was unusual to sit his bike in this spot and not to see at least some rat-tailed ostriches, a small herd of grazing ponies or a few of the flying rabbits, but the only living creatures he finally sighted—and even these so far away to east or west that he needed to make use of his big binoculars—were a couple of scurrying, tailless rats and a high-wheeling raptor or buzzard, lonely in the clear sky and so far up and away that he could not clearly identify it.

He began to really worry, then, while he negotiated the inland slope of the dune, knowing from his hunting experiences in the other world that when animals failed to follow usual patterns of behavior, there was always an excellent reason for such deviance. Rather than just speeding up and over and down the succession of low dunes that lay between him and the seaward margin of the plain, he now stopped upon each low crest to examine the country ahead for possible danger. And, on the crest of the last one, he drew his carbine from its scabbard and chambered a round, replacing it in the tube with one from his supply.

He rode slowly and most warily across the seemingly deserted plain, assiduously avoiding the higher, thicker stands of plumed grasses and bushy shrubs, trying to keep at least fifty yards distance of unobstructed terrain between him and anyplace that might give concealment to any large predator. Tom had said that the Teeth and Legs were shaped like him but taller, larger and heavier than him, so that gave him at least a little idea as to just how much in the way of concealment might be required to hide one of the things.

At midday, he halted in a carefully selected spot that gave him a view of seventy-five to over a hundred yards on all sides. There, while keeping close watch on the horizons and peering with binoculars at any closer declivities or stands of plants that might mask the presence of a large beast, he ate hurriedly out of his supplies, topped off the fuel tank of the bike and painstakingly rechecked his weapons—carbine, drilling, revolver, the Ka-bar knife at his belt and the Gerber Frisco shiv in his boot, even the flare projector, for in a real pinch it too could serve as a close-range weapon.

But he thought that he was to make it completely across the plain without so much as sight of one of the monsters, for the sheen of sun upon the spring-fed pond at the inland margin of the plain was in easy sight and he was headed toward it, angling a bit to the east in order to avoid a declivity some five or six feet deep and some twenty feet long by ten wide, when suddenly, it was there. Up, out, over the lip of the hole it came with a bound, covered the intervening yards with but one or two racing, leaping strides, a black-skinned, five-fingered hand tipped with black, flat, blood-dripping nails reaching for Fitz at the end of of a long, hairy arm.

Warned by his peripheral vision, the man swayed to his right and gunned the bike, which leapt forward, momentarily leaving the ambusher in a cloud of dust and fine particles of sand. But it was only a thing of the moment; a swift glance over a shoulder told Fitz that much. Impossible as it seemed, the incredibly long legs of the dark, hairy predator were covering ground at at prodigious rate. Tom had been right, then, Fitz no longer doubted it; that thing would not take long to overhaul the bike even at top speed, which speed he dare not maintain for long over the rough, uneven landscape, in any case.

Making a quick decision to take advantage of the small lead he still owned, Fitz braked hard and spun the bike about at the top of a low rise in the terrain, drawing the carbine from out its scabbard while still the dust and sand thrown up by his wheels was in the air all around him. The hirsute pursuer stopped in mid-stride, paused, then came on a bit more slowly, clearly wary of such unusual prey conduct.

Breathing and moving deliberately, Fitz brought up his weapon and nestled the toe of the butt in his shoulder, just below the clavicle. He released the safety, observed the hairy apparition over the length of the barrel and considered just where it would be best to place the first—hopefully, the first, last and only—shot. Months of target practice with the piece had given him understanding of and thorough respect for both the weapon and the cartridge—the hollow-nosed, soft-point weighing two hundred and forty grains, leaving the muzzle at a speed of over one thousand, seven hundred feet per second and with an energy of something more than sixteen hundred pounds. Compared to the personal weapons with which he had fought World War Two and the Korean War, this carbine was truly awesome in its potential lethality.

Even so, the relatively short-barrelled weapon did have limitations of accurate fire at distance. This might have been helped had Fitz succumbed to the blandishments of the gun shop that had sold him the piece, then customized it to his personal specifications, and allowed them to install a scope, but he had thought then and still thought now that a carbine was basically a rather short-range weapon, at best, and that a scope was just one more thing he could have break or go out of kilter at a bad moment and of which he knew nothing about repairing.

Recognizing the value of predators in Nature's scheme of things, he did not really want to kill this one, but if it came to a question of his life or its, he would. Nonetheless, he tried a warning shot, hoping that the roar and muzzle blast of the Remington magnum would terrify the whatever-it-was into finding other prey. He aimed the shot just above the thick-haired crest of the thing's head.

It did stop for a brief moment, just long enough for Fitz to jack another round into the smoking chamber and eject the empty case, but then it came on, relentlessly. He set his jaws and compressed his lips in a tight line; there was no help for it, then, he'd have to kill the beast.

He saw dust puff up as the big, heavy slug struck the animal's body, some eight inches below the left shoulder. To his way of thinking, that should have been a true heart-shot . . . but the Teeth and Legs obviously did not know it, for it just kept coming, gnashing its fearsome fangs, the cuspids looking to be big as a tiger's. So he worked the carbine's action, aimed and fired again at the same spot . . . and with no better results.

Taking a deep, deep breath to try to lay the panic that could easily be fatal under these tight circumstances, Fitz fired yet again, aiming for the head, but hitting the neck and throat, the mushrooming slug visibly tearing out a chunk of flesh and exiting on a fanning spray of blood. The creature squalled and staggered, but still came on, though more slowly. It now was only twenty-five yards away, if that.

"What the hell does it take to kill you, you bastard?" Fitz cried aloud as he chambered yet another round. This time, all else having failed, he aimed much lower. Maybe, if he could knock a leg from under the monster . . . ?

The big bullet had luck riding on it. It struck the left knee and demolished that joint. Again squalling, the runner spun to the left and fell. But it caught itself on its hands and still came on at Fitz, using the two overlong arms and the sound leg for a fast, three-legged gait. However, its position gave Fitz a shot that had been unavailable while it had remained erect on two legs. It having attained the very base of the low hillock, Fitz sent a bullet smashing through the beast's spine, between its shoulder blades, driving it belly-down upon the sandy plain and stopping it for good and all.

The only other sound that the creature made as it lay there, bleeding and twitching, was a long, rat-

tling expiration of air, just before it voided its dung
and its black-pupiled, reddish eyes began to glaze in
death.

Fitz could only sit on the seat of the bike and
watch, trembling like a leaf in reaction to the nerve-
shattering experience. He now knew that the .44
magnum carbine was not truly the powerhouse of a
weapon he had thought it to be, not for all animals,
and that knowledge was, to say the very least, un-
nerving. He momentarily debated the idea of returning to the ship for the Holland and Holland elephant
gun, but decided not to do so, in the end; that would
have meant camping the night somewhere out on the
sandy plain, the hunting ground of these all but
unkillable things.

When his legs once more felt up to the job of
supporting him, Fitz swung his leg over the handlebars, stood up and used the carbine to put one more
slug into the base of the creature's huge skull before
daring to go down and examine it at closer range.
Yes, *he* knew that it now was dead, but did *it* know
and admit that fact?

Even up close, however, he was at a loss to say just
what the long-legged, long-armed, hefty, hairy, very
toothy beast was. Although the long-fingered hands
had opposed thumbs like his own, there still was
something about them that put him more in mind of
apes or monkeys than of man, and the feet were even
more reminiscent of the pongids, being only slightly
thickened and flattened duplicates of the hands, the
thumbs of them thicker, a little shorter and a little
less opposed. But both hands and feet were equipped
with flat, thick, sharp nails that looked fully capable
of serving the purpose of claws.

The general color of the beast's coat was a dark
agouti. Its flat rump was padded with thick, hairless

calliosities, and above them sprouted a hairy tail a good two inches in diameter. That this dead creature had been a male of its species was readily apparent to Fitz. Its head was as big as that of a full-grown lion, though with longer snout, and Fitz doubted that any lion would have been ashamed of the array of orangy-white fangs and other teeth. There could also be no slightest doubt that the thing had been a meat-eater, either, for its dung was full of undigested bits and pieces of bone.

All things about the dead monster considered, Fitz could think only of something vaguely resembling a baboon. Only, who ever had seen or heard of a baboon that stood about six feet tall and hunted singly rather than in a packs?

A cold chill then coursed down Fitz's back. God, if these things do hunt in packs . . .? What if this was only one separated from the pack? If it takes five shots to kill each of them, hell, I'm dead meat.

In the seat of the bike, he stayed in place only long enough to fully reload the carbine, then turned the vehicle about and headed for the hills as fast as he dared to go.

As his bike climbed the rising ground beyond the pool that marked the verge of the sandy plain, the grasses gradually became shorter, less coarse and tough, greener. Shrubs became taller, denser, more colorful, and trees, real trees, began to appear here and there; thanks to his Boy Scout training, he could recognize a few of them—doveplum, myrtle oak, turkey oak, sweetbay and others he failed after all these years to remember. On the lower reaches of the slope, nearer to the sandy plain, there were a few palms of some sort, but there were none as he ascended higher, just more and larger hardwood trees and some pines of several kinds, junipers and cedars.

As the first slope gained altitude, more and thicker growths of underbrush grew among the tree boles until, finally, he was proceeding only by hacking out a way just wide enough to pass the bike and its attached sidecar, while thanking his stars that he had thought to pack along a machete and a pair of sturdy work gloves to save his hands.

But the heavy brush only ran for a distance of some dozens of yards; then, as abruptly as if cut with a sharp knife, both the incline and the brushy woods gave over to a level plateau on which stately trees sprang up from short, almost lawnlike grass. There was no natural crowding of these trees—oaks, maples, elms, a few chestnuts and ginkos and, within his sight, one huge mimosa covered with a pink froth of flowers—they therefore looked less like a true forest than a carefully tended park.

Startled by the noise of the engine, two deerlike beasts looked up, then burst into full flight, quickly disappearing among the tree trunks and folds of gently rolling greensward. They were clearly not the white-tails of his own world and hunting experience, however; he got a good enough glimpse of the departing creatures to at least tell that much. For one thing, both of them were spotted, though obviously adult, and they bore antlers more like those of a moose than a deer or elk.

Nor were the cervines the only animals to be seen and heard in the parklike expanse. Squirrels scampered up trees, to turn and scold at him from safe altitudes; brown voles and striped chipmunks scurried through the grass and dove into their burrows among the spreading roots of the trees; while high in a persimmon tree, a scaly-tailed opossum blithely ignored the noisy, smelly intruder and went about gorging himself on the rich, yellow-orange fruits.

And there were the birds. He knew that he never had before seen so many different kinds of birds in one place at one time. They flew, they perched, they hopped and stalked through the grass, stopping now and again to peck at something that had caught their avian eye among the stems of the grasses. They were of every conceivable color and hue and of all shapes and sizes—flycatchers, larks, swallows, wrens, thrushes, warblers, sparrows, finches, doves, woodpeckers, clouds of multi-hued parakeets, a tiny hummingbird hovering with blurring wings to sip from mimosa flowerlets, a brace of huge, blue-and-yellow macaws assisting the opossum in stripping the persimmon tree of ripe fruit.

Farther along toward the line of steep, pine-covered hills that filled the northern horizon in the near distance, small green parrots fed on the green-and-purple fruits of berries of some strange tree, and a flock of grey pigeons marched in a skirmish line through the grass beneath and around that tree, policing the area of any scraps that the parrots dropped, the sunbeams flashing on the bright, metallic bits of color that flecked their drab bodies.

Closer still to the upthrust of the hills, the grasses grew higher and, within them, scurried quail and small, fuzzy rabbits. A family of one large and a half-dozen smaller raccoons dove beneath the thorny foliage of a clump of blackberries upon which fruits they had been feeding at the approach of the growling bike, while from out the other side of the spreading thicket, a creature a good deal larger—honey-colored, possibly a hundred pounds in weight, looking a bit like a bear, save that its legs were too long and slender and its body was not hefty enough—hurriedly exited and scampered into the brush of the hillside nearby.

The hill was indeed steep, so much so that by the time he reached its summit-ridge, he was afoot and laboriously pushing the bike by its handlebars. The hill beyond looked even steeper and Fitz decided to look for a place where he could park the bike, then go on afoot. In the trailless wilderness, he needed a place that he could find again with relative ease and one that would, if possible, give concealment and at least a measure of protection from the elements to the machine as well as to those items he would not be able to pack on his back.

Just beyond the summit of the hill, the slope went gently down into a narrow valley, vale, really. A tiny rill threaded its way between grass and wild grain that stood a foot to a foot a half high and it, like the higher grasses below, was aswarm with quail and small rabbits.

Thinking of a belly that soon would be in need of filling, Fitz stopped the bike just beyond the stream, unlimbered the drilling and dismounted. After picking up a pocketful of smooth pebbles from the rill banks, he strolled out into the grasses, holding the gun at the ready in his right hand while he tossed pebbles at likely looking spots, trying to rustle up some quail for his supper.

With a startling burst of noise and a brilliant flash of color, a pheasant-sized bird rose up fast, very fast. But Fitz was a wing-gun of vast experience and, fast as was the big bird, his reactions were just as fast. The drilling boomed once and the barely risen bird dropped in a flutter of gaudy plumage.

"Pheasant-sized, hell," thought Fitz, as he held his kill up by its legs for closer examination, "this *is* a pheasant, I've seen pictures of them. But how in the devil did a Chinese golden pheasant get here . . . wherever here is?

"Some of the animals I've seen have been ordinary North American varieties. Of course, quite a number haven't, too; those deer, for one instance, not to mention that godawful thing I barely killed in time to keep it from killing me back on the plain. I've never ever seen, read or even heard of such a nightmare beast, anywhere in the world. Then, there're the flying lizards, the gliding jack rabbits, those ostrich-like things with scaly tails and feathery fur and, just now, that critter like a long-legged bear that's been dieting.

"Wherever here is, it's got the damnedest collection of odd fauna of anyplace I've ever heard or read or been."

Some yards up the slope of the next hill, while hacking at vines and undergrowth to make a path up which he could push, pull or tug the bike and side-car, Fitz uncovered the mouth of a cave. With all the vegetation cleared away, the opening proved to be some two yards in width at its widest and almost that in height. A thin, crumbling, shaly ledge projected out about two feet beyond the opening, which he could immediately see would give added protection from rain to any inhabitant.

Examination of its interior did not show recent signs of any large dwellers, only droppings of beasts no larger than a good-sized rat and even these were dried out and crumbly. A dark smudge, ever so faint, on the top of the opening and the bottom of the ledge, above, might have been soot from a campfire, but if so it was so old as to not really matter. None-theless, he took the elementary precaution of scour-ing the hillside about for good-sized chunks of stone to partially barricade the opening when he was ready to sleep.

While still some daylight remained, he did his

necessary chores—cleaning and plucking the pheasant, cleaning and lubing his bike and then filling the fuel tank, cleaning and oiling his weapons. The machete, he could hone by firelight. When his initial fire had died to coals, he spitted the bird carcass over it on a green stick supported by a pair of forked sticks, then filled a cup with water from one of his canteens and nestled it into a bed in the coals.

With starlight filtering down through the trees and the fire banked for the night, Fitz blocked the cave entrance with his boulders and the bike, then inflated his air mattress and pulled off his boots and outer clothing. The carbine, the drilling and the machete he laid within easy reach, but the pistol and both knives he took into the sleeping bag with him. Exhausted from the long, hard trip, full of spit-broiled pheasant, bouillion and sweet tea, he was soon asleep.

Sometime in the night, half-asleep, half waking, Fitz *knew* that there was someone or something in that cave with him. Slowly, he opened the side zipper of the sleeping bag; ever so slowly, he put out his hand toward the two shoulder guns, the machete and the flashlight. But instead of cold metal, the searching hand encountered warm, dense, plushy fur and elicited a basso purr.

"Damn it, Tom," he gasped, "you scared the shit out of me! Can't you at least show the elemental courtesy of letting me know you're coming? Or do you really *want* to get shot again?"

"Of course not, would you?" replied the cat. "But you see I cannot communicate with you so long as you are sleeping, and I cannot—or would not, rather—awaken you as I did there, in that other world and back in the place on the beach, for I now weigh as much or even more than do you, and you would surely have shot me with your revolver had a heavy bulk suddenly landed upon you."

"Well," muttered Fitz, "you could at least say something, clear your throat, anything, rather than scare me half to death by just slinking in and lying down and waiting for me to wake up on my own, like you did."

"You still don't understand," said the cat. "You think that I'm saying words to you with lips and tongue the way you and your kind do, but I'm not. I am meshing my mind with yours, just as I would do with another cat or most other creatures. You do not truly hear me with your ears, but within your mind.

"You, of course, do say noises that convey thoughts, but I know your meanings from your mind even before I hear those noises with my own ears. Really, you need not make the noises at all, just form the things you wish to impart to me and I will immediately know them, old friend. You will know all this and so much more soon, as you begin to regain and know your inherent powers."

Ever willing to try new things, Fitz slightly thought his words, "I would like to know just what these powers you keep carrying on about are, Tom? Or Tomasina, or whatever. Why don't I just call you Puss? That's a generic, nonsexist term."

"Puss will be all right. It is derived of a Nile Valley name for one of their gods, and Egyptian of that period was almost an old language. But you may still call me Tom, too, if you will be more comfortable in so doing; I don't mind.

"As for your powers, you will know them when your mind and body are ready to make use of them. Simply living here in these hills and valleys, partaking of the waters, breathing the air, eating of the foods, would eventually fully awaken your sleeping powers. But there may not be time, enough time, to take the slower route, and this is why you must find the Dagda, for he can accelerate the process, can quickly make of you what you truly are and have always been."

"Well, if it's so damned important that I find this Dagda, lead me to him. We can leave here as soon as it's light enough to travel, the two of us, together," thought Fitz.

"No," answered the cat, "I am forbidden to do such a thing, it has always been so. You must find the Dagda, you and you alone, unaided by me or the Keeper. The search and the dangers and trials you will undergo in that search will prove you worthy of what awaits you at its end, will prove that you are truly what you are.

"I may shadow you and your progress, I may visit with you and even give you counsel and encouragement now and then, but I may not guide you directly to the Dagda at his court. You must find him and it at your own risk and peril, being cleansed of impurities and molded into what you must be by your dangers faced and overcome, even as the fire melts and cleanses the copper and tin to make fine, unsullied bronze."

"But Puss," protested Fitz, "I don't even know which direction to travel to find this Dagda, and if these hills go on as far as they seem to, it—that search—could be a lifetime project for me. I'm already well over fifty years old."

There was a hint of a patronizing smile in the cat's thoughts, then, "You do not know just how old you really are, old friend of mine. In a way, you are incredibly ancient, yet in another you are but a little boy-child. I am forbidden to tell you all that I might tell you here and now, but I can say this: do not believe all that you learned as unshakeable, indisputable fact in that other world, for many things—both there and here—are not always what they seem to those without any powers . . or with few and ill-developed powers.

"As for finding the Dagda, any direction that you travel from here—save back, the way you came—will lead you to him. Dangers and trials will lie in your path, but each will be for you another step closer to your goal. The survival of each of them will help you in the development of your powers. While you may suffer in many strange and terrible ways in undergoing these trials and dangers, you will not die, unless . . ."

"Unless?" prompted Fitz. "Unless what?"

"I have said . . . almost said too much, my friend," answered the cat, "so I can say no more, at this meeting, save this: Although I am not to guide you, I am allowed to extend to you a certain amount of protection and good advice in what is yet to you an alien land filled with perils you as yet do not, cannot fully imagine or comprehend. Knowing me as they well do, it was wise of them to forbid me, personally, to give you other than counsel, so they have chosen one who will travel with you as long as you are without effective powers and so need him. He will join you at some time within the next couple of days. You will easily recognize him; he is big and blue.

"Now, I must depart and you must sleep."

When he had awakened in the chilly dawn, raked off the covering earth from the coals and heaped dry squawwood atop them, Fitz began to sort those things he could take and those things he could not or would not need to pack upon his back. Strangely, despite a very hard, very strenuous day yesterday, he felt fitter than within recent memory, but even so, he knew that there was a definite limit to what even men in their prime, in the peak of condition, could be expected to carry on a hike over rough, roadless terrain. He estimated his own maximum at about sixty pounds and chose accordingly.

Food and condiments, weapons. Although he loved and respected the power of the carbine, he knew that he needed a game-getter more than it, for in a real life-or-death emergency, he would still have the revover which fired the same cartridge and, with its six-inch barrel, could maintain accurate fire to substantial ranges. So he zipped the carbine in its case and stowed it in the cargo sidecar, along with the fuel and tools for the bike, eliminating something more than six pounds from his eventual load.

Ammunition. Shotshells and .22 caliber magnum rimfires for the drilling, a box of the frightfully heavy cartridges for the revolver. He felt a little like a posturing fool to pack in fifty-five rounds of .44 magnums . . . until he recalled that thing he had had to kill yesterday.

A complete change of outer clothing, two sets of underwear, three spare pairs of boot socks, toiletries, first-aid items, a small sewing kit and a scissors, an eight-foot by four-foot tarp of a light canvas with metal grommets at corners and along edges, fifty feet of three hundred pound test rope, insect repellent, a roll of toilet paper, a folding spade, a belt axe, a compact set of pot, pan, plates, cup and utensils, a packet of fishing gear, an Arkansas stone for the axe and machete blades, a folding lantern and candles for it, a butane pocket lighter and four aluminum replacement tanks for it, a box of lifeboat matches. The flare projector, of course, along with two each green and red star flares for it. Flashlight and spare batteries, salt tablets.

He considered the air mattress, then decided against it. The weight and bulk of the thing simply did not justify it. Besides, while he would be able to patch holes or smaller rips, a really large one would make the thing so much useless garbage to be left behind on the trail. And there were other ways to soften the ground under him, using natural, on-the-spot materials.

On his belt, in addition to the revolver and two cased speed-loaders for it, he carried his Ka-bar belt knife, a lensatic compass, two cased one-quart canteens, one of them with a cup, the machete and the smaller, more rugged pair of binoculars.

When he hefted pack, bedroll and belt together, however, they seemed lighter than any sixty or even fifty pounds, total, so he added a few "luxuries"—a small spool of wire for making snares, a pair of sharp-nosed pliers, a swiss army knife, a camouflaged poncho, another pair of boot socks, a spare set of rawhide boot laces and, on momentary impulse, a steel slingshot and its bag of ball-bearing projectiles. He had always been good with a slingshot and, should he lose or damage the drilling, the slingshot might well provide him with small game to fill his belly.

When he had used the compass to ascertain the exact position of the storage cave, he scratched the coordinates onto the back of the compass case with the point of a knife, then blocked the entrance as well as he could with the available boulders, before piling brush and branches over all. Then he urinated over as much of the brush as he could, hoping that the strong odor of humanity would keep animals away for at least a little while; it was all he could do.

He settled the straps of the pack-frame comfortably on his shoulders, slung his drilling, knotted a bandanna around his head to catch sweat before it reached his eyes, took up his hiking stick and set out due north, up the slope. It seemed as good a direction to travel as any.

*   *   *

That night, in another, higher vale, he dined on
rabbit, a small tin of beans and tea, then banked the
fire and sacked in, his bag atop a rectangle of tight-
packed conifer tips, his pack out of the reach of
prowling scavengers by way of suspension from a
high tree branch on the end of his rope. Sleeping,
unprotected and companionless in the open, as he
was, he took all the weapons into the bag with him.

The grey cat did not visit him that night. What
finally awakened him was the sunlight . . . and pain.
He opened his eyes with a squall to see some very
odd visitors about his camp. There seemed to be
twelve or fourteen of them, none of them taller
than he, but invariably sturdy, hale and strong-looking.

Some were blond men, some darker haired; all
had fair skin, though much-weathered and mostly
very dirty. All but one wore hide brogans, tight
trousers and shirts that hung to mid-thigh, the cloth
of both looking to be the color of unbleached wool
and coarse of texture. Over the shirts, most of them
wore sleeveless leather jackets, a couple of these
jackets being faced with overlapping scales of what
looked like horn or bone. All wore identical head-
gear, however—a conical steel helmet with a metal
piece projecting down between the eyes to protect
the nose. For weapons, they all wore a long-bladed
dirk at the rear of their belts with the hilt canted to
the right or the left, two or three held odd-shaped
axes and the rest had spears five or six feet long. It
had been the butt of one of these latter that Fitz had
been most urgently prodded.

The squat, red-haired ruffian standing beside the
sleeping bag had grinned at Fitz's squall of pain. He
did it again, but this time, now awake, his victim
only grunted, so he reversed the weapon, clearly
making ready for a downstab into chest or belly.

The tallest man, wearing a mail hauberk with sleeves and chausses and standing observant, one grubby hand on the pommel of a sheathed sword, seemed not about to do or say aught to stop his subordinate from coldly murdering Fitz, just for fun, so Fitz felt constrained to stop the proceedings himself.

Fingering up the quick-release of the bag's zipper, he threw it from off him, drew his revolver and fired a single round into the chest of the spearman. The force of the big round threw the body, flopping, a good five yards backward, to at last land well dead, though still bleeding copiously, a wide portion of the leather jerkin scorched black and smoking from the gunpowder.

For a moment, every one of the smelly strangers stood stock-still. The only sound was the thud made by the pack falling to the ground under the tree, as the man who had untied the rope suddenly let it go as if it had been a live viper. Then, with some cry of incomprehensible words, the man in the hauberk drew his sword, whirled it up and ran in Fitz's direction, shouting what sounded like the same words once again.

"Aw, God damn it, anyway," yelled Fitz in reply, then shot down the charging man, too.

At this, the strangers made a somewhat expedited withdrawal, running, scrambling through the woods in every direction, shouting in a foreign tongue, some of them, others seemingly just screaming mindlessly in sheer terror.

"Way to go, Daddyo!" came a voice . . . no, he realized, a thought transfer, "That's two of them Norman assholes down."

Following this statement, a full-grown lion strolled slowly into the clearing, a big, full-maned, baby-blue lion.

"You dig what they saying, man?" inquired the blue lion. "They all thinks they run up against one of old Saint Germain's black magicians. And that's cool, too, man, it means that bunch at least'll let us be from now on . . . maybe."

"Who the hell are you?" thought Fitz, bewilderedly. "And who were those poor, savage bastards I had to shoot? I don't understand any of all this."

"I'm a cool cat, man," replied the lion, matter of factly. "I'm the coolest cattest character you or anybody elst has ever seen. I'm Cool Blue, the meanest, rightest horn that ever blew a riff. I did my thing from coast to coast with all the top ensembs. And I'll be doing it again real soon now, soon's I can find out how to get out of this lion rig and get back to where I come from, man."

All at once, the baby-blue lion whuffed aloud and thought out, "Hey, man, I think that one in the rusty sweatshirt moved. You sure you cooled him right?"

"How should I know?" thought Fitz in answer. "That wasn't an aimed shot, it was just reflexive. I hope I *didn't* kill him. I don't take any pleasure in killing, you know."

"Oh, me too, man," the lion assured him. "Like, I only kill to eat, you know."

Upon examination, the man in the hauberk was not dead—although, to Fitz's nose, he smelled as if he should have been decently buried at least a week earlier. The .44 slug had almost missed him; in fact, it had glanced off the left side of the conical helmet, leaving a deep dent in the metal and rendering its wearer unconscious for a short span of time.

Upon fully awakening he groaned, then slowly sat up to sway on his rump. Picking up his helmet and observing the place whereon a hefty blow had obviously been dealt it, he whistled softly between his teeth, shook his head, then groaned feelingly once more.

He regarded Fitz with brown eyes that were full of pain, yet he somehow got his lips into a smile, slowly nodded his coiffed head and spoke words that could have been Greek for all that Fitz comprehended of them.

The blue lion's thoughts entered Fitz's mind. "Man, look, I won't be around all the time to help you out, so do this. See? See how easy it is? Now, like you can understand anybody, even if they like talk weird languages like this Norman dude, you know.

"What he said to start out, man, was like, you know, he don't remember what really happened, like. He knows you offed the other one, you know, but like he seems to think you beat him down with that damn machete or something, you know. Anyhow, he says he can't pay you a ransom, so he's gonna have to like serve you, man. Not too bad of an offer, man; at least you'd like have a cat to like guard your back, you know, when I'm not like around, you know. He's got guts, too, man, all these Normans has; not too many brains, most of them, but like a whole pisspot full of guts, you know. He's like strong, too, man."

"Too damned strong for my liking," thought Fitz to the lion. "He stinks like he's spent the last month soaking in a cesspool."

"Really?" replied the baby-blue lion. "Like don't throw rocks, man, you aren't that much less of a stinkpot than him, you know. I don't know how you and your kind stand yourselves, like I don't know how I stood my own self, you know, man. I tell you, a honest skunk is one hell of a lot easier to take than either you *or* him, man. You dig?"

When he had seen in Sir Gautier de Mountjoie's

mind what was the proper formula, Fitz took the young knight's oaths of fealty and service. Then, guided by Cool Blue, they all trooped off to a stream-fed pool. There, after Fitz had refilled both canteens, he stripped and bathed with deodorant soap, shampoo and a bath brush. When he had observed just what was rquired of him, Sir Gautier gritted his teeth and did the bidding of his new overlord, trying to forget how unhealthful and how patently unChristian was the act.

By the time they had walked back to camp, the sun had dried them both and Sir Gautier, signing himself reverently against possible evil, allowed his new overlord to spray his entire body with an icy-cold substance that left a not-unpleasant scent of Syriac oranges. While they had been absent at their bath, some something had come into the area of the camp and dragged off the dead body of the spearman, entire, but the spear had been left where it had lain and Sir Gautier was quick to appropriate it, as well as another spear and an axe which had both been dropped by the other Normans in the course of their rout, earlier that morning.

Cool Blue, who had been so grumpy about the disappearance of so much fresh-killed meat that his color had changed from baby- to royal blue, then faded finally to sky blue, left the camp while Fitz was heating a pot of water for tea and bouillon. Sir Gautier, squatting at fireside across from his new and most singular overlord, began to tell his story, speaking in Norman French, of course, but with Fitz understanding the young knight's thoughts.

Born of a Saxon mother and a Norman sergeant who had been knighted for his deeds upon the Field of Senlac, Gautier had been the youngest of the three sons who had had the good fortune and sturdy constitution to live to adulthood. He, too, had gained his spurs on the field, in battle against the wild, savage Welsh; he had gained an overlord there, too, that day—Sir William de Warrenne, Earl de Surrey.

But Sir Gautier had had only two years of comfort upon his knight's fee, before the Crusade was preached throughout all Christendom and his overlord had declared his intent to march with his host on Palestine and help to free the Holy City of Jerusalem from beneath the evil heel of the foul Unbeliever, so what was there for a faithful vassal to do but himself take the Cross and prepare to follow his master, for good or for ill, for wealth or for poverty, for life or for death, to the Holy Land.

He had no legal heirs. His young bride had died— her and the babe, together—in childbirth, and the few by-blows scattered about the countryside were only one-quarter Norman and so not worth the legitimizing. So, there being no other way to raise the cash necessary to his aims and aspirations, he had sold everything of value for silver marks and so brought along a full score of armed retainers to flesh out the host of Surrey.

At the sticking point, however, his overlord had not embarked, but had sent a younger brother, one Sir Reinald, as surrogate captain of his host. In France, they had joined with the mighty French host for the march across all of Europe to Byzantium. That march had been one disaster after another, with co-religionists— greedy, avaricious, and thieving, at best; murderous, at worst—robbing and killing the Holy Host on every hand. Horses, mules, draught oxen and asses had dropped like flies. The only two horses Sir Gautier had had left as his portion of the strung-out, miles-long column had passed into Byzantine lands had been commandeered by Sir Reinald to mount a favorite cook and his jester, leaving Sir Gautier and his remaining fourteen men all afoot.

It had not been until the long, brutal Battle of Dorylaeum that, in that battle's aftermath, Sir Gautier had been able to remount himself and his own, original survivors, plus those of another knight he had taken on following their master's death of wounds and thirst. The horses had been manageable and speedy enough, but of so light a breed that none of them proved capable of carrying a full-armed Western warrior for any distance or length of time, but they had been the only horseflesh then and there available so he had made do with them.

Before the young Norman could "tell" more, Cool Blue had returned, once more a baby-blue hue, but now with red blood smeared around his chops. "Like, man," he thought good humoredly, to Fitz, "your kind don't smell too good, but you don't make a bad meal. I caught the big, spotted cat stole that body from here, run him off and ate the most of that Norman spearman, you know. Like, once you get past the smell, you got it like licked, you dig?"

CHAPTER IX

Sir Gautier fumbled behind him for a spear and his sword, horror and rage on his tanned face with its blondish beard and moustaches. "Accursed, satan-spawn beast! You come back here and gloat of having eaten the flesh of my sergeant, Alain?"

"Like, sure thing, man. Why not?" thought the lion, completely unruffled, not in the least insulted or wary. "Like I should let good meat go to waste, maybe? Hunting's hard work, you dig? And like I didn't even get the best parts of him. The spotted cat had like scarfed up them before I got there, you know, and it won't all that much of him like to start with, you know."

At least, that was the way in which Fitz "heard" the discourse. Just how the hipster slang came out in 11th-century Norman French, he could not say. But apparently the baby-blue lion's "words" served to sufficiently mollify Sir Gautier that he ceased to search for weapons and glower murderously at Cool Blue.

At length, they began the day's hike, Fitz first having had to be quite firm on the subject of carrying his own load himself. That load was only less than sixty pounds, he estimated, everything included, while the knight's mail pieces and helmet alone totaled close to that, not even including his sword, two spears, dirk, axe or the rolled woolen cloak that had been left in the woods when the Normans had first invaded Fitz's camp. In the end, he had made a sling of one of his spare boot-laces and given the knight one of the canteens to carry.

As they walked on, up and down slopes, across vales and through streams of varying depths, Sir Gautier went on with the sorry tale he had commenced at fireside. Sir Reinald, brother to and surrogate for Sir Gautier's overlord, still safe on his estates in Surrey, had fallen during the course of the day-long engagement at Dorylaeum, and Sir Gautier had found himself and his followers beneath the banner of Sir Godfrey, Duke of Lower Lorraine. It had been that great man's orders, filtered down through a host of subordinates, of course, that had sent Sir Gautier and his following, along with a party of some hundreds of other knights, sergeants, men at arms, servants and straggling camp followers to seek out and explore a possible route of march through a succession of arid hills and wadis.

They had been able to find almost no water, and that little foul and brackish, so before long they all were afoot again, those not quick enough, ruthless enough to commandeer at swords' points the little asses of camp followers, which beasts seemed much hardier than the horses.

With food supplies low, game scarce and chary, no traces of foemen in sight or sound, and such few habitations come across all long abandoned and fallen into ruin, the party had split into smaller units and fanned out to east and west, though continuing the ordered trek. Then, of a hot, windless morning, all of the men rolling pebbles in their mouths in order to try to coax up the ghosts of drops of saliva with which to wet their bricky-dry throats, the knight and two of the other men spotted a wild, two-humped camel trotting away from them, up a wadi, and within moments the entire little party was in hot foot-pursuit of so much flesh and blood.

When, farther on, the wadi split into two channels, Sir Gautier and his men took one and the other knight, Sir Eugen, took the other with his followers, both knights agreeing to sound a horn blast whenever they cornered the camel.

The dry watercourse twisted and turned like a dying, spasming serpent, but Sir Gautier and his starveling followers stayed hard upon the track of the elusive beast, spread out across the full width of the wadi, close one to the other, lest the beast turn and break through their line and so escape them. They were in just such a tight formation when they rounded yet another turn and the ground abruptly dropped from beneath their feet. Sir Gautier felt himself to be falling; just how far he fell, he never knew, but at impact, all his senses left him.

When his consciousness returned, he thought at first that he had been killed by the fall and was just then in some part of Heaven. At a few yards to his one side, a high waterfall plunged two-score feet into a pool at the base of a vine-grown bluff. He and his men lay all together on a deep bed of dried pine tags between the pool and the tall forest of pine trees that marched down almost to the verge of that pool. A cool breeze soughed through this forest, rustling the branches of the trees.

To the hot, exhausted, footsore and very thirsty men, the setting was indeed paradisical. That the Lusatian knight, Sir Eugen, and his equally worn-down following might join them in this thoroughly unexpected but very welcome place, Sir Gautier sat up and winded his horn, paused, then winded it yet again. But there was no answering horn, none.

There proved to be fish and crayfish in the pool and in the stream that the pool fed, and by the time most of these had been caught and cooked and eaten by the ravenous men, Sir Gautier had, in the forest, cast a spear so shrewdly that he killed a fine big stag, giving them all meat enough for several meals. But all good things must finally come to an end. Sir Gautier recalled his duty, his honor, his sworn word to Duke Godfrey, and so roused his men and left the poolside to find the way back into that world of heat, flies, bad water, sand and dust. The Duke must know of this pleasant place on the long, hard road to the Holy City, Jerusalem.

He and they had been searching for the way back into the Syriac Desert ever since. During the six to eight months he estimated had elapsed since they all had wakened by that waterfall and pool, they had wandered countless miles of hills, vales, plateaus, valleys and even out a little way onto what his mental pictures told Fitz could only be the sandy plain.

"It looked more like that land from which he had come than any other we had seen," thought Sir Gautier. "So we filled our waterskins at a lake, then set off toward high, bare hills we could espy in the distance. But we had been marching on for less than an hour when we were attacked by a horrid monster, surely an imp from the depths of Hell. Giant and bear and ape it was, and ferocious as any desert lion, but we are Normans, all. We fought it and triumphed, killing it, but it slew four men in the fight."

Fitz shuddered. The mental image in the young knight's mind was of a Teeth and Legs. It had been bad enough to have to kill one of the things at long range with a powerful firearm; he doubted that he would have had the sheer guts to face one of them close up with only spears, axes and swords to keep its fearsome dentition out of his flesh.

Cool Blue had been "eavesdropping"; now he remarked, "You dig me now, man, 'bout these Normans? Like, I mean, they got miles and miles of guts, see, but they run kind of short, you know, like in the brains department, see. They'll like fight anybody or anything at the drop of a hat, you know. Crazy, man, crazy."

Fitz did not agree. He, rather, thought the young knight's decision to stand and fight showed not only courage but a rare quality of snap judgment, accurate snap judgment, the so-called command decision. If ponies, ostriches and motorcycles could not outrun a Teeth and Legs, then what faint chance would a group of unmounted men have had to do so? Unsophisticated, perhaps, by the standards of Cool Blue, Sir Gautier was nonetheless a mature warrior and nobody's fool, certainly a good man to have at your side if push came to shove.

But he wondered, too, did Alfred Fitzgilbert, how the Norman could have so misjudged the passage of time as to think that he and his men had sojourned less than a year here, when actually they had been gone from their own world and time for the best part of a millennium. He made a mental note to take this matter up with Puss, whenever she chose to make another visit.

However . . . and this one really bothered him: If the party of Norman Crusaders truly had been tramping about this place for nearly a thousand years, how

had their clothing, weapons and armor held up so
well for so long in such constant use? Thinking these
thoughts, he felt a pressing desire to see Danna, to
go back briefly to the other world, lest when he
finally did return, it would be to find that as much
time had passed for him as had already passed for the
unfortunate Normans.

An automobile drew up before the locked gates of
the house that had been home to Fitz, one sunny
afternoon. When several insistent toots of the horn
accomplished them nothing, one of the two men in
the front seat of the vehicle got out, stalked to the
side of the gate and rang the bell. Never having
actually seen the paunchy, jowly, red-faced man,
Fitz would not have recognized him as Henry Fowler
Blutegel, I.R.S.

After a moment, the smaller gate set inside one of
the larger ones sprung open an inch or so and a voice
from a box set on a post just inside said, "You may
come in now."

Once inside, the tax collector tried to open the
larger gates, but gave over when he realized his at-
tempts were in vain and waved the driver to enter,
shouting, "Bring my briefcase. And roll up all the
windows and lock all the doors, too. In a rundown,
red-neck neighborhood like this, they'll steal you
blind."

Followed by his driver-associate—a younger man
with black hair and sharp features, who walked with
a slight limp and bore purplish burn scars on one
side of his face and the backs of both hands—the
stout, red-faced Blutegel disdained to follow the walk-
way, cutting directly across the lawn to the front
stoop.

Immediately after he pushed the lighted button

mounted beside the door, a voice spoke conversationally from out another of the speakers. "It's open. Come in."

When the officious official strode in from the foyer, the first thing he saw was Pedro Goldfarb, relaxed in one of the leather armchairs, one leg up on the arm nearest the door and a snifter of pale liquor in his hand. The other chair was occupied by M. Dannon Dardrey, her hands folded in her lap.

"Sit down, won't you, Mister Blutegel," said Pedro, gesturing at the couch with a languid wave of his free hand. "Would you or your associate care for a bit of this excellent cognac? No? Then some whiskey, perhaps?"

"No . . . ahh, no thank you, Mister Goldfarb," Blutegel said, though his bloodshot eyes betrayed his very real craving for the offered spirits. "I'm not here to socialize . . . and you know it! Besides, if that liquor came from here, you may just be drinking what is—or soon will be—rightly the property of the United States of America."

Pedro shrugged, sniffed appreciatively at the rim of the crystal snifter and then held it up to the light, while remarking, "Too bad, Mister Blutegel, too bad. You're missing out on a rare treat in this cognac. As regards the other matter you just mentioned, I'm sure I do not know exactly to what you're referring. You demanded to meet with me and the new owner of this house and property, today, and I took time out of a very hectic schedule to accommodate you.

"You've met my associate, M. Dannon Dardrey, I believe. Well, she is the new owner-of-record of this property and residence, Mister Blutegel."

Blutegel sat down then, looking a bit stunned. "Well, Mister Goldfarb, where is your client? Where did Fitzgilbert run off to?"

Pedro shrugged again, swishing the cognac in the snifter, taking great pleasure from tantalizing the overbearing man, whom he knew to be an alcoholic. "I'm sure I don't know his exact location, Mister Blutegel. He owns interests in the Union of South Africa, you know, as well as in several countries in the Caribbean and Central America, or he might well be in Europe, possibly Switzerland . . .?"

Blutegel shook his head and said, sourly, "No, not Switzerland, I don't think. The Swiss are damned cooperative with us anymore, and I know for sure that Fitzgilbert and his wheeler-dealer buddy, Tolliver, didn't send any money to Switzerland. Those damned South Africans, now, they won't tell us one damned thing. The banana republics aren't too cooperative, either, but we're still investigating down there. I don't think it'll be too long before we know exactly how much money Tolliver and Fitzgilbert have illegally exported and cheated the United States of America out of.

"Was I you, Mister Goldfarb, I'd tell Fitzgilbert to hightail it back here and fully cooperate with me . . . it might go easier with him if he does."

Pedro set his snifter on the table, steepled his fingers and shook his head. "Mister Blutegel, the more I have to deal with you, the more you amaze me. You know and I know and you must know that I know that, lacking clear evidence of misdeeds on the parts of my clients, Gustaf Tolliver and Alfred Fitzgilbert, your paranoid suspicions and those of your superiors are not worth a cupful of cold spit in the tax court or in any other court of law."

Blutegel leaned forward, his face darkening, his voice becoming raspy, threatening, "Don't you go getting snotty with *me*, Mister Goldfarb! You don't know as much as you think you know, and we know more about you and your firm and these two clients of yours than you think we know, too. If we get a little bit more information and can provide evidence of collusion to defraud the United States of America between your clients and you . . .? Well, the next time we meet, you just might be singing a real different tune, mister big-time lawyer."

"You're insane, Mister Blutegel," snapped Danna. "Because Mister Goldfarb and I have refused to release privileged information to you, you . . ."

"You just mind your mouth, Mizzz Dardrey, until I tell you to open it up again. Hear me?" Blutegel coldly interrupted her, adding, "Unless you want Goldfarb here, and a whole lot of other people to know you're not as goody-good as you want everybody to think you are."

Danna inwardly cringed from his evil smirk as much as from the way that his eyes were undressing her, probing at the most private portions of her body, shamelessly.

"I can handle this blowhard, Danna," Pedro smiled. "He seems to be of the opinion that he's up to his usual work—terrorizing and trying to intimidate poor men and women who goofed in trying to do their tax-forms themselves, the kind of work that a professional bully like him does best.

"Mister Blutegel, you're a disgrace to civil service. How you've gotten away with the quasi-legal things you have done and still are doing or trying to do for as long as you have is a complete mystery to me . . . as to many another of my professional colleagues, I might add. Someday soon, some of us are going to make it our business to find out just what you have on whom that keeps you in this position of power that you so flagrantly abuse. I really do think that you will be much happier and more fulfilled out of government service, Mister Blutegel; for one thing, there will be less interference with your alcoholic avocation and you are certain to find employment to your complete taste, perhaps with one of the lead-pipe collection agencies."

"Who the hell you think you are, you sheenie bastard, you?" snarled Blutegel, springing to his feet, livid, both his meaty fists clenched. "I'm bigger and heavier and a whole lot meaner than you are, you skinny Christ-killer, and if you think I won't beat your Jew ass . . ."

Pedro had not moved a muscle, just watching and listening to the outburst of the raging fat man. Now he gave another of his languid shrugs and smiled condescendingly, "Oh, yes, Mister Blutegel, you're mean—and in more than only a single meaning of that word—and you're big and rather heavy, too. You are also a bit younger than I am. Even so, Mister Blutegel, it would be a cardinal error for you to physically attack me. Do you understand, Mister Blutegel?"

Blutegel gulped, hard. "You . . . you got a gun, huh?"

Another condescending smile. "No, Mister Blutegel, I don't need a gun, not for scum like you. Your weight is all big bones and adipose tissue, you see, with what little muscle you have left smothered under the fat. My adoptive father, Izaak Goldfarb, taught me savate when still I was a boy, Mister Blutegel. Later, I was a Golden Gloves boxer and, in the Marine Corps, I excelled in jiujitsu; moreover, I have remained in shape, in trim, as you so clearly have not. Are you beginning to get the picture, Mister Blutegel? Take a poke at me and I'll mop up the floor with your flabby carcass!"

Danna, hearing what sounded like a groan from

the other man, looked to see his scarred face twisted, his eyes both teary, one hand clasped tightly over his mouth and his body spasming.

"Now that that matter is settled, Mister Blutegel," Pedro went on, "I think that you owe Mrs. Dardrey an apology; I am sure that you do, in fact."

In still-angry frustration, the backed-down bully snapped, "I don't apologize to hooers, I never did, not even high-priced hooers, like her."

In milliseconds Danna was up, out of her chair, had strode over to confront the I.R.S. man and had delivered a ringing slap to his left cheek. "You slimy slug, no one calls *me* a whore!"

George Khoury, the other I.R.S. man, could not recall having ever seen anyone move as fast as Pedro Goldfarb did then, not even in the Nam. One of the attorney's arms swept Danna's body out of the way and the palm of the other took the blow of Blutegel's fist meant for her face. But Khoury himself arose fast enough to catch the stumbling, off-balance woman and steady her enough for her to regain her equilibrium.

With two of his skilled fingers applying unbearable pressure on certain nerve centers of Blutegel's body, pressure that caused so great a degree of agony that the beefy man could not even cry out, Pedro had no difficulty in easing him back into a seated position on the leather couch.

"Any more of that rough stuff, Mister Blutegel," he admonished, "and I'll feel compelled to hurt you, perhaps injure you severely. Is that clear?

"Very well. Now, what possessed you to hurl so egregious an insult at my associate, Mrs. Dardrey? Have you never heard of the word slander?"

"It's not slander if you can prove it, Goldfarb," the fat man gasped, hugging himself, his face still pale and lined with pain. To Danna, then, he said, "Okay, sister, you asked for it.

"Goldfarb, I've had a team watching this house and Tolliver's shop and house, too, ever since a man from another department tipped me off some time back that the two of them was up to something damned fishy and was probably tax cheats, too. I sent word out here to Fitzgilbert that he had an appointment with me, but he never kept it, didn't even phone so I could tell him another time to come in. He didn't answer his phone for over a week and didn't pick up his mail, either. When he finally did pick up his phone one day, he got right uppity with me for no good reason and told *me* when he'd come into the city to see me."

"I know about that conversation, I've heard the tape he made of it, but do go on, Mister Blutegel, please," said Pedro.

"Well, I got real busy that day, and forgot to call the team had been doing surveillance out here off. And that night, that Friday night, real late, a sports car comes up the street and stops here and Mizz Goody-Twoshoes, over there, gets out and rings that gate bell. Then Fitzgilbert comes out and lets her drive her car in and locks the gate back up and the two of them go inside here and don't come out again until Sunday night. I don't think they were just playing Parcheesi all weekend, either, because the logs say that all the lights were out a whole lot at night.

"Then, when we came to find out he'd signed his house and cars and furniture and all over to her . . . well, I just figured it was for services rendered, you know. Yeah, I think she's a hooer and I think it's lots of people would agree with me, too."

Pedro nodded wearily, "Yes, with a mind like

yours, I can see how you would think just so. You're a real Grade-A scuzz, aren't you, Mister Blutegel? All right, if you already know who the new owner of record was, why were you so insistent on meeting said owner out here, rather than in my office . . . or in yours, for that matter?"

The fat man shrugged, then winced. "What the hell'd you do to me, anyway?"

"Not one tenth of what I'd have done if you had actually managed to punch Mrs. Dardrey, Mister Blutegel. Now, answer my last question."

"Well, dammit," Blutegel almost whined, "she stomped over here and slapped me first—hard, too. I can still feel it where she hit me."

"Good!" snapped Danna, but said no more after a brief wave of Pedro's hand.

"The question, Mister Blutegel," prompted Pedro, with a grim undertone in his voice, and a hard-eyed stare accompanying the words.

"Huh?" was Blutegel's reply.

Pedro sighed disgustedly and said, "Why, if you already knew just who was the new owner of record of this property, did you insist on meeting said owner out here, rather than at an office in the city? But wait, you don't need to answer, I know your reasoning already: You thought that you could get her out here and pour on your accustomed tactics full throttle—threaten, bully, and possibly, in this case, use the information given you by your team of snoopers along with a few judiciously placed threats of public disclosure to extort some privileged information out of her. Am I correct, Mister Blutegel? Of course I am."

The chunky man had gone pasty white. He abruptly rose to his feet, grabbed his briefcase and headed for the door. "Come on, Khoury, you damn, dumb Ayrab, we're getting out of here."

But the man addressed remained seated after the front door had slammed behind his associate. "Mister Goldfarb," he said, "there's no need to try to cause trouble for Mister Blutegel, he's already in more than enough hot water. The only reason he's still working at all is that certain supervisory types, who've known him for years, are trying to help him make sure he gets his pension."

Pedro laughed harshly. "Now there's a misuse of taxpayers' money if ever there was one."

"Speaking only and briefly for myself, sir, I agree," said the younger man, "but then I haven't been at this for very long, either, and I just follow my orders, just like in the army, you know. Anyhow, he works under close supervision in the office and he's never allowed to do any sort of field work alone anymore, that's why I was with him today, you see.

"Please accept my apologies for the way he behaved here today. I know you know his behavior is not the policy of the Internal Revenue Service. He's a sick, aging, emotionally disturbed man with a severe alcohol problem, but in another year he will have put twenty-five years into government service, almost as long as he's been a citizen of this country."

"Blutegel's not native-born, then?" demanded Danna, surprisedly.

Khoury shook his head. "No, he's from Czechoslovakia, I believe; he came here just after World War Two. But with his lack of a foreign accent, even I didn't know he was an immigrant until a guy in the office told me.

"Look, I've got to go." The scarred young man stood up. "I've got the only set of keys to the car. I say again: I'm deeply sorry for all he said here today, but just let him fade away, huh? Don't go after his job . . . you just might get it jerked out from under him."

When the two in the house heard the doors slam, the engine start and the automobile drive off up the street, Pedro arose and carefully poured the cognac out of the snifter and back into its decanter, saying, "What I did with this, when first he came in, it was cruel, heartless to torment the man like that. But damn it, Danna, when I think of the relatively blameless men and women, the ones I actually know about, whom that fat bastard has bullied, terrorized, intimidated, made to crawl to him abjectly, torn every shred of dignity and self-respect from, my blood boils. He and people like him, they're examples of the savage barbarism that lies just below the surface of 'civilized' humanity. And I get even madder to think that he's being allowed to continue to practice his particular brand of sadism on helpless victims, despite all that the Powers That Be obviously know about him, simply so that he can qualify to draw a pension until he drinks himself to death. That Khoury chap can beg all he wants, but I'm going after Blutegel."

"Since I first met that man, Pedro," said Danna, speaking slowly, thoughtfully, "I've always thought that life and birth had miscast him, that he should have been a Nazi, Schutzstaffel or Gestapo. I just don't think he's a Czech; Blutegel is a German word."

Pedro replied, "Well, Danna, Germans live in Czechoslovakia, too, you know. That was why Hitler claimed he had a right to the first half of that country, back in the thirties, the Sudeten Germans, whom he said were being persecuted."

"Yes, yes, I know all that, Pedro, I was around then, too. But . . . but I've just got this . . . this very strong feeling, too." She sat with her forehead resting on her hands for a moment, then looked up and asked, "Pedro, would you mind if I spent a few days collecting photos and background on Blutegel?"

"Not at all," he answered, then asked, "But what do you intend to do with such a file when you get it all assembled, Danna?"

She took a deep breath. "Stick my neck out, probably. There's a man in Vienna, I read about him, he hunts hide-out Nazis. Maybe if he could see pictures of Blutegel—and I mean to get all I can, from just as far back as I can, too, and get his fingerprints, if that's possible—he might remember him from somewhere? Do I sound looney, Pedro?"

His elbows on the leather-topped table, his fingers steepled before his chin, with his full lower lip resting lightly on the two forefingers, he regarded her for a long moment, then said, "No, I don't think you irrational, Danna. It's a possibility, of course, that Blutegel's a ringer. There were just so many displaced persons let into this country in the wake of that war that any number of snafus could conceivably have occurred . . . probably did occur, if not in this case, then in many others. But what makes you think this of him, Danna? You say only that you have a feeling. Well, what kind of feeling? Tell me about it."

"If I do, then you *will* think I'm nuts," said Danna, then shrugged, "All right, then, here goes. Shortly after you accepted me into the firm, when I was working with Hiram and Myrna Page—remember? The couple who owned the small florist shop? The woman who suicided for no apparent reason. Well, I first went over to the Federal Building with them to see Blutegel, when I first walked into his office, Pedro, I . . . I could see what he really looked like, of course, but . . . but I could also see another him, standing in the same place, a younger him, dressed in a black uniform with shiny black boots almost up to his knees, black gloves on his hands and them flexing a black leather riding crop. And Pedro, that was my first meeting with Blutegel, I didn't know a bit of what a bastard he is, not then.

"I saw almost that same picture of him again, here, today, and I've seen it other times over the years. I've always had reliable intuition, Pedro, and I've more than once had good reason to regret it when I didn't respect and follow that intuition. I want to follow this one up. I feel that I need to, that if I don't, then no one else ever will. Do you understand?"

Pedro Goldfarb nodded. "I think so, Danna. You do whatever seems to you the right thing to do, and don't hesitate to call on me or any of the rest of our staff for help. You see, I, too, believe in obeying intuition."

Then he frowned. "But back to current matters: do you know where Fitz really is? Could you easily reach him if there was pressing need to do so, Danna?"

"Yes," she replied. "It might take a few days, but yes, I think I could reach him if it was necessary. Why?"

He used his hands to rub briskly at his forearms under his sleeves. "I can't say now, not in so many words, but there just might be a good and sufficient reason for a speedy return someday soon, so I needed to know. But that aside, you're developing a really nice tan, Danna. New kind of sunlamp?"

She smiled. "Thank you. Yes, you might say a new kind of sunlamp."

"You'll have to show it to me some time," said Pedro. "Look at me, I'm getting fish-belly white. The ones at my club aren't worth a damn. Sometimes I feel that cities were designed as a punishment for all humanity, Danna . . . and sometimes I get the feeling that humanity deserves every erg of that punishment, too.

"But back to you, Danna, have you gotten an overdose of *CHiPS* on television?"

She wrinkled her brows and asked, "What in the world are you talking about, Pedro? I hardly ever have time to watch any television, except the news sometimes."

"Buying guns and enrolling in firearms courses, buying a motorcycle and conning the salesman into teaching you how to ride it. I hear things, Danna, they come back to me from all over. Why these sudden interests in guns and motorcycles?" He snapped his fingers and grinned. "I've got it! You're going to organize a group of feminist motorcycle outlaws, right?"

"If you must know, and it would seem that you must," said Danna, "Fitz suggested that I learn both skills . . . for reasons that are really no one's business but ours, his and mine."

"*Ooowww!*" Pedro yelped, grasping his wrist and mock-wincing. "Okay, I won't pry again, I promise. But let me make a suggestion.

"Guns are not always the answer, or the best answer, in a given situation. Remind me on Monday and I'll take you to a place I know, it's called a *dojo*. An elderly oriental runs it and it's far from your common run of karate halls; he's well off and doesn't need to work for a living, so he only accepts students who appeal to him in some way."

"And you think that I, a fifty-five-year-old widow, will appeal to him?" she grinned maliciously. "Are you deciding you'd really rather be a flesh-peddler, Pedro?"

But he did not rise to the joke. In a serious tone he said, "No kidding, Danna. I think Master Hara will like you and I know you'll like him. Stick with him, and he'll teach you a lot—not just the self-defense and fighting skills, but the depths of philosophy that are the firm foundation of those skills. That philosophy can help you to awaken and develop within yourself powers that you never even suspected you had before. I know, my instructor was this very man, some years back, of course. Prior to my years with him, I wasn't even as much as half what I am now, today."

Later, after Pedro had left and she had locked up the gates, the front of the house and activated all the alarm systems, Danna packed a small cooler chest with ice, food, and a couple of long, green bottles of a Moselle. Cinching her waist with the gunbelt, she holstered her new Ruger Security-Six revolver and went out onto the back porch. At the foot of the steps, she filled a brace of gallon jugs with water from the tap and used them to balance the weight of the cooler as she crossed the yard, ascended the mound and entered the wall tent. It took two trips to get the items down the stairs safely, even with the new safety ropes Fitz had strung before he left.

Once in the sand world, by the driftwood log, Danna strapped the cooler onto the rack behind the seat and hung one water jug from each of the cooler's handles before starting the bike.

She had been spending most of her weekends in the sand world since Fitz had left. Unlike him, she had no desire to go exploring, but had spent her time lazing on the beach or on the ship she called her sand yacht. Just as Fitz had told her he felt constantly in the sand world, Danna too had felt a constant twinge of an uneasy sense that something, somewhere, was ever watching her; therefore, the only place in the sand world that she ever went without a revolver was when she swam in the sea.

Often, she brought along her briefcase and read and made notes and listed precedents known or to be researched in the stern cabin of the ancient wreck or stretched on a blanket covering the deck above that cabin. Despite the feeling of being watched, observed, she never felt as really good in the other world as she did in the sand world. She felt far more alive, vibrant, thoroughly healthy, even younger than her age. Also, she felt as if she truly belonged in the sand world, as if it were her personal world, created solely for her and Fitz, their private domain.

She missed Fitz terribly, of course, missed him by night and by day, in this world or in the other, but nights in the narrow cot in the center of the stern cabin were the worst, the hardest to bear. Often, she would extend a hand and caress the Very pistol that she kept on the low table near the cot and think of immediately going up on deck and firing the first star-shell to summon him back to her so-empty arms.

But she had not done so yet, of course. For considering the time differential of the two worlds, although a month had gone by for her—a month without Fitz. Could she really keep her sanity through two more months without him—it had been only some ten days or even less for him, and he could have done little of what he had intended within so short a time, she knew. It would not be fair to him to recall him so soon, so she had not. Even so, she still kept the flare projector close beside the cot, where she could reach out and caress its metal surfaces and think of Fitz during the long, lonely nights.

Fitz always insisted that night camps be made in open places—vales or clearings, with as little overhanging foliage as possible, so as to allow him to see a great swath of sky, preferably southerly sky.

"I'm watching for a sign," he had told both Sir Gautier and Cool Blue, in explanation. "If either of you, by night or by day, see a burst of color, red or green, in the southern sky, followed immediately by three stars of that same color falling from the place of the burst, tell me of it at once, it is very important to me."

As they were making camp one late afternoon, a doe, spooked apparently by something in the surrounding forest, bounded into their clearing and stood stock-still, obviously not expecting the clearing to be tenanted. Sir Gautier was deadly poetry in motion. In but a single, silken-smooth movement, he had leaned to pick up a spear, cocked his right arm and cast it with such power and accuracy that it transfixed the heart of the doe and she was dead even as she made one final, useless bound.

The meat was most welcome. Fitz had been getting a little tired of game birds, rabbit and squirrel meat, so venison steaks broiled on a grill (that Sir Gautier quickly and expertly fashioned of green sticks) over a bed of fragrant hardwood coals, basted with margarine and sprinkled with coarse-grind pepper, were a decided treat. Cool Blue, of course, got the lion's share of the carcass, but Fitz made certain that a joint was hung high beyond any animal thievery that they might have a bit more of the meat for their breakfast.

Fitz had wondered at the size of the grill and the spread of the bed of coals, then at the number of steaks Sir Gautier had insisted be set to cook. But once they were cooked, he ceased to wonder. Despite his hunger and the added spice of variety, three of the steaks were the most he could manage to cram down his gullet, but not so Sir Gautier. The Norman knight proceeded to wolf what his companion estimated to be at least seven and possibly nine pounds of cooked meat, followed with a double handful of berries and two cups of orange pekoe tea (of which the medieval warrior had become quite fond).

Following this—to Fitz, monumental—gorge, the young knight had lain flat on his back for a few minutes, belching and sighing with clear contentment, arisen to go off into the woods for a while, then returned to the fireside to use Fitz's axe stone on the edges of his sword and the machete, then the knife stone on the knives and the dirk. Before he finally rolled himself into his thick cloak, the Norman had grilled and consumed three more steaks, then polished off the last of the berries and the tea, grumbling about the lack of good red wine which should properly accompany venison.

But before his "bedtime snack," while he squatted with Arkansas stone and the Ka-bar knife (he always saw to his overlord's blades first, never failing to remark on the rare and fine quality of their steel—how tough and resilient they were, how well they held their edges in use and how little touching up those edges ever needed), he said, bluntly, "You are no evil wizard, Lord Alfred, but rather a decent and Christian man like your servant, Gautier de Montjoie. So please, I beg of you, Lord Alfred, tell me just how you called down thunder and fiery lightning and so slew my sergeant, Alain?"

Knowing the young, 11th-century Norman to be far from unintelligent, indeed, possessed of a quick and relatively open mind, Fitz nodded, drew his revolver and ejected all five of the cartridges.

Holding one up between thumb and forefinger, he tapped the nail of his other forefinger on the case. "Inside this brass cylinder, Gautier, is a powdery compound called gunpowder. When a spark strikes into it, it burns faster than the eye could follow and thus creates smoke and fire that must have room to expand and, in search of that needed room, they push this leaden plug out of the end of the brass cylinder.

"Now," he laid down the cartridge and picked up the silvery, stainless-steel revolver, "the brass cylinders are contained in the openings bored into this larger steel cylinder, here. This flat strap of steel inside this steel circle is called a 'trigger.' Observe, when the finger draws it to the rear, gears and springs you cannot see bring this forked thing back—it is called the 'hammer'—then let it fall with some force against this little steel button here in this groove. On the other side of the button is a very short steel rod called a 'firing pin.' When the button is struck by the hammer, the firing pin strikes the base of one of the cylinders and that creates the spark that ignites the gunpowder, the smoke and fire of which, expanding, cast out the leaden plug. The plug then continues up the length of this longer, slenderer steel cylinder, which is called the 'barrel.' The smoke and fire still are behind the leaden plug, pushing it with extreme force, so that when it emerges into open air, it will penetrate almost anything that happens to be in its way.

"The entire device is called a 'revolver,' Gautier, because this largest steel cylinder turns on a rod, see, to bring a fresh brazen cylinder beneath the firing pin each time the trigger is pulled. It is in no way magical, merely a man-made instrument for killing easily at distances greater than a spear can be thrown.

"As for your sergeant, he already had struck me with the ferrule of his spear and I believed he was making ready to thrust the point into me, so I shot him. A man must protect himself."

"My lord should not concern himself with the killing of an oaf of Alain's water," said Sir Gautier, shrugging. "He ever was impetuous, and I was often compelled to beat him for putting on airs not at all commensurate to his baseborn station in life. So he is no great loss."

Laying aside knife and stone, the knight rolled a cartridge in his fingers, examining it closely by the firelight. Then he handed it back and asked, "This powder, Lord Alfred, of what constituents is it compounded?"

Fitz had no idea of the formula for smokeless powder, of course, but he had to answer something. "Nitre, brimstone and charcoal, Gautier. Differing proportions for different purposes, but mostly nitre in all of them."

"Very interesting, Lord Alfred. Could you make one or more of these devices a good deal bigger, of a bigness sufficient to hurling good-sized boulders, there would be no motte in all the land could stand against my lord's war band, he could quickly become king of any land he desired to rule . . .?"

"So much," thought Fitz to himself, "for the myth of the hidebound, stubbornly conservative, superstitious and hag-ridden, unimaginative and unprogressive medieval man taught by historians of my time!"

CHAPTER X

Cool Blue had been stunned when Fitz had told him that almost eighteen years had passed since the man who had been transformed into the baby-blue lion had passed from one world to the other one.

"But, like, man, it just can't of been that long, you know. I'd of like *known*. Wouldn't I?" he added, a little plaintively, his shade of blue beginning to perceptibly darken.

"Man, like I knew exac'ly, almost to the like minute those fuckers kept me in the army, after they drafted me. And like you know, they wouldn't even put me in the Special Services. They had me driving a damn truck in Korea, for chrissakes, you know, like I'd been some dumbass bush nigger from Alabama, not a completely cool cat from Chicago, like I was, even then.

"What little bits of notes I could like blow out was all in my off-duty time, until some asshole like stole my horn. So it took me damn near a whole year after they finally let me go just to like get my lip back and get aholt of a decent axe again, you know. Hadn't of been for the fucking draft, like I'd of been way up there, one of the really big names, pulling down top gigs and good bread and I wouldn't of had to let none them loan sharks get their like claws into me, neither. Like, you know, man, it's all the fault of the fucking draft board and the Yew Ess Army that I would up here in this like lion get-up. You dig, man?"

"Frankly," said Fitz truthfully, "no, I don't understand the connection, Cool Blue. You must have been separated long before you came to this place."

"Well, like it was *them* fuckers interrupted my damn career and all so I had to like start all over again when I got out," "said" the now-navy-blue lion. "That took bread, like big bread, and like I wasn't hitting no really rich gigs yet, see. It won't no sense in going to no banks, 'cause I didn't own no co-lat'ral, banks only loans money to people as can prove they don't really need it. So I went the only place I could, to Fat Tony, the loan shark. He lent me the three grand and, like bang, I started in getting good gigs and all. But still I couldn't never get enough together to pay him no big chunks and with the vigorish and all keeping on piling up, it looked like Fat Tony was gonna be into me for the rest of my natcherl life, man.

"But then, man, like after a couple really groovy years, things went sour for me all of a sudden, like. You know, like two, three gigs welshed on me right together and I like had to miss some payments to Fat Tony, 'cause like, man, I just didn't have the bread. After the first time his goons come around and beat up on me, like I sold off ever thing 'cept my horn and give all the bread—I mean like *all* of it, man—to Fat Tony, but with more bread coming in so slow, like, I just kept on getting further and further behind.

"When one the deadbeat clubs finally come through with the bread they owed me, I hustled it right down to Fat Tony and he took it . . . but then he said I was setting a bad example to his other what he called clients and said I was just gonna have to *be* a example and he told his goons to take me out and kill me and dump me in the lake, but to make damn sure I floated so's they'd find me.

"Them fuckers, they beat the pure, living shit out of me in the back seat of their Caddy, too. And they told me that, before they did kill me, they was gonna jam a service station air hose up my ass and fill me fulla air so's I'd be sure to float. When they pulled into a all-night gas station, man, I like figured I didn't have nothing to lose if they had to kill me *before* they like filled up my ass with air, so when that bastard of a Nick the Knucks opened his door, I went across him like sixty and put my knee in his crotch on the way, too. Then I took off running like the hounds of hell was after me, and they was, too, you know.

"I wound up in this little-bitty park I'd never been in before, down by the lakeside, and after the beating and all that running and scared shitless, too, like I was, I was about to drop, like I mean it, man. I could hear the fuckers running and yelling to each other and then I seen this kind of tunnel-like up ahead with the sidewalk running right into it, but no lights in it, and like, man, that's where Cool Blue went. But when I heard them big feet slap-slapping off the sidewalk and coming my way, I started back to running, too, you know.

"But when I come out the other end of that damn

tunnel, I run face-first into a big old tree, and when I woke up, it was no park to be seen, no lake, neither. I was here, man, I was like *here!*"

"As a man," asked Fitz, "or as a lion?"

"No, man," Cool Blue "replied", "the lion bit came later. I was one beat-up nigger, but I was a man when I first come here. It's account of that fucking, black-hearted Count of Saint Germain and his bunch of wizards and warlocks that I'm running around this place on four legs, 'stead of two, him and his bunch and, 'specially, that oreo-cookie cooze he keeps around."

"Can you imagine that kind of shit, man? Here's this sister—dark-complected, good-looking, name of Sursy—puts the, like I mean the real make on me. And hell, man, like I'm, you know, I mean like as horny as any other cat. But when I like went after what she was damn near to like rubbing in my face, she ups and changes me into a pig, man, like I mean a real-ass pig, a boar-hog, right down to the little curly tail, you dig.

"So, like there I was, man, three, four hundred pounds of pork. She done said she wouldn't make it with me 'less I let her change me into what turned her on, see, so like I did. She did make it with me, like with the boar-hog I was then, I mean. But then the cow-cunted calico queen just left me, wouldn't change me back to a man, said I was gonna stay what I'd always really been.

"And, man, like it ain't no fun being a hog, I tell you. You starving hungry all the fucking time, you know, so you'll eat anything you comes acrost. And, man, like you don't know what heartburns and belly-aches is 'til you been a pig for awhile. Well, man, like I took it all for a while, living out in the woods, but then I went back into old Saint Germain's place and I started like tearing the living shit out of any-fucking-thing I could get my big old tusks into. I wasted two of his warlocks and like ate part of one of the creeps, man.

"Won't 'till then the Count, he come to find out what that Sursy, she done done to me, he thought I'd just wandered off somewheres. When he did find out, he turned her into a pink lioness and sent her away somewheres, then he turned me from a hog into this blue lion and told me did I ever come to find her, the minute we two got it on, we'd both be real human beings again. Like, I mean, you know, can you beat that, man?"

Fitz could not resist a chuckle then. "Well, Cool Blue, you were screwed and blued. Did you get tattooed?"

"Man, like it ain't none of it noways funny." Cool Blue sounded hurt. "I couldn't blow no horn if I could find one, I can't sing or even fucking whistle, all I can do is to like roar, man, the whole thing is like a real bummer, you know. Like, I mean, what'd I ever do to that fucking brownie-king, Saint Germain, anyhow?"

Fitz thought it rather pointless to answer the lion. He did wonder, very much, who this "Saint Germain" was, and what powers he might have besides transforming beatnik jazz musicians into baby-blue lions—if he could believe Cool Blue's story at all. At this point there were more immediate problems at hand.

At midday, they ascended to the top of a ridge to see below them not a valley but a vast, swampy flatland stretching into misty distance.

"Way you was headed, like, man, I was scared we was going to come up against the Dragon Swamp, man, and like we did. You don't want to go in there, you know, man, no way. And if you do, like count Cool Blue out, see. You dig?"

Fitz frowned, sweeping the visible portions of the lower ground with his binoculars. "It looks like a cross between an overgrown lake and a rain forest. How wide is it, Cool Blue?"

"Like hell, I don't know, man. I like never went into the place but once, and after I seen some of the monsters lives in there, I shagged ass out and I won't never go back. Man, it's dragons in there—real dragons, that breathes fire and smoke and all—and snakes so big you'd have to see the fuckers your own self to b'lieve it, and things you wouldn't think of to see in a nightmare or even on a bad trip on acid, man."

"Okay, then," said Fitz, "if you don't know how wide it is, Cool Blue, then how long is it? Can we get around it? Bypass it?"

"Yeah, man, you can, but like you're going to have to backtrack for a few days from here, 'cause like it spreads out south on both sides of where we are now, you know. Best thing is to go back south to the place I met you at or a little more, then cut west; it's like easier to travel that way, like along the valleys, than to keep going up and down hills and ridges, the way you been doing, see."

"Well, damn it, then," demanded Fitz in exasperation, "why the hell didn't you tell me this days ago, Cool Blue?"

The baby-blue lion yawned widely. "Like, man, you didn't ask me. I ain't no tour guide, you know, man. Like I'm just supposed to pad along with you for awhile and make sure you don't get your ass creamed, if I can."

Fitz turned to Sir Gautier. "Do *you* think we could get across that morass, Gautier?"

The Norman cast a jaundiced eye at the brooding

expanses of dark water and overabundant vegetation, but answered loyally, "Wherever my lord goes, there too goes his servant, Gautier de Montjoie."

Fitz squatted atop the ridge and considered the matter in all its many aspects. At length, he arose and said, "All right, Gautier, Cool Blue, we backtrack. Let's go, we have a half day left to travel in."

That half day, plus seven more days and nights, saw them at the clearing wherein Fitz had slain the Norman sergeant, put his mates to rout and gained his sworn servant, Sir Gautier. They camped that night there and, the next morning, Fitz asked the lion, "You say farther south than this, Cool Blue?"

"Yeah, man, like the hills is lower, south of here, but still not so low the Teeth and Legs would come up in them, see. They is baad news, man."

"Yes, I know, Cool Blue, I killed one crossing the Pony Plain," said Fitz. "I've got a plan, I think, but let's break camp now and get going. I'll explain things as we walk. Okay?"

Sir Gautier just nodded. The lion said, "Reet, Jackson."

Fitz had given everything careful consideration, had gone over and over it all during their week of backtracking. Puss had sworn that one direction was as good as any other, except for due south, for finding the Dagda, so if the western route, following the vales and valleys, was faster and less arduous than climbing and descending hill after hill after rocky hill, then he would do so.

However, as he had packed supplies for one and was now having to provide for two, mostly, he was running perilously low on everything. Yes, there were still a few things left in the cave with the bike . . . unless, God forbid, beasts or men had found and despoiled his cache. But even if they had not, there still was not enough left therein to last him and Gautier for more than a few days or possibly one week on the march.

Therefore, he had come to the decision to let Gautier help him get the bike down to reasonably level ground, then send the knight back up to camp in or around the cave with Cool Blue while he recrossed the Pony Plain to the dunes and the wrecked ship to restock. After that first crossing, he realized that the loaded weight and the extra wheel of the sidecar imparted vastly improved stability to the bike, so he would be able to bring back far more than he had on the previous trip north.

But he meant to first see if the cave's contents were as he had left them before he went into great detail with his two companions. Two days later, he found that they were. After he and Gautier had cleared the cave of the brittle, dried brush and rock rubble, Fitz unsnapped the canvas cover and lifted it from off the gleaming bike, sending a pair of big woods rats that had established residence there squealing and squeaking between the men's feet and out into the open. One got away, but Cool Blue pounced like some giant housecat. A quick descent of his muzzle, one crunch of his toothy jaws and a swallow, and he had effectively widowed the escapee.

"You told me that, as a self-respecting lion, you never hunted any beast smaller than a full-grown deer," chided Fitz, half-jokingly.

The lion sat and began to lick a huge paw preparatory to washing his face. "Like meat's meat, man. Hunting's hard work, you dig, and like you don't never turn down no freebies, see. Hey, where the hell the chopper come from, man? Like it's cool, the utter coolest!"

They camped the night atop the last low hill overlooking the Pony Plain. Fitz had emptied everything from the bike and sidecar except basic tools, some water, his carbine and ammo, knowing he would be at the ship, barring disaster or misfortune, well before the fall of the next night. Then, just as dawn was streaking the eastern sky, there was a bright, rosy flash high in the sky above the distant lines of sand dunes and from that flash fell three red stars.

Fumbling in his haste, Fitz dug frantically under the greasy tools until he found the canvas case that held the Very pistol. He started to fire, then thought to check the loaded shell. Replacing the green one with a red, he held the projector at a steep angle and fired the signal.

"Danna, I'm coming!" he breathed.

The plain seemed normal, with small herds of ponies, a flock of the rat-tailed ostriches and some smaller beasts in evidence. At the spot where he had slain the Teeth and Claws, there were only a few of the bigger bones and part of the skull and a few teeth remaining, all now marked by toothmarks and scouring sand, thoroughly desiccated by sun and wind. Well, it was only fitting that the monster that had fed for so long on the fauna of that plain should finally go to feed said fauna itself; that was simply Nature's way.

With the knowledge that Danna was waiting for him, the journey across the plain seemed to last forever. Why was she calling him back so soon, he wondered. Had the situation with the I.R.S. and Blutegel improved, was that it? No, more likely, considering the man involved, it had gotten far worse, he thought glumly. If only there was a safe place for Danna to be that was closer to the hills than the ship was.

"So, what do you want, Fitz, egg in your beer?"

Right now, he'd take the beer, gallons of it, iced and icy cold. Then the eggs, a gross of them—fried eggs, boiled eggs, poached eggs, coddled eggs, a five-egg omelet with cheese, cheddar cheese, lots of it, and minced onions and green peppers and garlic and shallots. He could almost taste a whole big head of steamed cauliflower with a sauce of Swiss cheese and saffron and pepper. Creamed spinach and rolls. Bread of any kind! Salt sticks, swirl rye, hot buttermilk biscuits melting in butter, with dark honey. *Anything but bloody meat!*

Funny, he had always eaten a good quantity of meat, when he could get it or had been able to afford it—steaks, chops, cutlets, roasts, patties, thick stews and ragouts, kebabs—but these past weeks of living on little save meat, with occasionally a few berries or wild greens and the rare fish, had awakened within him a distaste for even the thought of meat or blood. No, his hunger now was for vegetables, grain products, eggs, milk and cheese, spices and herbs. And he meant to have his fill of them, too, even if he had to go back into that other, overcrowded, stinking, paved-over and mostly hostile world to get them.

"But," he chuckled to himself, "I'd better not let Kassandra know that I'm in the least egg-hungry."

All journeys must come to an end and, just after midday, Fitz came to the first low dune. Another half hour, and he was wheeling the bike up the gangplanks into the waist of the sometime warship. And Danna was standing on the quarterdeck, above him, wearing only a dark, healthy tan and a metallic something that held her reddish-brown, now-longer hair back upon her neck. She looked far younger than he had recalled her and he knew that he never before had seen any woman so beautiful and appealing to him.

She came down the ladder and walked to where he stood and kissed him, thoroughly, but then she stepped back and said, "Fitz, come into the cabin with me, please. There's something . . . you've got to tell me if I'm going nuts or what."

In the cabin, the shutters still were bolted and the gas lanterns still were blazing out their stark white light. The ancient ship's table was laid with a plastic plate, some utensils and a wineglass. Beside the table hung a slender green wine bottle . . . that was what he thought at first glance, at least.

"I was in here last night, eating some cheese and bread and a glass of wine before I went to bed, Fitz. Then I somehow shoved the bottle too near the edge of that table and, when I moved to turn a page in the brief I was reading, it wobbled off and fell. I thought in the split second that if it broke, I'd have to go back into that other world tomorrow and get more because it was the last bottle here and I didn't want to go, because I'd have to dress and I just wished it would stop falling and not break or spill . . . *and it did, Fitz*. It . . . it's still there, I laid awake half the night just looking at it. Is it really just sitting there, six or eight inches above the floor, with nothing to support it, like my eyes tell me it is? Please, Fitz, tell me!"

Fitz squatted and ran his flattened hand around all sides of the bottle, beneath it and over it. Taking it by the neck, he lifted it easily, sniffed at the opening, then put it to his lips, threw back his head and drained the last few ounces of tepid Moselle down his dry throat.

Standing up, he held the empty bottle at waist height and let it go. It fell and clunked upon the boards. He picked it up and tried once again, and the same result occurred.

Intent on the experiment, he absent-mindedly meshed his mind with hers and thought to her, "Danna, when I next drop this bottle, try to remember just what you did or thought last night and stop it from hitting the deck. Okay?"

But she had paled under her tan, her green eyes were wide and she was backing the length of the cabin, both her hands held before her, as if to ward him off.

"My God, Fitz, what . . . you were *talking* to me—weren't you? Weren't you?—but your lips didn't move once. And . . . and still I heard . . . no, I didn't hear you, either! But I . . . understood you."

"It's called telepathy, I believe, Danna. That's how I've been communicating these last weeks, over there in those hills. I guess I just forgot and did it to you. But look, it's simple, love, I can show you how to do it, too. See?" He "showed" her.

An hour or so of experiments demonstrated that, not only could Danna stop the bottle in midair, but she could also move it vertically or horizontally in empty air, in any direction and for the length, width and height of the cabin, at least. But she could not seem, for some reason, to show him how to arrange his mind and his thoughts to emulate her feats. They tried her out on other larger, heavier items and found that size or weight made no difference, she could move them around and about at will.

After a long, refreshing swim in the cool sea, Fitz came back to the ship and ate such canned vegetables as remained in the larder and water—foul, chemical-flavored water from the other world. Then and there, he made a note to resupply the ship with bottled spring water rather than the jugs of chemical soup from the tap.

Sitting at the table with pencil and pad, making up a list of the things he needed from the other world, still nude from his swim, he dropped the pencil and it rolled off the table. With a muttered curse, he started to bend to retrieve it, then stopped himself and gave the mental method one more try. It worked this time. The yellow pencil rose, jerkily at first, then more smoothly, up and up and up.

"Danna! Look."

Forgetting the list for the nonce, Fitz and Danna played with the pencil and scores of other objects around and about the cabin like a pair of children with a new toy—he would raise something, she would then move that same object laterally or lower it and vice versa, or one of them would raise an object and then cause it to dodge others sent whizzing at it by the other one. After a while, they took their esoteric game outside, onto the beach, and soon had the air about them cluttered with colorful seashells, bits of driftwood and some empty plastic water jugs, as well as the original green wine bottle. They continued to play until the setting sun told them that it was nearing the time that they should leave for the other world.

Back in the cabin, Fitz rapidly completed the list, then hurriedly dressed. They had strung the water jugs together, intending to tow them, like so many balloons, across the beach and into the crypt, then up the stairs and across the backyard. Fitz had already raised the small fleet of jugs off the floor, but when he placed about his neck the stainless steel chain that held the back door key, all of the jugs tumbled back onto the floor, and when he tried to raise them once more, he found that he had not the power to do so.

Wonderingly, he lifted off the chain and dropped it and the brass key upon the table, then he tried again to raise the jugs. He overdid it and the jugs, all of them, zoomed up to ceiling height. He deliberately picked up the chain, and the string of jugs plopped back down onto the floor.

Calling Danna in from where she was waiting in the waist of the ship, he first showed her, then had her try to raise the jugs, with and then without the steel chain. It was the same for her as for him, with the steel chain in contact with any portion of their bodies, they were devoid of the power to move objects with their minds.

"Fitz, what in the world . . .?"

He shrugged, "Don't ask *me*, Danna. I'll tell you, let's see whether it's the steel or the brass, first, huh?"

They discovered, quickly enough, that brass, bronze, copper, silver, gold, aluminum, nickel or tin, none of them affected their performance, but anything iron or steel, if in contact with their skins, made their power to mentally lift and move objects completely disappear.

"Well," remarked Fitz, when they were done testing, "now, at least, we know why I couldn't do it when I first arrived, anyway. I was heavy with steel—revolver, knives, steel fittings on my belt, the steel frames of my sunglasses, and so on. And that's so much for my thoughts of raising the loaded bike with me on it over rough ground; I could probably still raise it and move it, but I'd most likely have to get off to do so.

"Okay, you have no iron or steel on now, so you lead the ducklings and I'll tow the heavy, clumsy stuff after you've raised it. I've got a brass chain in my house, as I recall, I'll replace this steel one with it as soon as we get there. Why does Pedro want to see me so bad, anyhow, Danna?"

"He didn't tell me that, Fitz," she replied, as she raised the jugs again and took their tow string in her hand, "he just said to get you back as soon as possible and gave me a wordless telephone code to tell him when you were back. You see, we're pretty certain that the phone in your house is bugged."

"*Herr* Blutegel?" he asked, grimly.

"Who else," she answered. "And Fitz, that title may be hitting a bit closer to the mark than anyone knows yet."

While Fitz towed the bigger bundles inside the house, Danna first lowered the jugs, then, grinning mischievously, tied the end of the string to the rail of the steps and raised the plastic jugs high up to almost the limit of the string's length before she, too, went inside.

Unbeknownst to her and despite the early hour—it was just about dawn here, in this other world—she and Fitz, too, had been seen by malicious eyes, and the moment she had closed the door behind her, Calvin Mathews picked up the plastic bucket of strawberries he had been picking in the garden of Fitz's next-door neighbors and set out for home at a rapid clip.

Inside, with the blinds tightly drawn and all the drapes closed, Danna used the telephone while Fitz used the shower. He had just come out of the bathroom when the telephone rang. Danna picked it up and switched on the speaker, that he might hear, too.

A cheery voice said, "Good morning to you. This is Chuck Taylor, here at the WTRI Studios. Your telephone number was chosen by our blindfolded guest, here on the WTRI AM Show, and if you can answer our question of the day, you'll be the lucky winner of FOUR . . . HUNDRED . . . DOLLARS. Now, what is a teledu and where does it live?"

"I'm sure I don't know," said Danna, sounding tired and disgusted, "and don't call back, this is an unlisted number, you turkey!" Then she hung up and looked at Fitz, smiling. "Pedro got the message and he'll be here at four o'clock."

Standing nude and damp in the doorway, he grinned. "Do you want to eat or drink . . . first?"

Still smiling, she kicked off her shoes, stripped off her shirt, then stood up and unbuttoned her shorts, letting them drop to the floor. "Fitz, dearest, I am not a nymphomaniac, but you have, after all, been gone wherever for fifty-one days and . . ."

"The hell I was," yelped Fitz. "No more than fourteen or fifteen days, at the most."

Around noon, over their brunch, he told her of the Norman knight, Sir Gautier de Montjoie, and of Cool Blue, the baby-blue (most of the time), telepathic lion. He told her of Puss, the leopard-sized, grey feline that also was telepathic and sometimes appeared to him as his long-dead grey housecat, Tom. He told her of the Teeth and Legs—the fearsome beast of which Puss had warned him and which he had had to kill out on the Pony Plain. He told her of the man, the Norman sergeant he had also had to kill. He told her highlights of his trek through the hills and vales and valleys beyond the Pony Plain, and he told her what little he knew of this entity he was supposed to be seeking, this Dagda.

"Fitz, weren't you ever told any of the old Irish fairy tales as you were growing up? Didn't you at least read some of them? The Dagda was supposed to be the King of the Fairies, of the Little People, the Ones Who Were Here Before, who called themselves the Tuatha De Danann. Do you suppose . . . authorities say that all of the old myths have at the least a tiny grain of fact at their root . . . could this strange dimension you and I have somehow managed to penetrate actually be what the myths referred to as 'Fairyland'? All these strange things . . ."

She sat up straight in her chair, shook her tousled head and frowned. "Oh, listen to me carry on. A respectable, respected, fifty-five-year-old attorney, and I sound like a fugitive from the funny farm. There are no such things as fairies, so there was never any such place as fairyland, they were all just tales concocted for children."

He shook his head slowly. "Danna, I know just what is going through your mind right now, because I felt that way at the start of all this myself. But Danna, I had to come to grips with the fact that these things are all real, they exist in reality—a strange world beyond a stone wall under my backyard, a casket of immensely valuable gold coins on board a wrecked, medieval ship on a beach where thirty-foot crocodiles come to nest, ostriches with long tails and fur, flying lizards and gliding rabbits, a leopard-sized reincarnation of my dead cat and a baby-blue lion that used to be a black musician in this other world eighteen years ago, a party of thousand-year-old Norman Crusaders who still think they're somewhere in Syria on their way to Jerusalem during the First Crusade.

"Face facts, like I had to do, Danna—it's all real, it's there, it exists. It's as real as this."

He laid down his knife and Danna felt herself rising up out of her chair, floating on empty air, some foot above the seat. Stunned by the singular experience, she said nothing for a moment, but Fitz did.

"Well, I'll be damned! I *did* it! *I* did it! Now, let's just see what else I can do."

As slowly as she, he too arose until they were again facing on the same level. He reached out, took her hand, then proceeded down the hall, towing her behind him, into the bedroom, where he gently lowered both of their bodies into their accustomed place on the rumpled, well-used bed. There, he floated his alarm clock over to him and set it for three-thirty, then floated it back to its place on the nightstand.

"Danna," he said, smiling, "not only is it all real, just think of the immense possibilities of this sort of a shared talent on lovemaking. Hmmm?"

Pedro Goldfarb arrived closer to four-thirty, muttering darkly about afternoon traffic and the patent stupidity of county road-planning commissions. Once seated in the parlor, he got immediately down to business.

"Fitz, there's little time to waste. Despite our cloak-and-dagger machinations, it's entirely possible that Blutegel *et alii* already know you're back out here. Despite the fact the he's in trouble with his service, the nitwits are letting him stay on to earn out his pension, so he still has a degree of power and he seems to have taken on the cases of you and Gus Tolliver as a very personal crusade; possibly, he means it to be his swan song.

"It's thanks to Gus, really, that you two are so deeply in the soup. The inheritance thing, I might've been able to clear up fairly easily and inexpensively for you, but Gus has a hatred of the I.R. S. that borders on the paranoid, I feel. He had to do the very things I advised him not to do. That he did it with his money was bad enough, but he did it with healthy chunks of yours, too.

"Fitz, the tax laws of the United States are incredibly complicated and even the collectors of them—the honest, candid ones—will tell you that they are not in any manner or means fair to the average taxpayer. But Fitz, the way to thread your way through this dangerous maze is to hire a good firm of C.P.A.s and/or a reputable tax attorney, *not* to do what Gus has been doing for the both of you—smuggling currency out of the country.

"Now level with me, Fitz, you don't yet know just how much could be riding on truth at this point. Did you sign any papers Gus may have presented you? Some of them may have been documents written in Spanish or Portuguese."

"No, Pedro, not that I recall," said Fitz. "I have at least one copy of every business-related thing that I signed, they're all in my files, and you now have my files. Why not ask Gus?"

Pedro leaned back in his chair. "Gus Tolliver and his wife are no longer in the United States, Fitz. The last call I had from him was from Rio de Janeiro, but he indicated at that time his intentions of leaving Brazil. Just where he is now, I couldn't guess.

"He said, as did you, that you had signed nothing involved in this sticky business. The good news of that is that, if we can prove it, you may be off at least one prong of Blutegel's hook. But, of course, the bad news is that you may well have lost the bulk of your profits from sales of your gold coins. I don't know, I always had the gut-feeling that Gus Tolliver was a completely honest, aboveboard man . . . but I've been wrong before, like any other human being." He smiled fleetingly and barked a short laugh, for no reason that Fitz could understand . . . not then.

"However, we shall see what we shall see about Gus Tolliver's honesty in due time.

"But back to the Blutegel matter: win, lose or draw, whether you turn out to have lost your funds or not, the I.R.S. stance is going to be that, as the money was earned in this country, then you owe federal income taxes on it. They are going to insist on a full accounting of all the transactions and then are going to sock you with an outrageous bill covering taxes, penalties and interest, and you are going to have to pay it, Fitz, all of it. It'll be either that or leave the country for good or go directly to a federal penitentiary for quite a spell. Yes, it's unjust that murderers, rapists, child molesters and proven spies spend less time behind bars than do persons convicted of tax evasion, but that's the way the stick floats, as they say.

"Now, I know how much cash you had in your open accounts and in your safety deposit boxes, but that's not nearly enough, not the kind of money you're going to need to pay all that I imagine the feds are going to demand of you. Do you have any more stashed away somewhere that you've not told us about, perchance?"

"No, no cash, Pedro, but I've still got some of the gold coins," replied Fitz. "But with Gus gone, who'd sell them for me?"

Pedro grinned. "Just about any one of at least a score of top-flight numismatic houses of whom I can think, offhand. Whether or not Gus ever got around to telling you, your coins have set records for sales figures. They're in such astoundingly good shape for their age that they've been tested over and over again because many collectors and dealers just could not believe until they did test them that they were authentic. Gus let some of the earlier-sold ones go for thousands less than his buyers resold them for. A new lot released at this time would bring you in substantially more than you got for the first lot.

"We already have your power of attorney. You give me the gold and I'll see that it's sold at top dollar for you. The monies realized will go directly into an escrow account until we get this mess cleared up for you. Now, where's the gold?"

Fitz led the way back to the utility room, picking up a big cleaver on his way through the kitchen. When he had opened the big chest-freezer and laboriously shifted a good half of its contents, he lifted up and set on the table beside the cleaver a two-gallon plastic cylinder that was clearly marked "stewed squid." With the plastic holder split away, he chipped at the brown-grey cylinder of hard-frozen fish until finally it split open to reveal a cloth bag of exactly the same color. Inside the cloth bag was a plastic bag containing some dozens of golden coins. He handed these to Pedro.

"There're maybe half this many more, but I can't get to them just now; they're not in this country. If you want them, I'll get them to Danna. Okay?"

The attorney shrugged. "You may not need them, probably won't, I'd estimate that there's more than enough value right here to bail you out of your problems . . ." he grinned, ". . . and with enough left over to pay the whopping fee I'm going to charge you, too, my friend. Now, I'll take that drink you so graciously offered earlier."

Once more seated in the parlor, he sipped at his whiskey, then said, "I don't know where you've been or what you've been doing there, and I don't want to know; but whatever you've been doing certainly seems to be good for you. You look years younger than you did when last we met—you could pass for thirty-five now, easily, and your tan's even darker. Danna's getting a tan, too, had you noticed?"

"Pedro, just how bad is the trouble I'm in?" asked Fitz. "There are some things I need to pick up in town. Dare I show my face there for that long?"

The attorney frowned, then brightened a bit. "This is late on a Friday afternoon, they'd play hell finding a judge and/or a federal marshall until Monday. Go on to town, if it's important enough to take a risk for, but please be circumspect. It might be best if you didn't let your neighbors see you being driven out of here, so take your Jeep and lie or crouch in the back with a tarp or blanket over you until you're out on the county road. Do whatever you have to do in that town fast, then come straight back, avoid any conversations. You have dark glasses and a hat with a brim? Good, wear them.

"Right now, as matters stand, you're in as much trouble as is Gus; Blutegel has seen you tarred with the same brush. He's going after you on the same grounds they used to nail so many racketeers. Yes, you could be arrested if you stay in the country too long or are careless about your activities while here, so don't stay and don't be careless, Fitz. That's my professional advice to you as a client. You asked, I told you."

Once Danna had driven the loaded Jeep into the garage and had closed the door, Fitz straightened up, got out and began to unload by hand before he remembered and commenced to float the items out of the back of the Jeep and into the house.

Danna, who had done most of the actual shopping in the larger places in town, had asked, "Fitz, why so much soap? You can't eat soap."

He had chuckled. "It's Sir Gautier, my sworn Norman liegeman. When I first met him, he smelled like an open sewer, but since he's discovered that regular baths won't kill you or unman you or turn your feet into cloven hooves or whatnot, he's become a regular bathing fanatic and he goes through one hell of a lot of soap."

With everything in the house, Danna began to open the glass bottles of mineral water, while Fitz stepped onto the back porch to bring in the plastic jugs, still swaying in the evening breeze on their string. And the shotgun boomed even as his foot touched the first step. Fitz dived for the ground, for all that the shot had missed him and plowed into the side of the house by the doorway. With the instinct of his decades-old combat training and experience, he kept rolling until the concrete foundation of the porch was between him and the source of the gunfire, then chanced a peek around the protective masonry.

Just on the other side of the fence stood Yancy Mathews, a cheap, battered, double-barrelled twelve-bore in his hands and the neck of a bottle sticking out of his pocket.

"You uppity fucker, you," he shouted, slurring his words a bit, "you think I's gonna fergit how you come to git me th'owed in jail and half worked to death out to the County Farm and all? My boy, Calvin, he seen you sneak in here with your stuck-up fancy woman this mornin' and he come tol' me. I hadda work today, all day, 'cause if I misses work even one day, them fuckers'll put me back out there on thet damn farm. I'm gon' kill your ass, *Mister* Fitzassgilbert!"

Fitz realized just how hopelessly drunk the man was when he put the gun to his shoulder and tried to hold it steady. Mathews tried to shoot at the corner of the porch, around which Fitz was peeking, but the load of buckshot instead plowed into the side of the mound. Cursing, the drunken would-be murderer opened the gun and began to fumble in his shirt pocket for shells.

Fitz made his move. Rising suddenly twenty feet into the air, he sped across the intervening distance and his feet came to earth only a half-yard from Mathews' mud-caked clodhoppers. He easily jerked the still-open gun from the pie-eyed man and hurled it over his fence to clatter into his yard. Then he disposed of Yancy Mathews, almost bloodlessly.

As he and Danna floated the last loads across the darkening yard, into the tent and down the stairway, she said, "Fitz, no matter what he is or what he tried to do to you, I think we ought to lower him out of that tree before we go back to the sand world. When he wakes up, he could fall and injure himself badly; that's at least ten feet up to that limb he's on, you know."

Fitz just laughed. "Danna, Yancy Mathews couldn't fall if he tried. He's not *on* that limb, he's just an inch or so above it, and he's on 'hold.' I'm releasing him from that right now, but there's still no fear, I took off his belt and put it around both him and the limb.

"Now, let's get everything through to the ship. I should leave for the hills fairly soon, but first I'm going to want you to help me test out the comfort quotient of this double-size air mattress I bought. If you don't mind and can make the time, that is, counselor."

Yancy Mathews came awake with a terrible hangover and someone nearby shouting at him. He cracked a single bloodshot eye to see old Collingwood, who owned the house next door to that fucking Fitzgilbert bastard, standing in his yard and shouting up at him.

". . . no-count drunk, that's all you ever been, you stump-jumpin', hillbilly sonuvabitch! What in tarnation you think you doin' up there in my tree? You come to steal apples, like them two thievin' brats of yourn does all the time, you in the wrong fuckin' tree.

"I tell you, you git down from there and outen my yard or I'm gone call Sher'ff Vaughan to send depitties to git you out. Put you back on the county farm where white trash like you b'longs! You no good white nigger, you!"

Stung to the very quick by such baseless slander, Yancy made to sit up in preparation for launching himself at the seventy-odd-year-old man and beating him to death. But when he moved, he rolled off the narrow limb and wound up under it, hanging from it by his belt and screaming in his terror. By the time the two deputies arrived, Yancy was almost hysterical and they finally had to cold-cock him in order to get him down out of the tree and into the car to be driven down to a place he had seen many a time before—the drunk tank of the county jail.

"I don't know but what all his boozin' has fin'ly rotted out his brains, if he ever had any," Collingwood had opined to one of the deputies " 'fore you fellers got here, he'uz trying for to tell me that Mister Fitzgilbert it was had flung him up in that there tree. And not only is Mister Fitzgilbert not got the built it would take to put a man as big as Yancy Mathews up there, they tells me the genulman has done been in Africa for the best part of two months.

"I sure lawd hopes you keeps that Yancy Mathews in the pokey a good, long time, like you should ought to of done last time. I tell you, a body can't go away to visit with his own daughter and his grandchillun for two pitiful days, but he's gotta come back to crap like this with the meanest drunk in the county up in one his trees.

"Was he up there all night? Hell, I don't know, depitty. I come in 'bout midnight, it was darker'n the inside of a cow out here. I just noticed him up there after I got up this mornin', for to fix my cawfee and tie some flies.

"You do eny fishin', depitty? Well, you wanna buy some flies?"

SPECIAL BONUS CHAPTER!

Here is a chapter from Book II in the *Stairway to Forever* series, MONSTERS AND MAGICIANS, coming from Baen Books in early 1989:

Fitz had just finished eating his spit-broiled pheasant and was carefully sipped at his canteen-cup of steaming, fragrant tea when, with the now-familiar faint tickling of the mind that bespoke telepathy, a "voice" declared, "I smell fresh meat and like, man, I'm hungry as a lion."

With that, a full-size blue lion strode from among the brush and bushes of the hillside into the tiny clearing before the rock shelter, facing Fitz across the firepit. His normal baby-blue hue was closer to a royal blue, which fact told Fitz that he was or recently had been upset about something.

The blue lion flopped down on the rocky ground,

pointedly eying the pint-size antelope hung in the tree. "Hunting like sucked today, man," he declared dolefully. "Old Saint Germain must of like let some of his damn pets loose around these parts, them fuckers like scare all the game away from wherever they're at, they stink as bad as snakes or alligators. I'm like flat bushed and my stomach's growling like I was still a damn old boar-hog, too."

Nestling his steel cup back among the coals, Fitz stood up, paced over to the tree, untied the rope, then took the lowered carcass over to the waiting lion. While the huge beast rent flesh and crunched bones, they continued to silently converse.

"Where's Sir Gautier?" asked Fitz.

"Well, like man, he nor me expected you back so damn soon. Like, you ain't been gone a whole day, you know. He went off to see could he find the rest of his Normans. He shouldn't have no trouble there, like, man, he can just follow the stink." The feeding carnivore added. "He should ought to be back in two, three days, like anyway. Hang around, man. You can spend the time like shooting some more of these; they're good eating, see, but the little fuckers are like too fast for me to catch one, usually. I'll be done with this soon, man, hand me down that bird up there too, huh?"

Fitz shook his head. "That pheasant's my breakfast, Cool Blue. Do you want what's left of the one I just ate?"

"Like is the Pope a Catholic, man?" was the lion's reply. "Like throw them over here; I'm like starving, tramping around these fucking boondocks all day for nothing but a few damn frogs. What'd you like do with the guts and the head and legs and all of this little thing, huh, man? Like they're some of the best parts."

But when Fitz had directed Cool Blue to the spot he had dumped the offal from his kills, little was left aside from bloodstained leaves and stray feathers. The lion's color became almost navy blue and Fitz ended by giving his companion the other pheasant, reflecting to himself that he could breakfast out of the supplies he had brought from the other world, Sir Gautier not being on hand to take a share. Then he banked the fire and zipped himself into his sleeping bag under the overhang, the entrance more or less blocked by rocks, the motorcycle and other gear, and the huge, blue lion sleeping just the other side of the firepit.

Hungry as the lion still remained, Fitz doubted that any edible creature would survive long enough to get across the small clearing to the overhang and him, so he went to sleep feeling as secure as if he had been in the soft bed in his other-world bedroom, guarded by multitudinous alarms and a twelve-foot cyclone fence topped with barbed wire.

He slept until he suddenly became aware that he was rolling down a grassy slope, vastly enjoying the feel of the coarse blades lashing at the skin of his nude body, just as he loved the feel of the hot sun and the sweet scents of the wildflowers and herbs that grew here and there among the grasses, the occasional puffs of warm, gentle winds.

At the bottom of the slope, he sat up and gazed out across a plain grown with higher, coarser grasses, dense stands of dark-green bushes and some scattered trees. In the dim distance, a small herd of wild cattle grazed and, closer to him, several cervines browsed on the fringes of a thicket of thorny shrubs.

Fitz had assumed that he was alone, but then a silent, unspoken, mind-to-mind beaming asked, "Are you hungry, Seos?"

"No, I have no hunger for food." Fitz sensed the return beaming of "his" body. "But if you do, become a deer; there are more than enough shrubs over there to feed another."

I am rather going to become a cat and eat a deer," 'said' the other. "What about you?"

"Sister-mine," beamed Fitz's body, "do as you wish, indulge yourself, for we two must return soon enough from this lovely place. I think I'll become a young bull and trot over to visit with the heifers of yonder herd."

"You would!" came the response from the other. "Just for that, I should become a lioness and make my meal of young bull flesh, this day . . . but I won't. But before you change, watch me make my kill . . . please?"

"Of course I will, sister-mine," the body beamed. "Then I will be able to use some of that kill in forming my young bull."

A few rods away, a slender but well-formed body rose up into the air, moved through the air at some speed and then sank, as lightly as a falling feather, into the depths of the thicket around which the cervines browsed. To the mind of Fitz, the sun browned body appeared to be that of a girl in her mid-teens, as totally devoid of clothing as was the masculine body he just now inhabited. Like "his" body, the female's was possessed of reddish-blonde hair, almond-shaped blue-green eyes separated by the bridge of a straight, slender nose. Her face of course lacked the curly, fair beard that his bore, but both owned full lips that smiled often to show the white teeth. Fitz guessed her height at between five feet even and five feet four, her weight at around a hundred pounds, tops. Her nipples were the same red-pink as her lips and the breasts, though smallish, stood up proudly. Though her hands and feet were on the small side, they were proportionate to her body which, at the distance from which "his" body's eyes had viewed it, had seemed almost hairless, apparent hirsute adornments only appearing at armpits and crotch. The fine bone had all looked to be properly sheathed in flat muscles.

While the cervines browsed on, unsuspectingly, the eyes of the body within which Fitz was visiting continued to watch the base of the thicket, knowing what to expect.

Then, with the suddenness of a lightning-bolt, a yellow-and-black, hook-clawed streak launched itself from out the dense dimness of the thicket, landing squarely on the back of a plump doe. One taloned paw hooked under the chin of the frantically plunging deer and drew the head up and back so far and at such angle that the spine was compelled to snap . . . as it quickly did. As the dying doe sank beneath her deadly rider, the rest of the deer scattered at flank speeds, making no single offer to fight, as was their natural way unless defending fawns or cornered by predators of any kind.

The cat speeded the death of the kicking, twitching cervine by using strong jaws and sharp fangs to tear out the throat, the torrents of deer-blood from the veins and arteries drenching her yellow-gold, black-spotted hide, dripping from her stiff whiskers.

To his own big-boned, hundred-sixty-pound body-mass, Seos began to gather and add a vast assortment of natural materials—animal (from the new-slain doe), vegetable (from the plants and trees and grasses all about) and mineral (from the rock-studded soil and that soil itself). Adapting and restructuring and shaping the constituents of all these in the manner first taught hundreds of generations before to the first hybrids by the Elder Ones, the blond young man slowly became transformed into a large wild ox—a bovine that later, much later, generations of humans would call aurochs or *bos taurus primigenius*.

The final creation was, to say the least, impressive in the extreme, to Fitz. In this dream as in previous ones of similar nature, he was not only participant but observer as well, and so he could view the formed beast as from a close distance even while he realized that he along with his host-body were actually a part of the beast.

Its color was so dark a brown as to look almost black, which caused the two-inch-wide white stripe down the length of its spine to stand out in startling contrast. The long, thick horns were a yellowish-white, save at the sharp-pointed tips where they were shiny black. Under the glossy hide, the creature was a mass of thick bones, steely sinew and rolling muscles, a good six feet in height at the withers, with the big head carried even higher, the cud-chewing mouth and wide nostrils edged with off-white.

Within that huge, weighty, very powerful and vital body, Fitz noted how much concentration was required on the part of his host, Seos, to maintain his creation in its present shape and to prevent his own mind from becoming submerged in the simpler mind of the beast. Fitz, from his vantage-point, could understand how such a thing was done but discovered that his own, human mind owned no words or even speakable concepts to explain it.

Then the young aurochs bull set out across the rolling plain at a slow trot, leaving the "leopard" to her bloody feast just inside the confines of the thicket, admonishing him telepathically with "Have your fun with those heifers and cows, brother-mine, but be

careful, too; big as you now are, you're still not as big
as some of the king-bulls I've seen, here and there.
There still are but few enough of us and I fear that
our sire would be most wroth were I to arrive back
upon our island with only your well-horned body."

In great good spirits, Seos replied, "You be careful, too, my sister-mate. That form you now inhabit
is such as to set any male leopard to full arousal, and
I think our sire might be equally wroth were you to
throw before him a litter of furry, fanged and clawed
grand-get. Hahahaha."

Despite the flippancies of the exchanges, Fitz knew
that there was real and abiding love between the
sister and brother (who also were sexual mates, in
the ages-old tradition of their hybrid race) and both
love and awesome respect for their sire, Keronnos,
ruler of their small group of Elder Ones-human hybrids, resident on the rocky but verdant island in the
midst of the sea.

The mind of Seos was as an open book to Fitz, and
the man-bull was completely oblivious to the presence or delvings of the "visitor" within him. In the
memories of Seos, Fitz could see that island—soaring
peaks flung high above broad, long plains, little,
deep-green glens between hills, large and smaller
streams of crystal-clear water flowing from the mon-
tane springs to cascade down rocks and race down
hillsides and flow upon the plains and feed the lakes
and ponds before finding ways to the purple sea—
was able to know that, before Keronnos and his kin
had come upon and settled it, there had never been
humans or even primates thereon. Even now, after
the passages of hundreds of winters, there were few
on the large island—though only a bit over twenty
miles average width, the island's length was more
than eight times that distance—for, though the hy-

brids lived very long as compared to pure-strain humans, their birthrates were very low.

In hopes of partially rectifying these problems, Keronnos and all of the others had taken to seeking out among the smaller clans and tribes of humans in the lands and islands scattered around and about the sea, using their inborn mental talents to try to spy out supposedly pure humans and find those who might own within them enough of hybrid descent and undeveloped but developable talents to make decent breeding-stock. Those chosen had been taken up and borne back to the island, set down upon it and given all that was needful for them to lead happy, healthy and comfortable lives—hunting, fishing, gathering wild plants, breeding kine and sowing crops in the rich, volcanic soil of the island—while the hybrids got children upon them or from them, guided them into breeding among themselves in ways that would concentrate and enhance their own heritages of talents, and undertook the awakenings and training and discipline of the ever more talented young.

Even so, people of any strain still numbered few upon the island and the hybrids still flew out over the surrounding lands and islands in search of promising humans for the carefully controlled breedings they had undertaken.

But this day, this trip to this land, Fitz realized, was not such a search-mission, it was rather in the nature of a romp for the sibling mates, Seos and Ehra, a vacation from out the tight strictures of their sire and the other teachers of the young for, although mature enough for most purely-human pursuits, even for breeding, as hybrids their mental and emotional maturity lagged far behind their bodies' so that, in effect, they were only over-grown children. Not only did they naturally embody all the faults and failings of human children of similar mental and emotional development, they could add to them superhuman abilities and, as their sire and other mentors knew only too well, this combination could, without discipline, sometimes produce devastating if not deadly results, so such unsupervised jaunts into distant lands were rare and precious to the hybrid young.

Seos made a good, believable bull, for it was far from his first inhabitance of a bovine body. Where not sown with grain and other crops, the plains of the island gave graze to herds of cattle which, although somewhat smaller, less rangy and much less ferocious, were still obviously the near-kindred of the huge, fierce wild oxen that still roamed many of the lands surrounding the sea. Therefore, Seos had been able to observe, move among and model the cattle almost since his birth.

Fitz could see in the mind and memories of Seos that there were other beasts and birds he enjoyed— sometimes he became a huge eagle or a monstrous white swan, sometimes a fierce mountain ram, once, a wolf, again, a bear or a boar or a desert lion. On occasion, he and one of his brothers had become long, sleek, black-and-white porpoises and swum through the sea off the island, chasing schools of plump fishes into the waiting nets of human fishers from one of the island communities.

But of them all, among all creatures he had been, Seos still most preferred being that which he now was—three-quarters of a ton of big bones, muscles, sinews, speed, ferocity and such horn-tipped strength that not even the hungriest lion, the biggest bear would dare to attack him. Indeed, of all the predators in nearby lands, the mature aurochs in his prime and uninjured seldom fell to any save the increasingly rare long-tooth cats, pack-hunters such as wolves or hyaenas or humans, or the almost-extinct dragons. But a herd of aurochs could usually stand off and drive away even these.

The big ox that was Seos-Fitz moved slowly, sampling a few mouthfuls of the herbiage along his way, tail swishing and skin twitching against the voracious, blood-hungry flies that swarmed about him. Along with the mind of his unsuspecting host, Fitz too was aware that, for all his impressive looks, the created bullbody was not quite solid, durable; for the parts of the doe not considered easily edible by Ehra in her leopard-body had simply not provided enough building materials of the proper kinds for Seos to use in creating a good, workmanshiplike construction.

Abruptly, as the bull crested a low-crowned hillock, he could first smell, then see, just what he needed. At some time within the last few days, a largish hoofed animal—either a good-sized antelope or a short-necked giraffid, from the appearance of what the killer-predators and scavengers had left of it—had been slain and mostly devoured in the tiny hollow bisecting two of the grassy knolls. Now, all the flesh and organs were gone, as too was most of the hide. All that remained, presently being gnawed at and worried by a brace of jackals, were some of the larger bones, three hooves and a pair of long, pointed horns still attached to the remainder of the skull.

A snort and a few steps of a mock charge, huge head and black-tipped horns lowered in a business-like manner, were sufficient to send the jackals scurrying up the opposite slope. Fitz wondered to himself what the matted-haired scavengers thought to watch their feast silently and utterly disappear into nothingness.

At length, everything finally absorbed into the created bovine body, the bull that was Seos and Fitz descended the knoll, trotted across the stained, much disturbed level surface whereon so much feasting had so recently taken place, then set his now more solid bones and muscles to breasting the upward way, the two small jackals scuttling before him, ratty tails tucked between thin shanks. Fitz realized that, had Seos intended to spend more than a few hours in the creation, he would have sought around and about, located more carnal refuse and picked over kills and used them to give full size, weight and solidity to the bull; but this was but a romp, an outing, for he and Ehra must fly back to the island soon enough.

The bull, unlike Seos, did not see colors, only shades of grey, and his vision was only clear within a relatively short distance, but his olfactory sense was exceptionally keen, as too was his hearing; even from this far away, his ears still could detect the snarls of the Ehra-leopard, but even had the Seos part of the bull-mind not known just what the cat was, the animal-mind could identify the sounds for the warnings of a feeding feline, not the coughs and growls of a hunting-stalking-attacking cat. And besides, no mere leopard would have dared to essay killing an aurochs bull.

No, he need fear precious few creatures in most lands. True, the smell of lion had lain heavy about that kill on the remains of which the pair of jackals had been gnawing, but having fed so recently, it was doubtful if any save a very large pride would be hunting again so soon. Long-tooth cats liked hillier country than this, as too did the most of the land-dragons, while water-dragons never were seen this far from the sea or at least a sizable river, riverine swamp or deep lake. Smaller predators were only dangerous to such as Seos now "was" in numbers and could often be heard or scented from a distance, especially the two-legged packs.

Fitz could see in Seos' memories the two types of "dragons"— the water-dragon was a large crocodile and the land-dragon looked like nothing more than a lizard, but what a lizard it was. Could Seos' memories be believed, the thing must have been as long as the crocodile—between twenty and thirty feet!—and, although not apparently armored, of a lighter and more slender physique and with a long, tapering tail. The thing stood at least four feet at the shoulder, with a toothy, snaky head on three feet of thick, dewlapped neck, and every line of its scaly body spelled speed. Seos also recalled that there had been a related species—though larger—on the island when first the hybrids had settled it, but as the things were an ever-present danger to anything that lived and breathed, they had hunted them down and completely wiped the species out there. Pure-strain humans feared and hated the things, too, and banded together to exterminate them whenever or wherever they were found, so the monsters were becoming exceedingly rare, rarer even than the long-tooth cats, in lands inhabited by humans or hybrids, nor did it help their chances of survival that the larger of the monsters had an inborn proclivity to chase down, kill and eat the smaller whenever they could.

The young bull had been moving into the wind, deliberately, so that he was ever downwind of the herd and could scent it before his own scent was available to them. This was the cautious thing to do, for if the king-bull grazed with or close to the herd on this day, he was certain to take rather ferocious exception to a strange, younger contender for the favors of his cows and heifers. And it developed to be

as well that he had so done, for closer in to the herd
he smelled, not the scent of a mature king-bull, but
the unexpected—the reek of two-legs, men—and,
when he was come close enough to actually see the
cattle, it was clear that they were some generations
from the pure, wild strain. These had obviously been
bred smaller, with shorter legs and horns, though
still were they closely enough related to their larger,
wild progenitors that their scent was the same.

Here and there about the far-flung periphery of
the herd stood stripling boys and a few older men,
some of them leaning on the shafts of long, stone-
tipped spears, chewing on stems of grass and watching that their charges did not graze too far from the
rest of the herd, while keeping a sharp eye out for
any possible dangers.

As the Seos-bull came within sight of the herd, so
did he himself come within sight of some of the
watchers and these, too far away to themselves do
anything about him, signalled to those closer with a
series of meaningful whistles. To them, the advent of
a wild bull was as dangerous and serious a menace as
the appearance of a lion or bear or wolf, for the very
last thing they wanted was to have the original size,
hornspread and savagery bred back into their carefully-
nurtured strain of cattle.

Running at full tilt around one end of the herd, an
older man—likely about forty, thought the hybrid
part of the Seos-creature, with grey in his hair and
beard, a profusion of puckered, off-color scars on his
hairy limbs and torso, missing an eye and the most of
an ear and moving with a slight but very noticeable
limp, of late middle age for a pure-strain human—
took command of the striplings nearby, with a few
panted words and gestures, he rapidly formed them
into a semicircle facing uphill and the strange bull,

each of them now with a tall shield on his left arm and his spear presented and menacing. Then he set his troops in motion with a harsh, barked word, advancing on the deadly-dangerous interloper, hopeful of running him off without a fight, but certainly prepared to do whatever it took doing to keep him from their herd.

One of the striplings at the tip of the offensive crescent stopped long enough to take a hide sling from round his neck, load it, whirl it and accurately send a round stone against the near side of the head and the Seos-bull with such force as to bring a bellow of pain from the bovine creature. Seos knew that he had but two options, then: fight and kill all or most of the herd-guards—for they stood no chance of killing him since he was not real, fully-formed, flesh-and-blood, only a clever semblance of a beast—or beat a hasty retreat. He chose the latter course, turning and cantering off in the direction of a stand of forest from which came the good, cool smell of fresh water.

A few spears were hurled after him, but the flights of the shafts were short, none of them intended to strike or flesh in the Seos-bull. The herd-guards leaped and cavorted in an almost-dance of victory, they shouted and shrieked and screamed in their guttural language, anything to relieve the tension and express their patent relief at being spared a combat which, had it been well and truly joined, would assuredly have resulted in the messy deaths of more than one boy or man and the crippling or injury of others. Full-grown wild aurochs of either sex never died easily, the butcher-bill for the hunters was always high, and not a one of the herd-guards was so young or inexperienced to not be fully aware of the grim facts.

* * *

The girl half-reclined atop a high rock that was the point of a narrow peninsula of bank jutting out into the stream. The gathering of edibles was usually good in the stream bed and along its banks up here, above the falls, but the crystalline water that flowed over and among the rocks was icy-toothed cold, telling of the high-mountain snows that spawned the stream, despite its meandering journey across the sun-dappled high plains, and so, periodically, she always found it necessary to find a place to sit or lie in the warm sunlight until the feeling was come back into her feet and legs and the skin of them was no longer all ridges and puckers.

She might have not suffered from the cold in the warmer, deeper waters below the falls, but there she would have been in danger from the water-dragons, which toothy, ever-hungry monsters now and again swam up from the sea to sometimes take their bloody toll of bathers—young and old and of both sexes—despite the best efforts of the priest-chief, the regular sacrifices of goats and all the prayers of the gods of their tribe and of this land.

Besides, her revered father often remarked on how much more tender were the greens from upstream, how much tastier were the shelled creatures she expertly plucked from among the rocks, and pleasing her tall, strong, powerful and wise father was of paramount importance to her, for it was through his loins that she and all her siblings were distant descendents of true gods.

The gathering had not been too good, this day— only some dozen of the shelled water—creatures and even them not so large as many a one she had taken hereabouts in times past, though a fair amount of tender sprouts of various greens—but she had lucked onto a something that she knew was certain to bring a broad smile to show through her father's thick, sun-yellow beard.

The round, smooth rock was about as large as her two clenched fists together and might have passed for only another, stream-bed rock had not a small chip been sometime broken from off one end to show the white stone within—very fine-grained and about the hue of the fat from a mountain-sheep. Her father already owned two axes shod with this incredibly hard and tough and long-wearing stone; he treasured them as he treasured little else, and she knew that he was sure to be inordinately pleased to gain the wherewithal to fashion another.

On impulse, she sat up and looked down into the water at the side of her perch, hoping to see yet another of the rare stones, but the rocks seemed all alike and she ended staring at, studying her own reflection in the relatively still pool.

Sighing, she shook her head of thick, black hair. She had always wished that she could have looked more like her father, as did some of her sisters and brothers, and less like her mother—who had been taken in war against a clan of nomads who had tried to seize and hold tribal lands, pushing up with their herds from the southwest, years ago.

All the warriors of the scattered settlements had gathered under the priest-chiefs and had met the invaders on the plain nearest the sea. After a day-long battle, most of the male aliens lay speared or axe-hacked and dead on that plain, with dust settling on their wide-staring-brown eyes and their black, oiled, curly beards. Then the priest-chiefs and their still-hale warriors had descended on the camp of goat-hair tents, pitilessly slain the old, the infirm and the ugly, then taken the remainder for slaves or concubines or, in the case of the prettiest, more biddable young women, wives.

The girl's sire had taken two attractive sisters and, though one had died in childbirth after a few years, he still felt well served, for he had by then had three sons and a daughter out of her, while her sister still remained healthy and fecund, throwing another child every couple of years as a woman of any value should.

She was just upon the point of arising and descending from the rock back into the knee-deep water to work her way back downstream when she noticed movement in the woods that came almost down to the edge of the stream-bank opposite her and she froze, for wild beasts often came to the stream to drink. She had seen the tracks of their hooves and pads imprinted in sand and mud and atop flat rocks, but seldom the beasts themselves, for most of them moved by night. And she had no slightest desire to meet one of them here and now, armed with only a small cutting-stone and a couple of scraping-stones, especially not one that looked so big as what was on the move through the gloomy shadows under those trees.

The Seos-Fitz-bull knew in its hybrid mind that the spearmen would not pursue him, follow after him, for their responsibility was to the herd and it was their assigned duty to stay nearby it, protect it and keep it from straying beyond easy protection. Of course, they would most likely put hunters on his trail, soon or late, for his huge body represented much meat, fat, horn, sinew, hide and other very valuable items, but by the time the hunters got around to undertaking the tracking of this particular bull ox, he would no longer be in existence in his current form.

Although the periphery of this wood was of the

same thorny brush as the copse out on the plain
where Ehra-leopard had killed the doe, within, it
was true temperate forest—mixed deciduous and ev-
ergreen trees such as oak, maple, ash, pine, larch,
walnut, elm and chestnut. Once under the shade of
the huge-boled old trees, the bull's hooves sank
fetlocks-deep into a mold of damp, dead leaves,
wherein a host of insects, worms, mice and shrews
crawled and scuttled about their daily lives. Squirrels chattered and scolded from the trunks and limbs
of the trees and a vast profusion of multihued birds
occupied every level and flew through the air between those levels. Without exception, the denizens
of the forest ignored the interloping bull, knowing
that they had nothing to fear from him so long as
they kept from beneath his big hooves.

Unable to take a direct route to the enticing smell
of the water because of the erratic placement of the
trees, the bull still continued to veer in that general
direction and, at last, even his nearsighted eyes could
detect the sheen of sun on a stream. Pacing slowly
and deliberately out from the shady concealment of
the forest, the bull waded out into the stream and
dipped his mighty head down to drink of the clear,
cold water, ignoring the cloud of insects that came
swarming from every direction to buzz and drone
about him.

But no truly wild beast survived long without being
always on the alert for danger in all its forms and not
even this created facsimile of a wild ox was or could
properly be an exception to the universal rule; therefore, when the bull, even as he drank up the water,
heard the ghost of a sound, sensed a flicker of motion
above and to his right-front, he abruptly brought his
dripping muzzle up, snorting, one hoof unconsciously
pawing at the water-rounded cobbles that covered
the streambed.

On the point of bellowing his awful challenge, the Seos-bull caught sight of the creature above him, atop the rock. Even with the lack of color perception, he could identify the young woman as a stunning beauty of a human female. So much, in fact, did the observance of her lissome form attract and arouse the man within the bull that the hybrid mind let slip its control of the creation it inhabited and first small, then larger and even larger portions of it began to slip away, slough off into the current to be borne away downstream, an unexpected feast for the water creatures, large and small.

As for the girl, crouched upon the rock with her baskets of gatherings, the cold, trembling, whimpering fear of the great, deadly and known-vicious wild ox rapidly became lost in a degree of awe that left her unable to move when she witnessed the quick transformation from beast into a tall, fair young man, resembling in so many ways her god-descended sire. In the inchoate turmoil that her mind was become, she knew that this could be, must be, none save one of the true gods.

The last of the short-lived bull-creation dropped off into the stream, Seos waded through the icy water to the side of the rock, lifted himself into the air to its top and stood on the sun warmed surface, devouring the recumbent girl's toothsome young body with his eyes.

THE MANY WORLDS OF
MELISSA SCOTT

*Winner of the John W. Campbell Award
for Best New Writer, 1986*

THE KINDLY ONES: "An ambitious novel of the world Orestes. This large, inhabited moon is governed by five Kinships whose society operates on a code of honor so strict that transgressors are declared legally 'dead' and are prevented from having any contact with the 'living.' . . . Scott is a writer to watch."—*Publishers Weekly*. A Main Selection of the Science Fiction Book Club.

65351-2 • 384 pp. • $2.95

The "Silence Leigh" Trilogy

FIVE-TWELFTHS OF HEAVEN (Book I): "Melissa Scott postulates a universe where technology interferes with magic. . . . The whole plot is one of space ships, space wars, and alien planets—not a unicorn or a dragon to be seen anywhere. Scott's space drive and description of space piloting alone would mark her as an expert in the melding of the [SF and fantasy] genres; this is the stuff of which 'sense of wonder' is made."—*Locus*

55952-4 • 352 pp. • $2.95

SILENCE IN SOLITUDE (Book II): "[Scott is] a voice you should seek out and read at every opportunity." —*OtherRealms*.   65699-7 • 324 pp. • $2.95

THE EMPRESS OF EARTH (Book III):

65364-4 • 352 pp. • $3.50

A CHOICE OF DESTINIES: "Melissa Scott [is] one of science fiction's most talented newcomers. . . . The greatest delight of all is finding out how she managed to write a historical novel that could legitimately have spaceships on the cover . . . a marvelous gift for any fan."—*Baltimore Sun*   65563-9 • 320 pp. • $2.95

THE GAME BEYOND: "An exciting interstellar empire novel with a great deal of political intrigue and colorful interplanetary travel."—*Locus*

55918-4 • 352 pp. • $2.95